PREEMPTIVE

DOUGLAS GRANT

ISBN: 9781941142219

For my father, with gratitude
for his tireless support in this endeavor.

PROLOGUE

Jennifer Simmons rode the subway to work the morning of the big day. She did this against her husband's wishes. Her husband, Peter, needed to go into work early to prepare for a presentation he was giving later that day, and she had insisted that he use their weekend car. She would catch up with him later.

He had been on the phone almost every minute since he had slammed down on the alarm clock's off button. He was conversing with a co-worker throughout every step of his morning routine, save shaving and showering, going over some last-minute details before a workday that would prove to be momentous. She watched him from the bed as he was getting ready. While she had not completely awoken from her slumber, he was anxiously moving about, overly excited from his caffeine intake. He raked his left hand through his curly dark hair, sighing into the phone. He then tried to put on his pants, but with one hand already occupied, he tripped over a pant leg. He cursed as his stocky frame collided with the dresser. How she loved him.

He had tried to persuade her to ride along with him, but she had refused, saying that he needed at least five minutes to collect himself, and she knew he never used his cell phone while driving. She smiled with the thought. It was another sign of the strong discipline that she loved about him. The two worked together at Cantor Fitzgerald and usually shared a cab together, but on this particular day she needed time to herself to think.

The short ride to work was one of the few times in her insanely busy day when she could simply relax. Besides, she had enough to think about over the next couple of days. When added to her workload, new concerns threatened to overwhelm her. *Overwhelm me with joy,* she thought.

She felt a small, girlish giggle escape, one that she hoped had gone unnoticed. She never lied to Peter, and was glad that he'd been too engaged on the phone to hear her. She had to wait until the right time to tell him. Until then, she'd have to practice better self-control.

Peter always insisted that she take cabs rather than the subway. She didn't lie to him today. She just never raised the issue. Having once been the victim of a mugging on a subway platform, he was adamant about her using cabs. This morning, she couldn't help it. She felt a strange energy that she wasn't accustomed to and thought that perhaps in becoming part of the morning bustle she might use it up. Riding the subway with her fellow New Yorkers would be a nice change of pace.

When she'd finally, slowly slipped out of bed, she went into the bathroom and splashed water on her face and rinsed her mouth. She pulled back her long black hair and tied it into a bun. She knew Peter was on his way out, and she wanted to see him off, even though she knew she'd be seeing him shortly. She felt a bit of remorse for having kept the news from him for so long already, but her blood warmed with the thought of the look that would be on his face when she told him tonight at dinner.

The night out was to be celebration for jobs well done at work, a way to pat themselves on the back for months of tedious dedication to their professions that led to important moments in their careers. But tonight would turn into a double celebration with her announcement. She suspected that she'd break down and cry for joy. This would be one of those rare moments when they could simply sit and bask in one another's glowing presence. Then they'd go home and she'd surprise him with the lacy and essentially transparent lingerie she'd splurged on at Victoria's Secret for this occasion. After that thought, she projected her imagination months into the future and wondered if Peter would still find her sexually attractive.

Take it easy, she reminded herself. *One thing at a time. One day at a time.* She was nearly on the verge of tears now, standing there, staring at herself in the mirror, mouth burning with the taste of peppermint. *Tighten up, Jenny*, she demanded of herself with more resolve. She could hear Peter moving about in the den, and knew she had to hurry if she was to catch him. He was nit-picking with Lewis on the phone as he hurriedly grabbed his briefcase and headed for the door. She stopped him at the foyer.

"Hold on a sec, Lew." He turned to her. "I'm late. I've gotta get the hell outta here. He says that everything's in order, but I can tell from the way he sounds that we've got a big mess waiting for us, and ... what?" He turned back to his phone. "I don't care if you *can* hear me. When I call back in ten minutes, you'd better have talked him into it. Ten minutes." He hung up, showing an exasperation that was too early in the morning to be a good sign for such an important day. He looked flustered and edgy. "I'm sorry; I've gotta go." He gave her a quick peck on the cheek and rushed out the door.

"Wait!" she called after him.

"What?" he said as he turned to face her.

She felt foolish. The news was to be a surprise, and she would save it. But she felt that his kiss was insufficient to begin this day. But she didn't close the ten feet now between them to get a more endearing one.

"I'll see you soon," he reassured her with a loving glance.

If you only knew. "Okay," she said, smiling at him radiantly. He returned her smile with a fleshy, lopsided grin and then dashed down the hall to the elevator. She immediately regretted not having told him that she loved him, and did not want to embarrass herself now by shouting after him, standing there in her bathrobe. She watched him get on the elevator. The doors closed. She second- guessed herself again, even though he already knew what was in her heart. *Oh well, plenty of time for that*, she told herself. She needed to get ready. She looked like hell.

After a long shower and a rushed breakfast of a bagel and cream cheese, she left their apartment and ambled down Sixth Avenue, mentally planning the next nine months of her life on both broad and specific levels. After a while she decided that her head had no room for business, no matter how important. Besides, she knew her business would soon be at hand.

Manhattan's heartbeat was accelerating. Yellow cabs cut each other off, only to be met with outraged horns. Traffic lights jumped from red to green and buses shot plumes of exhaust into the air. Policemen conversed with citizens on the corner while they tried to simultaneously monitor their posts. Peddlers cried out the names of their products. Pedestrians moving north and south came to abrupt halts at crosswalks, while those moving east and west resumed their journeys, some hurried, some relaxed. Steam rose from manhole covers on the streets. Pigeons' heads bobbed on stone ledges. Digital billboards scrolled from one advertisement to the next. Residents of penthouses gazed down from their privileged positions. The sun continued its climb over the buildings of the East Side.

Jennifer descended the stairs that took her into the under levels of this great city that she lived in. She loved life in New York, and she could not really see herself living anywhere else. Her brother Derek, on the other hand, would no doubt soon be seeking an escape with his bride, Miranda, to Colorado or Montana, or anywhere rural enough to be without a building higher than two stories. Derek and Miranda's desire for such an escape stemmed from their exhaustion with a lifetime in this city. New York City, to them, was a giant, unyielding machine that never stopped pumping out the lure—and sometimes the reality—of money and success. It had become the antithesis of everything the couple now sought in life.

But before any move, she and Derek would have to return to the ongoing, unresolved discussion concerning their younger brother's future. Zack was fresh out of high school, and neither she nor Derek could imagine what was in store for him. Zack had issues, after all, and they needed to be addressed sooner than later.

Before she boarded the train, she stopped to purchase a newspaper. Once aboard, she sat down to be alone with her thoughts, unhindered by outside stimuli. First, she would check on her and Peter's stocks. She flipped through the pages.

One article caught her attention, and it made her frown. It was about a recent bombing in Palestine that had killed thirteen people. She found this so saddening, so contrary to what she was feeling today. Although she had found success in her life, and was a hardworking contributor to her company, she found it deplorable that she was so often ignorant of what went on in other parts of the world, places torn by conflict and dying economies. *We have it good, very good, right here in America.*

The occasional indifference she felt about events that took place on the other side of the world would have to be remedied. What would her parents, who'd served in the Peace Corps, think if they were alive today and saw that societies plagued by violence and sorrow seemed to hold little interest for their daughter? She cared. She'd prove it somehow.

After checking the stock market, she folded the paper with deft snapping movements and placed it on her lap. She closed her eyes. For a while she contented herself by listening to the rhythm of the subway car speeding along its tracks. When she lifted her eyelids, she looked across the aisle to a woman with a toddler in her lap. Although the woman was black, she held certain similarities to Jennifer. Both had straight black hair and slim figures. Both women looked physically tired, a trait that could be seen by observing the tenseness in their facial muscles and the lines underneath their eyes. The similarities ended there.

In this instance, the woman sitting across from Jennifer was tired from dealing with her antsy son. She was trying to prevent him from removing his blue and orange Mets hat and unzipping his tan jacket, and she was making only a minimal effort to hide her frustration.

"Boy, if you touch that one more time I will spank your bottom in front of all these people. Just you try me!" the woman warned. Her whole approach to the situation seemed a little harsh to Jennifer, but she could not hide her smile. One day might she be as tense as this woman was, with an even greater load of responsibility? *It won't seem funny soon enough.* Sure, it was alright to be amused by it now, but when everything came together, would she still feel the same? *Ah, well, I'll have Peter to share the burden with. No, not the burden*, she thought, *the blessing.*

She'd finally be able to share the news with someone. Well, she'd shared it with Zack. She didn't keep anything from Zack. He was both her friend and confidant. Although they enjoyed a wonderful relationship as siblings, at times she felt a motherly sort of love toward him. Despite his inner conflict, his unattainable peace of mind, he was always there to lend her his ear or be a shoulder to cry on. Peter was there for her in these ways as well, but he had not been in her life as long as Zack, and she needed them both.

Zack had seemed shocked when she'd told him. Their family had slowly but surely been diminishing with time, and he seemed surprised that it could grow. But it would. She, Derek, and Zack had picked up the pieces of a broken family, and now it seemed as though those pieces were being put back together.

She felt suddenly emotional. She was on the verge of tears again, staring at this beautiful little boy being fussed over by a mother whose well of patience had nearly run dry. Someone, somewhere, must be smiling upon her if she could be this happy.

The train arrived at her stop. Climbing the concrete steps, she smelled the pleasant aroma of hot pretzels coming from a vendor's cart. As she reached the street, she marveled at what a clear, blue, and sunny morning it was shaping up to be. All around her New York breathed with liveliness and activity. She knew she'd made the right decision in taking the subway. Through her own personal bliss, she felt more connected to the people around her than she ever had before. She delighted at seeing the concentration on the faces of bicyclists zipping by, or the hurried gestures of a customer purchasing a magazine from a newsstand. Considering all the tragedy their family had endured, and almost become accustomed to, she often forgot that there was another end to the spectrum, a light at the end of a long, dark tunnel. *Well, here it is.*

She turned a corner and there they were—the twin towers of the World Trade Center. No matter how many times she beheld them, the towers never failed to instill in her a sense of awe and power. As she crossed the plaza heading toward Tower

One, she felt pride in the life she'd made for herself. How many people could say they worked in a place like this? *Well, actually a lot,* she reconsidered. Thousands of people worked in the twin towers. Still, she felt privileged. She'd worked hard to be where she was today. She'd earned it.

When she stepped off the elevator, she was relieved to once again find solid footing. She made her way to the offices of Cantor Fitzgerald and took a quick look around. Peter was not there. She'd wait. If he'd found even ten minutes to have a smoke, he'd be up on the roof with the tourists, a habit he indulged in all too often. She never joined him up there. The offices were high enough for her as it was, and it wouldn't do to let him see her succumb to one of her fits of acrophobia. His time on the roof was *his* time to himself. Regardless, she doubted he'd found the time this morning. The way he'd carried on with Lewis on the phone earlier was an indication that he'd have little time to spare over the next few hours.

She stepped into her office and closed the door. Sitting down at her dark oak desk, she focused on addressing the details of her workday. *Okay, time to put your game face on. Down to business.* Reaching into her purse, she retrieved a mini tape recorder that Zack had given her two Christmases ago. She loved the gift and used it two times a day: once before she started to work to list everything she had planned for that day, and once in the evening to confirm whether or not she'd accomplished what she'd set out to do. It was her personal business journal, but also her occasional diary that sometimes recorded her reflections that were not of a business nature. She spoke into the recorder:

> Tuesday, September 11, 2001. 8:05 am. In just a few short hours, Peter and Lewis are going to have their meeting with the Sullivans, during which they're going to present their plan. They seem a little apprehensive, but I have confidence in both of them. If everything goes smoothly, they'll be done before lunch. After that, I intend to spend the rest of the day contacting the interns we had this summer. We'll need a new underwriter soon,

and it would be nice to have some prospects lined up. If time permits, I may try to get Dan down at Procter and Gamble to upgrade my computer with that new software he was telling me about last week, but I don't know if today will work for him. Also, I've got to finish these spread-sheets, and...

She paused and clicked off the recorder. She allowed herself to indulge in some more of that girlish giggling. She realized she sounded silly. When she'd gotten it out of her system, she continued:

Peter and I are going to dinner tonight. He won't tell me where yet, but I think it's Cappricio's, that place that we went to last year in the East Village. Assuming there won't be problems with the ten o'clock meeting, the dinner will be a little more than just a breath of fresh air. What Peter doesn't know is ... what he doesn't know is that I'm pregnant. I don't know why I'm having trouble saying this to myself. At any rate, tonight I'll tell him, and we'll celebrate in style. I'm overjoyed right now, so I'll just leave it at that. It's only 8:00 am, but so far this has been a really wonderful day.

After she placed the recorder in her desk drawer, she gazed out her window and took in the metropolis. A single tear escaped her left eye and ran down her cheek, taking part of her mascara with it. It didn't trouble her in the least. At this one, precious moment, everything was perfect, and the future couldn't seem any brighter.

CHAPTER 1
FEBRUARY 28, 1998

Benazar Rashid was sitting in a cave. He didn't even know why he'd chosen it. He didn't recall how far from his farm it was. He'd started the fire he sat close to now, but he barely remembered that either. Apparently, one part of his mind had brought him to this place while the other part was focused on something else entirely.

The war had pushed him to the edge of instability. The traumas, both physical and mental, had conceived demons within him. He'd been warned about this before. They threatened to destroy him.

He looked older than his forty-seven years. His leathery, sun-burned face was disfigured from several scars. His missing front teeth accentuated his years, as well. His black hair and beard were long and unkempt. His body had been emaciated from his time in captivity, and although after his release he had eventually regained his strength and health, he had never looked the same as he had before his capture.

Sitting with his legs crossed, he stared at the fire in front of him and watched the burning embers dance in front of his eyes. He was on the verge of an epiphany. He *knew* it; he could feel it.

His son, Hakeem, had no idea he'd left the farm in the middle of the night. Hakeem would have been shocked. Everything he'd taught Hakeem about defending their land with his life meant nothing right now if he'd left his son there to fend for himself.

Benazar felt certain there was a good reason for his being here. He just didn't know what that reason was yet. He was sure that if he opened up his mind the answer would seek *him* out. He was patient. He allowed his dark eyes to lose focus and just stare into the blue, orange, and yellow flickers of the fire.

Afghanistan was rotting from within. Even someone as reclusive as he was could see this. The situation worsened every day. The Soviets had withdrawn. Technically, the Mujaheddin had won. And the current state of affairs was what the aftermath of that victory looked like. It disgusted him.

Betrayal. He'd suffered it many times before. Each time it happened, it made him stronger. It gave him an even clearer focus. It reinforced the feeling of righteousness he had in everything he'd done. But this last one left him feeling purposeless. For the first time in his life he didn't know what to do. His drug running was destroying his people. The guns he sold would eventually be turned on his own. He told himself that he did it to survive in this land, hoping that ends could indeed justify means. But in his heart he knew that there were no ends. Without knowing how, he'd become part of the problem. The thought tortured him.

Staring for many minutes into the fire, he could see shapes begin to form above the red embers. They morphed into people from his past and his present. Many of them, in one way or another, had been instrumental in the destruction of this place he called home. But the one face he saw that ignited a fire within his veins was that of the man who embodied the power that Benazar believed had caused the nation's downfall. He was the source—the one responsible for the ultimate betrayal: Agent Stuart Flanigan. His one-time ally. His bitterest enemy.

Benazar was not alone in his beliefs. The country swelled with men who thought as he did. The resentment, the need to see justice served, cut these men to the heart. They wouldn't forget. They'd bide their time.

What set him apart from these men was his perception. They saw enemy activity as a crime against Islam. He, however, saw it as a crime against humanity. He considered his the greater cause, yet in the end they all had the same desire: retribution.

He wasn't above petty vengeance. He'd embraced it more than once. But it wasn't merely vengeance he sought this time. He wanted to wake up the whole world. And the world had turned its back on Afghanistan. The world had forgotten it. But Afghanistan wouldn't be ignored. Men needed to be held accountable for their actions.

No, this wasn't just about vengeance. He'd make them see what he saw. He'd make them see what *they* had created in serving their own self-interests. He'd open their eyes.

Diplomacy had failed. Blood was all that their enemies would understand now. The United States was the driving force behind all of it. It was a democracy made up of registered voters. Its people couldn't blame their crimes on corrupt governors, dictators, or warlords. They were *all* guilty, every single one of them. And they were completely ignorant of the horrors his people faced on a daily basis, yet it was they who were responsible for his people's misery. Now they would have to answer for it. There was only one way to make them understand. And he was one of the few people who truly knew what it was they had coming.

For a moment he caught a glimpse of Hakeem's thoughtful face in the shifting mosaic of forms he saw in the fire. At one time his son might have had a promising future here, but not now. Hakeem had been swept up in the new reality that was the product of bullets and rocket fire. His son's life had been rendered as meaningless as his own. Yet, he regarded Hakeem to be a better man than he. He was a rare gem in this land of barbarians. He was an optimist, a pacifist, and an intellectual. Benazar had grown too old. Perhaps it was his son's time to carry on his legacy.

Benazar thought he might actually be able to see how the future would play itself out. There would be a period of waiting. Necessary preparations would be made; then would come the moment to strike. Then the people would see the truth as if it had slapped them in their faces. But then ... then everything would get worse here. Martyrdom for everyone. It was the ultimate sacrifice, the price paid for pursuing the truth. He could live with that. But would he have that for his own son?

One way or another it was going to happen. Nothing could stop it now. The choice now was to sit idly by and watch events unfold, knowing that all were doomed in the end, or they would become part of the manifestation, embracing their fate.

He'd do whatever was necessary, sacrificing anything and anyone, to do what needed to be done. This land and everyone in it might burn to ashes, but history would look back on this time and realize the mistakes that had been made by a select few, and what those mistakes had cost.

The challenge lay in bringing Hakeem into the fold. It was his best qualities that would work against him. He wouldn't understand, not at first. But Benazar was convinced his son would eventually see life for what it really was. It would cause Hakeem unbearable pain. Hakeem might come to lose all hope. But one day ... one day Hakeem would see that he was capable of changing the world for the better, even if that meant laying down his own life. When he realized that, he would understand that he was meant to be part of something greater than himself, and when that happened he'd understand that all the hopes and dreams he had carried with him up until then had been inconsequential.

Benazar sat by the fire for hours. When it finally died out, he thought he understood everything with a clarity he'd never before attained. He understood the value of alliances, and that meant connecting himself once again with individuals he didn't trust. He understood that a violent storm was coming, that nothing would stop it, and that it was better to meet that storm head on, on his own terms. Most importantly, he understood that everything he knew would soon be coming to an end. This didn't necessarily mean his death, but his day was quickly passing. The dream he'd bled for had never been realized. Something inside of him was broken, and it would never be fixed. He suspected that's how the country was perceived by the few people who still spoke its name.

He rose to one knee, and then slowly pulled himself erect. He had no idea how far away from his farm he was or how long the journey back might take. He felt fatigued and feverish. He glanced back at the smoking fire pit and wondered if his father had also suffered lapses in memory when the visions had visited him. He hoped the genetic trait would pass over his son the way it had his brother. Their cryptic messages were enough to drive one mad.

He left the cave. The sun had not yet risen. The horizon to his right was beginning to welcome the coming sunrise with streaks of blue and violet.

East. The way home was east.

CHAPTER 2
March 29, 2002

No one else knew it, but it was the basic little pleasures that got Zack McCrady through each day. He made no effort to mask the way he felt. But he had his own way of expressing himself, and he had never really told anyone that it was these small, simple sights that brought smiles to his face and that kept him moving forward.

Today it was the faintest hint of buds forming on the tips of the tree branches, signifying the end of winter; that made him grin. It was not as if he was unique in this regard. Everyone relished the onset of warm weather and blooming foliage after a harsh winter. But not everyone was dependent on these small pleasures to keep them in good mental health. Zack was.

Coasting leisurely down First Avenue on his Diamondback freestyle bike, Zack felt warm inside upon seeing the trees' annual rebirth. It was a feeling he hardly recognized. Deciding to embrace the unexpected but welcome feeling, he pedaled faster. He was making good time on his deliveries today, and up until now he had been in a sluggish mood. He was surprised at how easily his spirits had been uplifted. *Let's just see how long it lasts.*

When at last he reached Thirty-first Street, he found a pole to lock his bike to and set out to locate his customer's building. He found it and looked it over. He'd never been here before. It was a pretty nice place. He hoped that meant he'd be making a generous gratuity for himself.

The lobby receptionist gave Zack the once-over when he entered the building. Zack, with his unruly, sandy blond curls, torn hooded sweatshirt, and baggy jeans, was obviously not the typical New Yorker that this place was used to receiving. *I'll still take the money.*

"Hi. Bob White. I'm here to see Tom Horton in 606."

"Okay, just one second." The burly man at the desk called up to the apartment for confirmation. Hanging up the phone, he said,

"He's expecting you. Go right on up."

"Thanks."

"You have a nice day, sir."

Zack hadn't even finished knocking on the door when his customer pulled it open. He might as well have already been jacked up. He was one of New York's suave yuppie types that looked like a model for *GQ* magazine. His apartment had the combined scents of leather furniture and expensive cologne. From his tailor-made Armani suit to his shiny, slicked back hair, this guy definitely looked the part. Zack couldn't care less. Mr. Suave, here, was still buying powder from him.

He invited Zack in. Sitting down on the couch, Zack put his backpack on the floor and unzipped one of the compartments. One by one, he removed little glass vials and placed them in a row on the coffee table. Each one had a different label. Holding up two of them, Mr. Suave said, "I'll take these."

"You know how much," Zack said.

"All right, I'll be right back," Mr. Suave said, retreating to his bedroom, presumably to get money.

Zack surveyed the apartment. For all the flashy furniture and appliances, this place was little more than a closet space. Zack's place was bigger than this, and he figured that Mr. Suave had to be at least in his late twenties. He grinned.

When his customer returned, he handed over the money, which Zack then began to count. He was halfway through counting when he looked up to find Mr. Suave staring at him with a curious look on his face.

"What?" he inquired. *What the hell is this guy starin' at?*

"Your name's Zack, right?"

Not good. A customer did *not* need to know his name. "I don't think I know you."

Mr. Suave only started nodding and pointing. "Yeah, you're Zack McCrady. You probably wouldn't remember me. I'm Tom. I briefly dated Jenny when we were back at Fordham together."

Zack felt as though he had been gut-punched. It was nothing new. It felt exactly the same every time his sister's name was unexpectedly mentioned. He suspected it would remain that way for the rest of his days.

There was an awkward silence that hung in the air between them for several moments. Finally, Zack said, "I guess I don't remember you." He avoided eye contact.

Mr. Suave, uncertain where to take this conversation, offered, "Look, man, I can't tell you how deeply sorry I was to learn that Jenny was there that day. She was as angelic as they come. Everyone who knew her loved her."

Here was an example of what he'd had to listen to for the last seven months. No matter how good their intentions were, no matter how hard they tried to make him feel better, he always wished that they'd just kept quiet and let his wounds heal. He *hated* being the object of pity.

"Hey, that's great. Now let's stick to the business at hand," Zack said, his voice low and cold.

Mr. Suave looked mortified. He hadn't been expecting that. He looked away as he thought to respond. Zack continued to count his money.

"Look, I'm real sorry. I just wanted you to know—"

"How sorry you are," Zack cut him of sharply. "Yeah, you already said that. You're sorry. Everyone's sorry. Don't be sorry. It's not your fault. It is what it is." He stood up abruptly, put his money in his pocket, and slung his backpack over his shoulder. Heading for the door, he muttered disgustedly, "This guy's gonna tell *me* that everyone loved her."

"Hey, man, what's your problem?" Mr. Suave asked, holding Zack's attention. "I don't know how to tell you this, but you're not the only one to have lost a loved one that day, y'know? Are you forgetting where exactly it is that you live?"

So, maybe Mr. Suave was a lawyer. Who knew? If Zack could have killed him with his penetrating look of hate, then he would have struck this prick dead where he stood. "If I ever see your address on my list of deliveries again, you'll be gettin' Ajax to put up your nose." He slammed the door as he left.

Zack's blood boiled as the elevator descended. His mood could easily change as easily as flicking a switch. All the warmth he'd felt earlier was now gone. There was only that cold feeling that made his stomach tense up as if he were actually expecting someone to punch him. It was a feeling that chased him around. It was always just around the next corner. It was never welcome. Worst of all, though, in Zack's opinion, was that it was slowly but surely consuming him, changing him for the worse. He'd become so accustomed to it that it was now part of who he was.

Someday he'd have to make a choice. Would he accept the cold as a part of him, a result of how all the rotten misfortunes that happen in life can change a person? Or would he resist the cold, the bitterness, and stand as strong as his sister had? He suspected he knew what choice he'd make. He'd have to put off admitting it to himself, because he really didn't like the answer.

* * *

Like the trees Zack had spotted budding on First Avenue, the trees of Central Park also welcomed spring's rejuvenation. It was here that Zack headed after the altercation with Mr. Suave.

Figuring that practicing a few simple bike maneuvers would help to settle him down, he pedaled back and forth from the park's east side to the west side, practicing on curbs, benches, and railings. He'd finished his deliveries early today. Now all he wanted to do was blow of some steam until dusk.

Zack grew weary after a short time and decided to go cash out with Marco. He was in the middle of the park when he decided it was time to go. He knew he wouldn't be able to leave without stopping by the carousel. It was there he now headed.

Zack could not say that there had been a great many inspirations for him over the years, but *Catcher in the Rye* had been one the stronger influences on his life. He had read it in school two years before, and he could easily say that it had helped change him for the better. There were so many different ways Zack had been able to relate to the novel's young protagonist, Holden Caulfield, and the parallels he was able to make between himself and Holden had enabled him to fix a couple of the problems in his life.

The end of the novel, set at the carousel Zack now saw before him, was the part he'd especially related to. When Holden watches his little sister, Phoebe, trying to grab the brass ring on the merry-go-round, he wants to be right there to catch her if she should fall. It was all he wanted to do—catch Phoebe. There were so many times in the past where Zack would have liked to have been there to catch his sister. Never mind that she was twelve years his senior. Never mind that it had been Jenny who had raised Zack after their mother had died. Never mind that Holden comes to the realization that he needs to let Phoebe fall. Zack had always felt that brotherly need to protect her.

Too many people had tried to keep his family down on too many occasions, but Jenny and his brother Derek had always kept their heads held high, never complaining. Sometime in his early childhood, he could not recall exactly when, Zack had decided that he would be there for his sister to catch her if she fell. But until the day of her death, she'd never let anyone knock her down. She'd accepted the challenges of what he considered to be a greedy and corrupt society and succeeded at every turn. He'd always been in awe of her ability to roll with life's punches. Perhaps that was why *Catcher* was so appealing to him. He could relate to the way in which Holden was so protective of Phoebe. And yet he'd never really needed to protect Jenny. She'd been too tough.

It seemed to Zack as though fate had scoffed at him when Jenny had ultimately met her end. What in the world could he possibly have done that would have prevented that? She, Peter, and everyone else had been doomed from the moment those hijacked planes had left the ground.

Now, sitting on his bike, watching the children get their last rides before dark, he wondered if he was only worsening his mood by thinking about it. When he did, he concluded that relating to Holden Caulfield no longer helped to put his mind at ease the way it once had. Jenny was gone. He couldn't be there to catch her. He felt the cold creep in, and knew that now even this place would no longer comfort him the way it once had.

He reached into his pocket and withdrew a Xanax. He needed to take everything down a notch. He was sipping from his water bottle when his phone rang. Caller identification told him that it was Marco. "I was just about to head back," he said as he answered.

"Yeah, well you'd better be back in twenty minutes. You and I are gonna have some words when you get here." Marco's tone was flat, never a good sign.

"All right, I'll be right there." Hanging up, Zack gazed at the carousel for a long time. The rearing and lunging horses were slowly coming to a halt. He didn't know if he'd be returning anytime soon. The cold had found him here, followed him from his last delivery. This place, like everything else around him, had been forever tarnished by that infernal day back in September.

He turned and left the park. With traffic picking up this time of day, he'd never reach the village in twenty minutes.

*   *   *

Marco ran a boutique in the heart of Greenwich Village. He had a wide variety of items in his store, including vintage clothing, records, CDs, comics, posters, jewelry, pipes, and bongs. It was in a room in the back, behind closed doors, where Marco ran his most lucrative business.

Zack was on his way toward the back of the store when he met Jamar, who had just come from the back. He was Zack's best friend and the one who had gotten him this high-paying job. He was tall and built, an intimidating person. He was grinning and running a pick through the puffy Afro he was currently sporting. He glanced back at the room he had just come from, and asked, "Yo, what the hell happened?"

"Nothin'. Why, what's goin' on?" Zack had no idea what he was in for.

"Stand tall, man, that's all I'm gonna say," Jamar said, laughing, as he headed for the front.

"Hey, c'mon, tell me. What the fuck?" Zack didn't want to walk blindly into this. But Jamar had basically told him that he was on his own.

"I'm gettin' somethin' to eat. I'll swing by later," Jamar said over his shoulder. Then he was out the door.

Zack wanted to get whatever he had coming to him over with. He sauntered into the back room with an expression of pure innocence. Marco turned to face him. He was even more intimidating than Jamar. He was a powerfully built Latino with plenty of gold jewelry around his wrists and neck. He wore black pants and a wife-beater that revealed the many tattoos that covered his thick neck, chest, and arms. However, it was the look he gave Zack now that really worried him.

"What do you think this is?" Marco asked icily. When Zack opened his mouth to reply, Marco charged over to Zack so that he was less than a foot away. The two were almost nose-to-nose when Marco began shouting. "What the fuck do you think this is? You arrogant little shit! Who the fuck gave you permission to mouth off to my customers?"

Now it was all clear to Zack. Mr. Suave had filed a complaint. Cursing himself for getting carried away earlier, he now just stood there and mopped it all up. He could feel saliva hit his face as Marco continued to tear into him. "You're lucky Jamar has your back; otherwise, I'd throw your ass out in the street right now. Goddamn it. Is this how you repay me for promotin' you?"

Marco was referring to Zack's recent move up the ladder. Previously, he had only been able to deliver pot. Now he was entrusted to move cocaine, ecstasy, and a wide assortment of prescription pharmaceuticals. He had just turned eighteen, and it was rare for Marco to put his faith in someone so young. But he'd put his faith in Zack.

As Marco carried on, Zack tuned him out. He made a face like he was listening, but his mind was elsewhere. He was good at doing that.

Eventually Marco calmed down. When he did, he said, "All right, now listen up, you stubborn bastard. You now work under a three strikes and you're out rule. After you tried to rip off that Jamaican up on Eighty-second Street last month, this makes strike two. One more and you can carry your ass down to Russo's joint and sling his shitty pies. I don't care. We all feel real bad about what happened to you, but you need to either get over it or leave that morbid ass attitude of yours at home. There's no place for it here. I'm tryin' to run a business, and I'm not gonna have you out there draggin' my good name through the mud just 'cause you can't get a grip on yourself. For now on, I'm gonna be watchin' you real closely. Now give me my money and get the fuck outta here."

Although Zack felt like he was leaving Marco's with his tail between his legs, he wasn't the least bit contrite about what had happened earlier with that asshole on Thirty-first Street. He did want to keep his job, though. From here on out, he would have to try to keep from being so quick-tempered. He supposed it was a step toward maturity, but he was more concerned with all the money he would lose if he got fired.

Marco had said something about feeling sorry for what had happened to him. Once again, he loathed being pitied. It made the pain of the loss feel so raw. Hoping to restrain the cold, that awful dark feeling, he popped another Xanax into his mouth. It was dark out now, and time to go home. He was always tired after such an active day. He unlocked his bike and headed back.

CHAPTER 3
MARCH 30, 2002

"When's the last time you talked to Zack?" Miranda asked Derek while rinsing off their dishes from dinner. She turned to look at him, playing tug-of-war with their black lab, Bella, on the kitchen floor.

"Friday, why?" he replied loud enough to be heard over Bella's growling. Derek and the dog continued playing.

Miranda turned of the faucet and let out a sigh. "Oh, I don't know. Maybe because it's been almost a week since you've spoken to him, and that seems like too long. Maybe because you keep putting of that talk you're supposed to have with him. I feel like I worry about him more than you do these days."

Derek fell out of his playful role with Bella. He looked up at his wife, exasperated. "What's going on? What are you talking about?" Looking into her eyes, he said, "You know how worried I've been about him. But you know how he gets. We had a few choice words on Friday, and he hung up on me. I not only needed to give him time to cool off, but I needed some time to rethink my whole approach to this situation. It just seems like we keep going in circles, and I don't really know what to do differently."

Derek always had trouble conveying his feelings on this subject to his wife. He and his brother had always had a turbulent relationship. Aside from their family resemblance, the wiry builds and wavy sandy blond hair, the two were practically complete opposites. They never saw eye to eye on any matter. When they got together, their contradictory natures often led them into heated arguments during which cutting comments would be exchanged that could not be taken back. More often than not, Derek would look back having rued most of the words he'd said, as had been the case last Friday. Watching Miranda now, with her chin lowering and expression softening, Derek thought about how lucky he was to have her.

"I know," she said, "it's just, the poor kid. He seems so detached. You can't just allow him to drift off, or he might not come back. I mean, God, Derek, I don't know why I have to keep on your ass about these things."

Her concern moved him deeply, and he felt real guilt. Standing up and going to her, he took her in his arms and kissed her softly on her forehead. He held the embrace for a few moments, playing with her shiny auburn hair, and then turned and walked into their office. She began to load the dishwasher when she heard him on the phone.

"Hey, punk, what's going on? Oh yeah? Sounds like you have company. Did I catch you at a bad time?"

Miranda did not intend to eavesdrop, but she heard anyway. What she heard made her proud. Here was Derek, swallowing his pride in an attempt to reach out to his troubled younger brother.

"That's cool. Hey, listen, let me buy you lunch on Saturday," he proposed. There was a pause. "Well, I picked up a shift at the restaurant on Sunday, and—"Another pause, followed by, "You know what, forget it. Sunday it is. Huh? Well, I was kind of hoping we could go to McSorley's. Trust me; you're going to like it. How's noon sound? Cool. You know where it is, right? Yeah, not far at all. I'll talk to you then."

She heard Derek hang up the phone. She understood where her husband was coming from better than she let on. Although Zack would say that his brother carped at him excessively, she knew that Zack was overly touchy and did not respond well to efforts made to give him any kind of advice or guidance. She had seen Derek remain patient when Zack was being unreasonable.

Brothers, by nature, were often quarrelsome, but now, more than ever, this pair needed to stick together, and Zack had a knack for becoming bellicose at the worst possible times.

If only Jenny were still alive. She had somehow miraculously been able to bring her brothers into balance after their mother's death, and the brothers would always put their differences on hold whenever she was around for fear of hurting her. Now that the loss of Jenny was the primary reason behind Zack's struggle for peace, Derek did not know how to proceed in helping him.

Zack was out of high school. There was no talk of college. There was really no talk of the future at all. He was constantly depressed and would too often shut out those closest to him rather than let them see his pain. However, through this self-imposed isolation, Zack was more exposed than ever.

This was one of the reasons the couple had indefinitely postponed their move to Crested Butte, Colorado. Realizing that this was not a good time to leave Zack by himself in New York, they had at first considered renewing their lease at their apartment in Flushing Meadows on a monthly basis. They had originally planned their move for the beginning of 2002. But with Zack's continued regression and the weight to bear after a death in the family, the two had made the decision to sign another year's lease, but at a roomier one-story house in Bayside. *Another year in New York.*

She sincerely hoped that Zack knew that he was loved. She knew that despite the cold, hard demeanor her brother-in-law tried to project to other people, he was, on the inside, a fragile person who had endured a lifetime's worth of emotional trauma. He, like his sister, had refused to be broken. Although now it seemed he was in danger of that happening. She prayed that her and Derek's love would be sufficient to prevent it. Because without Jenny, without her gentle and loving presence, Miranda knew that Zack might, after all these years, break at any time.

* * *

"Was that your bro?" Jamar asked Zack after he had hung up. He was sitting in a chair with his back to Zack. Their friend

Tiffany was wrapping Jamar's thick strands of hair into tight braids. He would occasionally wince with pain and call over his shoulder, "Damn, girl, you pullin' too tight. Take it easy on my damn scalp." Returning his attention to Zack, he asked again, "That Derek?"

"Yeah, we're goin' to lunch on Sunday at that place our dad used to take him." Zack did not seem interested in taking the conversation any further than that.

Jamar snorted and chuckled. "And I noticed you didn't even blow up on his ass. You're makin' progress."

Jamar was not going to leave it alone. That was fine. Zack took a pull of his beer and said, "If I was you, I'd worry more about those gay braids you got hangin' off your head."

Tiffany turned toward Zack and arched an eyebrow. "Now, I know you ain't over there talkin' shit with that mangy-ass mop you got sittin' on top your head," she stated bluntly.

Everyone in the room laughed, including Zack. He loved having his friends over. It was great to just do nothing but sit around and drink. And they were all good at doing that. He was beginning to stagger with each step, and his speech was already slurred. He really wasn't a big drinker. In fact, his tolerance for alcohol was so low that he was often the object of ridicule from his friends when he got bombed too quickly. Derek would have worried about that, but it would have been for nothing. Zack only drank to be social. He had never turned up a bottle of liquor with the intent of forgetting about his problems. He drank with the sole purpose of having fun with his crew, and that alone was enough to temporarily make his problems go away.

Jamar addressed them all, "Look at Gatsby over here spillin' his drink. He's actually kickin' it with us." He gestured to Sam in the corner. "Pass that blunt to my man over there."

Zack could not help but laugh at hearing the nickname Jacqueline had given him. He was often referred to as the Great Gatsby when he had people over. He often took of during his own parties for long periods of time. On top of that, he was the only one in his group of friends who had his own place, so there were always randoms coming by, friends of friends, who had no idea who he was.

He grinned as he inhaled deeply on the blunt. Such little pleasures got him through each day. He was trying to hold onto this moment as his friends interacted. He looked at Jamar, who was wincing even harder now. "Tif, please, not so hard."

She used her long, purple fingernails to pull her own braided tresses out of her eyes. "If you'd hold still and stop makin' me laugh, it wouldn't hurt so much," Tiffany retorted. She turned to one of the other girls. "Hey, can we turn the music up?"

Two of the group picked up the coffee table and moved it to the side of the room. People began dancing. Zack took the initiative to turn up the stereo and then joined the others at the center of the room. Everyone was buzzed and having a good time. More people were getting up from their seats. Sam was answering the door for new arrivals. One by one they each crammed into the apartment.

Zack turned and fixed his glassy eyes on Jacqueline. She had sought him out through the crowd. Slim-figured and tan, she wore a yellow tank top over jean shorts and sandals. Her hair was dirty blonde with bright blonde streaks. She said nothing, but smiled and put her arms around his neck. The bass from the music bounced heavily of the walls as the two moved. Zack looked over the faces of the crowd. Moments like these, no matter how many of them he tried to cram into short increments of time, always seemed too few and far between. All he could do was try to have a good time.

Sam interrupted his fun by tapping him on the shoulder. "Yo, it's your neighbor across the hall." Zack peeled Jacqueline of him and went out into the hall to greet Ms. Goldcamp. He was hoping to keep this short and simple.

"How are you tonight, Ms. Goldcamp?" he asked with exaggerated politeness.

"Well, I'm not sure, Zack," she said in that condescending tone that always managed to get under his skin. Her voice was high pitched and nasally, and Zack always found it to be unbearably whiny. "I was actually wondering if you were planning on having one of your all night shindigs, because the bass from your music keeps me up all night and I have to get up at 6:00 am to go to work. I guess I wanted to know a little bit ahead of time whether or not I'll be calling the police tonight. I really don't know how they'd react to that cloud of marijuana smoke pouring out from under your door."

Zack bit his lower lip at her sarcasm. This was a woman who had 911 on speed-dial, and knew all too well what a cop would do after he came knocking on Zack's door. Rather than shy away from her threats, he put on a phony smile and said, "No need for you to call your friends in blue tonight, Ms.Goldcamp. We'll turn the music down, and keep our cigarette smokin' to a bare minimum."

He knew that she considered him a mere hoodlum, the bad apple of the family she had come to know over the years. If push came to shove, he would play the part. But for the moment, the subtler approach was the better one. She began to offer him some unwelcome advice as he turned away from her and closed the door.

"Who the hell was that?" Jamar asked.

"Ah, you know, just some Jehovah's Witnesses tryin' to convert and save me. I kicked their asses to the curb." Zack decided to call Ms. Goldcamp's bluff. He pointed to Sam and said, "Yo, turn that shit back up. Let's booze."

* * *

The police did not pay a visit that night. It was in part because everyone had drunk themselves into a stupor early and had lost their partying spirit when it had come time to pass out. At 2:15, the only people left were Zack, Jamar, and Jacqueline. The three were smoking a joint and trying to carry on a conversation. They appeared to be babbling, but the topic of their discussion was serious enough. They had been praising a local graffiti artist whose work they all admired when Jamar began telling them about some graffiti he had seen on the wall of a Chinese restaurant's bathroom earlier that day.

Jamar quoted what he had read: "We should gas every last one of those sand niggers for what they've done. It's us or them. Fuck the towel heads. Bomb them back to the Stone Age."

This was typical of the way one of their conversations took a turn after a long night of partying. For some reason, Zack and Jamar always had these serious discussions about life when they were the most intoxicated. Jacqueline did not join in the conversation. She simply contented herself by listening to what the other two had to say.

When Jamar had finished relaying the quote, he said, "We been fuckin' a lot of shit up over there. We got the Al-Qaedas on the run. We've pretty much taken control of the whole situation."

"Yeah," Zack said.

"I'm pretty sure we've smoked them all outta their caves and wiped 'em out."

"Yeah," Zack said.

"It's just too bad we're probably gonna end up takin' this thing too far and blowin' it up bigger than it had to be. It's like a damn gangster movie or something."

Jacqueline was now confused. She sat up a little straighter, and asked, "What does that mean?"

"It means," Jamar began, "that it's bad guys versus bad guys. Ain't no righteousness about it. We went over there and fucked up plenty of innocent lives to get revenge for what happened to us. Don't get me wrong; we did Afghanistan a favor by chasin' off the Al-Qaedas. The Taliban shoulda never harbored them in the first place. The Taliban used to be legit. Now they both fucked.

"But us? We acted first and asked questions later. Who knows how many people died in the crossfire? I'm just sayin' I don't trust the military to do the right thing. The media will keep tellin' us what we want to hear, lettin' us know what *they* want us to know."

Zack sat in silence and listened to Jamar's ranting. He agreed with some of what Jamar said. He disagreed with a lot of it though. He knew Jamar was intelligent, despite what his high school GPA said. But Jamar was far too opinionated. He always had all the answers and asked too few questions. Zack was often the same way, but at least he could admit that to himself. He did not mind being obstinate. It was part of who he was. Zack agreed with Jamar about the country's current situation being like a gangster film. In Zack's opinion, too, America was the bad guy.

Al-Qaeda had been the ones responsible for his sister's death. He had never seen or heard anything about them before 9/11, and now it seemed they no longer posed a threat. Zack's rage regarding

these faceless killers was boundless, but it seemed as though the problem they'd represented was now under control. His sister's killers were either dead or on the run. They would pay with their blood if they hadn't yet. But they were only half of the problem.

Zack had dark feelings he could not put into words toward his own government. It had been the military that had angered the men who would later become terrorists. He imagined some aspect of the country's foreign policy had not fallen in place with the ideals of an Islamic faction. He had never even heard of Osama Bin Laden before the attacks, and now he was public enemy number one. How could the government have something like this happen? The World Trade Center had first been bombed in 1993. How was this not a wake-up call to the whole country? The government shrugged it off as if it was of no consequence. They had not taken the threat seriously enough in his opinion, despite their military might and intelligence capacity. An attack on the same place ten years later was successful. This, to him, was deplorable.

Through most of his life, the government had kept his family on its toes, always making life difficult for his mother or sister, always trying to take away what was theirs. The way he saw it, they should have spent more of their time uncovering terrorists who were living among them than badgering him and his family.

He was more confused on the matter than he would admit. On the one hand, he had untapped and seemingly limitless rage toward strange people from a strange land whom he'd never meet face to face. On the other hand, he had unchanneled rage toward his own government for being blinded by its own arrogance. Strangely, these feelings seemed to cancel one another out, bringing him into an unhealthy sort of balance.

Derek wouldn't understand his feelings. He would say that Zack was anti-establishment, unpatriotic. Zack had been getting into trouble with authority his whole life, and Derek would consider Zack's feelings merely to be part of his refractory nature. He would say to Zack that America is proof of a society that truly works, and that now more than ever it was a time for all Americans to stand together. Well, the way Zack saw it, his sister and her husband had been the victims of someone else's war. They had paid the price for their leaders' mistakes. He would not stand behind the nation's leaders now, and he would *never* fight for this country, at home or abroad. He would let them fight it out themselves. The down side to that was that he was left with little to believe in.

As if reading Zack's thoughts, Jamar put his empty beer bottle on the coffee table and looked up at Zack. "So, tell me, what you gonna do when you twenty-five and this whole thing has turned into a full-scale war? What you gonna do when they come knockin' on your door tryin' to enlist your ass? Cause I can tell you my black ass is gonna be up in British Columbia, hidin'." Jamar was grinning, but Zack knew the question had been serious. Jamar wanted to know if Zack was willing to put aside the differences he had with a government he so often despised to stop those who represented the individuals who had taken his sister from him.

Zack was through tackling life's biggest issues for the evening. He shrugged and said, "They can knock on the damn door all they want, cause I'll be up in BC with you, snowboardin' and drinkin' twenty-twos of Labatt's."

"Ha-Ha!" Jamar laughed as he clasped hands with Zack. "Damn right!"

Jacqueline chuckled and Zack shook his head and held his goofy looking grin. He picked up a smoking roach and handed it over to Jamar. "Just hit this."

"No, I gotta roll," Jamar said excitedly as he rubbed his hands together. "I'm gonna head down the street and wake me up some trim."

More laughing came from Zack and Jacqueline. Zack said, "Alright, man, be safe. Say hi to Tanya for me."

"Me, too," Jacqueline said as she leaned over to hug Jamar.

"Late." Jamar grabbed his skateboard and headed for the door. Jacqueline leaned back into the sofa and turned to Zack. After a few moments, she began stroking the back of his neck. He knew what was in store for him. He just wished that their relationship had not gotten so weird.

Jacqueline had been his first love. He'd lost his virginity to her when he was sixteen. They'd been close friends for two years prior. He was fairly certain that he'd been her first sexual experience as well, but it hadn't been long after the two had consummated their relationship that she had become promiscuous with some of the other boys in their circle of friends. He'd hated hearing thirdhand about those whom had been with her. He and she had remained close friends through it all, and sometimes they even talked about it. Mostly, it had been awkward. He just wished that events had unfolded differently.

Only after he'd lost Jenny had Jacqueline started coming by more often. He really didn't remember when exactly it was that she'd resumed being there for him in *every* way. He could only guess at her reasons. Even though the sex was great, the whole situation made him uncomfortable. This was why it always felt weird now.

She began to kiss his face and neck. "Do you want me to stay tonight?" she asked softly. Her breath felt warm and good on his cheek.

He put his forehead to hers so that their noses were touching. "What am I gonna do, say no?"

Tilting her head to the side, she smiled and leaned into him. She kissed him softly for a long time, then got up from the couch and walked into his bedroom. She left the door slightly ajar.

Zack sighed as he laid his head back on the sofa cushion. He spent the next few minutes smoking the roach and staring up at the ceiling. These parties always made him feel better. Everything would be different when he and Jamar moved to Brooklyn, but they would still throw down. He needed to. He needed his friends. The love and support they gave him provided him with the strength he needed to carry on. He thought about how he'd been able to keep the cold away for some time now, and hoped that his present mood would last. He knew he'd be in an even better mood in a few minutes. For the moment he was content. He was calm, at peace. This was rare. It was also most welcome. He thought ahead to the lunch he'd be having on Sunday with his brother and hoped that Derek wouldn't do anything to foul up his good feeling.

CHAPTER 4
APRIL 2, 2002

Russell McCrady met Sally Lawson in 1967 when they were both twenty-two years old. They met at JFK Airport when embarking on a journey to Morocco. Upon meeting her, he couldn't hide the awe that he felt that such a breathtakingly beautiful woman, who was as charming as she was lovely, was about to join him on a trip that would consume the next two years of his life. She couldn't believe that a man could so easily and perfectly intertwine such a wonderful sense of humor with such a fierce intelligence. They'd enjoyed one another's company for the duration of the long flight. By the end of the flight, they were holding hands. During layovers, she would sleep with her head on his shoulder. Nothing like it had ever happened to them so fast before, and it was as scary for the both of them as it was wonderful. Remarkably, it was a love neither of them had been looking for. He had recently had his heart broken when his previous girlfriend had left him, and she too had been deeply hurt when her ex-lover had proved to be unfaithful. Neither of them had been ready to enter into a new relationship, but it wasn't long after their arrival in Casablanca that they acknowledged their love for one another.

From there the relationship prospered. They spent two years participating in numerous community service projects that helped to improve the quality of life for the citizens of several remote areas in Morocco. Their love grew, and at the end of the two-year period, on their last night together in a foreign land, Russell proposed to Sally. He'd previously written to her parents, who resided in Hoboken, New Jersey, asking for her father's permission to propose to Sally. Russell was not only granted permission, but he was sent a diamond engagement ring that had been in her family for generations and was being kept for such an event. Sally, deeply impressed by his chivalric behavior in contacting her parents, had tearfully accepted his proposal.

By the time they had returned to the states, they were both twenty-four and ready to return to life in America as they had remembered it. He was a graduate of NYU, with a degree in pre-med. She was a graduate of Hunter and had a degree in business. They were married in the spring of 1969. Sally was two months pregnant at the time. They began their new lives together living in a tiny apartment in the city's Upper West Side. He had taken out loans sufficient to attend medical school at Columbia University, and she began work as an advertising representative. Jennifer was born in November of that year. The birth of their daughter managed to lift their relationship to a new level that both previously would have thought impossible.

The year 1973 was a good one for the small family. It was not only the year that Russell finished medical school, but it was also the year their second child was born, a baby boy they named Derek. Russell opened a successful office downtown where he began to practice pediatric medicine, and Sally had already proven herself a valuable asset to her company. They purchased a two-story house in Queens, and for the next ten years the four of them lived contented and comfortable lives.

Russell's practice continued to prosper. He was a respected physician. Sally and Russell hired a nanny to take care of Jenny when they were both at work, but after Derek was born she and Russell decided that his practice had grown to the point where it was financially feasible for her to remain at home and raise their children. Sally's heart and soul had been in her work, but her passion for her profession was not enough to overcome her need to be there to raise her children. Russell knew how much her work had meant to her, and her sacrifice for her children strengthened his love for her. She was a wonderful mother, and Jennifer and Derek's best qualities reflected her care. Russell had been there for his children as well, but constantly returning home from fourteen-hour workdays had always kept him from being with them as often as he would have liked. It was a regret he felt he could do nothing about. So they had wonderful weekend getaways skiing up in Vermont or enjoying the beaches on Long Island. Once a year, the family would take a cruise to somewhere interesting and relaxing. It had been a grand era for the McCrady family.

The year 1983 was a bad one for the family. It was a year when disaster struck. There was much about the event that neither Jennifer nor Derek would ever understand fully, but it had begun when Russell had taken a weekend to go skiing in Stowe, Vermont, with some old friends from NYU. Sally had just announced a few days earlier that she was pregnant once again, and she was going to spend the weekend shopping with the kids. He considered canceling the trip in light of the news, but she told him not to be silly, to go have fun with his friends, and to be ready to go shopping for the baby when he returned.

He never did return. That weekend, he had gotten separated from his friends on the slopes. He had lost control and hit a tree head on. He was dead when the ski-patrol found him.

Sally had needed to search deep within herself to find the strength to go on alone, a strength she feared she might not possess. The idea of bringing a posthumous child into the world terrified her, but she found strength when she looked down at her swollen belly. She feared that if she were to let depression claim her, it would have terrible repercussions for her unborn son. In the long, hard search to find this power to endure the pain, she found it in Jennifer and Derek, who had been trying to be strong for their mother from the moment the tragedy struck. With their love, the family had successfully managed to cope with the loss. But Russell's passing only marked the beginning of the family's troubles.

Russell had not been dead for two months before the lawsuit struck. At the time, it had seemed unthinkable that it could happen, but Sally was presented with allegations of malpractice on Russell's part. She would never get the whole story from Morgan Hutton, Russell's friend from NYU, who was the family's lawyer for years. Apparently, Russell, along with fourteen other doctors in the New York City area, was facing a class-action malpractice suit on the grounds that certain prescriptions he had recently written for a drug new to the market hadn't officially been approved by the Food and Drug Administration. After the prescriptions were written, the medicines were delivered straight from the pharmaceutical lab to the patients' homes. Dangerous side effects from these medicines had developed, and the families of the patients had been outraged. The whole court case quickly created a media frenzy and was regarded by the public as an appalling scandal.

Sally did not know what had truly transpired among her husband, his patients, and his colleagues. She would never know; she didn't want to know. She would have stood by her husband even if he'd made such a mistake. But her gut instinct, combined with what little information Morgan had been able to provide her with, brought her to the conclusion that Russell and the thirteen other physicians had somehow been deceived by the pharmaceutical company, and had been duped into prescribing medicine that was not truly ready for public consumption. In the end, the court had favored the plaintiffs. The pharmaceutical company, as well as the physicians, had been held accountable. Sally spent the months leading up to Zack's birth with stress eating away at her, while Morgan did what he was able to from his office.

Over 85 percent of Russell's life insurance money went toward the lawsuit. Payments on the house could not continue. By the time Zack was born, she and the kids were renting an apartment not far from where she and Russell had started out together. Jenny was now fourteen. Derek was ten. Times had been hard for all of them, but there was still love and mutual support in their lives. Sally couldn't believe how tough her kids were. She could barely keep it together herself. She got her job back at the ad agency. Care for Zack was provided by her mother, Russell's mother, and Jenny. The whole ordeal had worn

Sally's spirits thin, and carefree days for her were rare, but life went on.

In 1993, Zack was ten. The apartment he lived in with his mother was far less cramped than it once had been, for his siblings had moved out. Jenny went of to Fordham in 1987, and graduated four years later with a degree in business. She lived with three other girls in a Soho loft. She found a job as a technical underwriter for Metropolitan Insurance, and was doing well for herself. Derek was twenty and was finishing up his sophomore year at Hofstra, with a major in education. When Russell's mother had passed on two years earlier, the insurance money the family had inherited was put toward Sally's children's educations. She also bought the apartment she and Zack lived in. The problems of the past were left behind. They seemed distant. But then Sally was diagnosed with cancer.

The doctor found a malignant brain tumor in Sally. Treatments began immediately, but there was little hope. Metastasis had begun. Her health insurance was barely sufficient to cover the hospital bills. There was little her family could do. Russell's mother was dead, and there was no one else on that side of the family to provide support. Her own parents had previously secured a second mortgage on their house to pay her brother's lawyer fees for a brush with the law.

Before the year was out, Sally was confined to a hospital bed, with death a nearby inevitability. She looked so withered and pale in her final days, so unlike the beautiful woman who had once moved with the grace of a dancer. Her bright and beautiful smile was the only remaining testament to the woman she had once been. She smiled at her children on the night of her death, holding their hands and whispering to them. She told them always to look out for one another, and that they needed to stand together. They had listened to her say there were no guarantees in life other than the unconditional love of family. She assured them that with this love, even a deathbed could not diminish the happiness she felt. She felt fortunate to be able to tell them this before she passed on. Not many people were lucky enough to say good-bye to the ones they loved. That night Sally fell into a sleep from which she never awakened. Except for her emotionally exhausted parents, Sally's three children were alone in the world. Jenny and Derek had already fully matured into adults. Zack, however, was left on a long road to maturity, one he would have to travel without a mother and father, and with all the bitterness of a confused, pre-adolescent child.

Derek reflected on those difficult times as he sat waiting for Zack to arrive at McSorley's. The McCrady family struggle had been long and hard, but he had never really considered before how much harder it must have been for his young brother. Although Zack had never met their father, had not experienced the pain of the loss, Derek realized that the absence from the beginning may have been just as painful. The only father figure Zack had ever had was Morgan, and Morgan had a mysterious falling out with the family some time ago. Zack had never experienced the good times that Derek and Jenny had early on. In fact, Zack's earliest memories were probably of a mother with too much of a burden to carry, who made ends meet at the expense of her own happiness. The stress that their mother had tried to hide from them for so long had definitely not gone unnoticed. There were always financial difficulties to be dealt with, and little Zack never really understood what it was that kept his mother fighting to keep her composure on a daily basis. Derek knew how much Zack mistrusted the government, and all authority for that matter. He decided that Zack's feelings stemmed from his childhood. From the time Zack was born, he had somehow known without an adult's understanding of how the world works that those in authority had caused problems for his mother, looking to take her for all she was worth. It hurt Derek to think of his brother standing by, powerless to relieve his mother from her pain, and never really comprehending why people were always causing such trouble for his family. Were the McCradys not good people? Their mother had worked so hard; why had their troubles kept piling up?

As Derek imagined walking in Zack's shoes, it enlightened and disturbed him at the same time. It enlightened him because he suddenly began to know his brother in a way he had never known before. It disturbed him because although he could relate on some level, he knew that Zack was on a self-destructive path and needed to be swayed by whatever means possible. The situation was a delicate one, and it needed to be treated as such. Jenny's passing had pushed Zack too far away. Derek knew what a fragile state Zack was in; he too had experienced the tragedy. But Zack's whole take on the situation was troubling.

Zack was into drugs. That was something Derek was sure of, and that deadbeat friend of Zack's, Jamar, was liable to get them both thrown in jail. He was contemplating how to address these matters when his waitress approached. "You wanna go ahead and order, hon, or do ya wanna keep waiting for your friend?"

"No, I guess I'll just wait. Maybe—oh wait, here he comes." Derek grinned as his brother stepped through the doorway. At that moment, as they made eye contact, they were just brothers, neither of them plagued by problems or years of loss. Zack sat down at the table and put his backpack on the sawdust-laden floor.

"What's up?" he asked Derek with a grin of his own.

"Not a whole lot," he replied turning back to the waitress. "Bring my brother a dark beer, and I'll have another, too."

Zack's grin widened. He was amused that Derek was going out on a limb to get him a beer, however small the gesture seemed to him. He reached into his shirt pocket and withdrew a photograph. It was a picture of Bella from when she was a puppy.

"I found this when I was cleanin' up the other day," Zack said, handing it over. "Look how cute she looks." Derek took it from him and nodded with appreciation.

"Thanks. Miranda always complains that I never took enough puppy pictures of her." Derek was always grateful for whatever small amount of bonding they could have together. This was a good start. The waitress returned with four beers on a tray and placed them on the table.

"You ready to order?" she asked as she brought out her pen and pad.

"Just bring us two liverwurst sandwiches on rye with chips. That should be good. Thanks," he said as she retreated.

"What the hell?" Zack gaped at Derek.

"Trust me, you're gonna love it," was Derek's reply. "That's all Dad and I ever got here."

Zack took a look around the aged, memento-laden room. "This place is kind of a dive, huh?" Zack said as if not too impressed.

Derek wished that Zack would make more of an effort to appreciate a tradition that their father had tried to create with him.

"I know you know about this place. It's the oldest pub in New York, and we're lucky that there's not a line out the door to get in here," Derek countered.

"Do they always bring you two beers when you order one?"

"Yeah, it's some kind of weird custom they have here. And they only have one light and one dark beer. It's good beer though." He raised his glass to toast Zack. "To Sunday."

"Cheers," Zack said as he touched glasses with Derek. "So, Dad used to bring you here a lot, huh?'

"Yeah, but I was too young to drink. We came for the food. So you'd better like your sandwich, because you're an heir to the tradition." Changing the subject, he asked, "So how's work?"

"Work's work," he muttered. "I'm tired of dealin' with assholes." He looked as if he was thinking about something else. There was a long, awkward silence as Zack continued to stare of to the corners of the bar, as if he wanted to be alone with his thoughts. His eyes fixed on something, and his gaze became fixed.

"So, Zack," Derek proceeded to break the silence, "let's talk about how you're gonna get on with your life."

Zack continued to stare at whatever it was that held his interest, but shook his head as if he now understood some sad truth. "Okay, here we go. All small talk bullshit is over with. Time to tackle the bigger issues," Zack said, sounding like a game show host.

Derek glared at him. "Look, first of all, talkin' about our father is *never* small talk bullshit. Second of all, just what the hell reason do you think I need for invitin' you here? We hardly ever talk anymore. I'm your brother, Zack, and aside from Grandma and Grandpa, I'm all you've got. We need to talk about this."

"What's to talk about?" Zack's eyes did not move from where they were fixed. "We both know I'm not goin' to school anytime soon. You and Miranda are being really foolish if your only reason for hangin' around here is because of me. Jamar and I will be livin' in Brooklyn soon, and assumin' the whole country doesn't get nuked in the next few years, I'll continue to work and make money." Derek saw Zack's hand go up to his mouth as he popped some kind of pill into it. Derek's fears had proven justified. Zack had become agitated, and now he was popping pills. Derek didn't know whether Zack had done this intentionally to spite him, or if it had been an unconscious action in response to stress. Either possibility bothered him.

He was even more upset by Zack's rudeness and refusal to face him. He leaned over the table to get a better view of what Zack was staring at. What he saw was a pregnant woman, laughing with her friends and drinking water instead of beer for the sake of her baby. Zack's jaw was clenched tightly. Was it this sight that was bothering him so much, and if so, why? Why didn't he just look away?

"Zack, what is it?'

"Jenny…," he managed to spill out, his voice scratchy.

"Jenny what?" Derek was at a loss to explain what was going on. Zack had never seemed so far gone. What was previously apprehension in Derek now turned to fear for his brother. He did not know whether he would be able to help Zack. The situation seemed to deteriorate every time the two spoke. He needed his wife here to back him up. He felt like he was in over his head.

Zack finally returned to his brother. He now looked determined. He tried to keep his voice from cracking as he opened his mouth to speak.

"Look, Derek, I know someone like you would say that everything happens for a reason. So, if you really believe that, then consider this: maybe we weren't meant to live the lives Mom and Dad had intended for us. Maybe all this crazy shit that's happened to us was for a reason. Maybe you and I were meant to walk our own separate paths through life, alone. Maybe we'll both find what we're looking for when we stop screwin' up each other's lives. I've lived by myself in that apartment for two years now. I know how much you hate New York, so please, do us both a favor and just leave. Please leave. I'm tired of feelin' like someone else's baggage." Zack had never looked so sincere.

Derek softened up a little. "I'm sorry, but I can't do that until I know you're okay. I'm not even convinced that you're emotionally stable. We promised Mom that we'd watch out for each other, and I intend to keep that promise. In fact, there's someone I know through Morgan that you might be able to talk to. He might be able to really help you."

Zack's eyes had widened with the suggestion that he might be unstable, and he flinched at the mention of Morgan's name. He appeared pained.

"Wow, Derek, to think that you know me so little after all this time, it just..." He paused as if to consider what to say next, but the waitress saved him the trouble.

"Food's here," she interjected as she set it down. "Let me know if you need anything."

"That was fast. Thanks, we will." Derek looked straight at his brother, but Zack wouldn't face him. It was characteristic of Zack to just up and leave at such a moment, so Derek was glad that he had not chased his brother off yet.

"Zack, I—"

"Forget it."

"No, listen—"

"I said to forget it," Zack growled. It was obvious he did not want to be challenged. He proceeded to wolf down his food without pause, as if to create an excuse for the silence between them. He was finished in less than three minutes. As soon as he was done, he stood up and put on his backpack.

"You were right, the liverwurst here is pretty good," he offered with little enthusiasm. "Thanks for lunch. I'll talk to you soon. I gotta go."

"Zack, wait."

"I gotta go." And with that, he was out the door. Derek had lost another squabble with his kid brother without realizing when or how exactly the conversation had gone off in the wrong direction. He turned his head to look back over at the pregnant woman, laughing up a storm with her friends without the aid of a beer buzz. He did not know what it was about this woman that had bothered Zack so much, but he was convinced that it was something that Zack was keeping secret from him. He hoped to God Zack hadn't knocked up that Jacqueline girl he'd started running with again.

He sighed. If this sight had moved his brother in such a way, then it was definitely not something that he should be left in the dark about. He supposed it was possible that Zack might one day share his thoughts with him. He sincerely doubted it, though. Zack was better at putting up walls than breaking them down.

It dawned on Derek that Zack probably confided more in Jamar than in him. The more he thought about it, the more it made sense. This bothered him. He was more concerned now. If he didn't take appropriate action soon, he wouldn't just fail Zack, but he'd fail his mother as well. He ran his hands through his sandy blond hair, a gesture that usually meant he had a lot to consider in a short amount of time. Zack had suggested that they were both following separate paths. Maybe it was supposed to be Derek's path to watch out for his kid brother, even if it meant sacrificing his own plans.

CHAPTER 5
APRIL 4, 2002

It was a dark, dreary Tuesday, and after finishing his deliveries all Zack wanted to do was go home, get high, and watch a DVD. Before he reached the apartment, he stopped by the corner store to get some snacks. He grabbed a bag of Doritos and a two-liter bottle of Coke. He'd stuffed some candy into his pockets, but it wasn't really stealing if you paid for half of it. When he got to the counter he started counting out change. He waited for about twenty seconds before he realized the clerk hadn't yet acknowledged him.

The clerk was someone Zack knew. He was of medium height and build, with a swarthy complexion, bushy hair, and a long goatee. Zack had gone to high school with this person. He remembered him as being somewhat intelligent, but nowhere near friendly. He always gave Zack dirty looks when he came in. He was a jerk in Zack's book.

Zack didn't know if this guy, whose name he remembered was Mo, was related to the owner. Although the owner barely spoke a lick of English, he'd been running the store for as long as Zack had been coming here.

At the moment, neither Mo nor the owner was paying the least bit of attention to Zack. They were watching the television behind the counter, and it seemed as though they were having some kind of argument. Zack craned his neck to see what they were watching: more news from the Middle East, more reporters, more mass arrests.

Zack couldn't understand the dialogue between the two men. It was in their mother tongue, whatever the hell that might have been. If he had to venture a guess, he'd say that they appeared to agree on a larger topic, but were in disagreement over some minor details. He could feel the anger rolling off of them.

Mo's hands waved wildly as he gestured toward the screen, his voice rising with each word. The owner shook his head, spat something Zack couldn't understand, and crossed his arms over his chest. They both looked utterly disgusted.

Zack didn't have all day. He slapped his hand on the counter. Both men turned their attention to him.

Zack held his palms up. "Can I get this stuff today?" he asked. He'd tried not to sound too much like a smart-ass, but sometimes it just came out of him.

Mo's response was not what Zack expected. "I'm going to make you a deal," he said, his voice heavily accented. "You can leave today without paying for the candy and cigarette lighters and whatever else you stuffed into your pockets. You can even take the chips and soda if you want. But don't ever let me see you in my uncle's store again."

"What?" Zack asked, caught of guard.

"Don't think I don't remember you," Mo said. "We were in school together. I remember what a slippery little degenerate you are."

"Hey, who the fuck do you think you're talkin' to?"

"Is it because of who we are? Because of where we're from, maybe? Is that what gives you this sense of entitlement?"

"You'd better watch your goddamned mouth! You're way out of line!" Zack was taken aback. Mo had read too much into Zack's petty thievery. But now Zack was pissed that this was the conclusion he'd come to. "If I have somethin' to say to you, I'll say it. I don't need to steal your shit to prove a point."

"That sounds like an admission to me," Mo said.

"I don't give a shit what it sounds like to you," Zack said. Still, he wasn't about to empty his pockets.

"Look, we have you on tape. Just get out."

Zack turned to go. He was secretly admitting defeat. He was willing to let it go, but what Mo said next got him really steamed. "That's a nice bike you've got," he said. "I used to have one just like it, until a rotten bigot just like you stole it. Maybe I'll follow his example and get myself a new one."

Mo's uncle said something to try and calm him down and diffuse the situation. But no one was there to calm Zack down.

"You motherfucker!" he shouted. "I wanna know who's responsible for lettin' you ungrateful pricks move here. I wanna know who made the decision to let you stay here. You wanna have your cake and eat it too, huh?" Zack pointed out the window. "If you don't like it here, the airport's that way!"

"I'm calling the cops," Mo said calmly, looking at his uncle but speaking in English.

"Fuck you, and fuck your store," Zack said. He left the Coke and Doritos and slammed through the door.

He was watching the store as he unlocked his bike. He half expected Mo to come out after him. He'd be ready for him if he did.

Zack was tall and lanky, with a ropy musculature. He'd been in many a fight, and he never took any crap from anyone. It didn't matter how big or tough Mo seemed. If push ever came to shove, he'd knock him flat on his ass.

He got on the bike and took off. Remembering that he'd been trying to relax and unwind before he'd gotten all fired up, he took a Xanax out of his pocket and popped it into his mouth. He hurried home. He was eager to lie on the couch.

*   *   *

When Jenny had been declared Zack's legal guardian after a long custody battle with the state of New York, she had been as tired as her mother had been after dealing with the malpractice suit years earlier. The state was either going to send Zack to live with his grandparents, who could hardly handle the responsibility, or place him in the care of foster parents. Morgan's legal fees, despite the discount he gave Zack's family, were always steep. It had cost Jenny a pretty penny to keep Zack under her care.

In the end they'd won. Morgan's efforts and their money had paid off. Jenny was forever indebted to Morgan, wondering how Morgan could work so many miracles in so many different fields of law.

Zack had never been able to see past the legal fees, though. He knew money made the world go round, but he'd always suspected Morgan had somehow taken them for a ride. It had been such a ridiculous dispute to begin with. It just didn't add up.

After their mother's death, Jenny bid farewell to her life in Soho and moved back into the apartment with Zack. She stayed there for another six years. Then in 1999, she told Zack that Peter had proposed, and that they were to be married that spring. She conveyed to her brother that the losses their family had suffered had taken their toll, but in light of hard times the tragedy had bred three tough survivors. They'd learned to fend for themselves.

This was why, in order for Zack to do some growing up, she was going to let him continue to live in the apartment by himself. It could teach him independence and responsibility. Their childhoods had all been cut abruptly short, Zack's more than Jenny's or Derek's, and that was a fact they'd just have to accept. Life went on.

Derek had been against the idea from the beginning. That was to be expected. But Jenny was the leader when it came to family affairs, and she outranked him and had overruled him. She'd told Derek that Zack needed his freedom, and although it required a great leap of faith concerning their younger brother, it would be a positive experience for him and would help him mature.

Lounging on the couch now, watching a Fugazi video, Zack wondered if he'd done right by his sister. He stared at his entertainment center. Every component of it was the best that money could buy. He thought about where the money had come from, and admitted to himself that she wouldn't have approved.

Derek had definitely disapproved. He'd been suspicious of Zack's new electronics the last time he'd been over, and had voiced his suspicions candidly. Zack had dodged his questions.

Despite what Jenny might have thought Zack couldn't change the way everything had turned out. He'd achieved success through the only means available to him at the time, and he was good at what he did. Not that it required a great deal of skill.

He was in the middle of taking a bong hit when someone knocked on the door. The noise was too soft for it to be one of his friends. Spraying some aerosol into the air, he peeled himself of the couch and shuffled to the door.

"Who is it?" he inquired through the thick wood.

"It's Nomar, Zack," came a voice with an accent similar to Mo's, but not quite as thick.

Zack turned the deadbolt and opened the door. Nomar was as tall as Zack, but of a slightly thicker build. He always struck Zack as rather scholarly with his round glasses, Polo sweaters, and khakis— not to mention that he was soft spoken and mild mannered. At the moment his hands held a baking pan covered with foil.

"What's this?" Zack asked.

"This is raisin bread pudding that Aunt Rabia has made for you," Nomar said, presenting the pan to Zack. He was smiling warmly. "She once shared the recipe with your mother. She knows how much you enjoyed it."

Zack took the pan in his hands and inhaled the aroma of fragrant spices.

"Aunt Rabia is getting on in her old age, but you were in her thoughts, so she made this for you. It's something of a parting gift. We know that you'll be moving out of here fairly soon. You and your family have been good neighbors to my aunt over the years, and she wants you to know that you'll be missed."

Zack hid his skepticism. Aunt Rabia was in her late eighties. He'd been convinced that all she could do was sit on her balcony and stare off into space. And now she was making bread pudding? Nomar must've had a hand in helping. After all, helping her was what he was there for.

"I know I've only known you for a few years, but I feel the same way," Nomar added.

Zack was beginning to feel bad about what he'd said in the corner store. Rabia Pezeshk had always been a warm, caring person who had strange observations that made Zack laugh. She'd come here from Pakistan and had been living upstairs across the hall since his family had first moved in. Nomar had only moved into the building a year or two ago when he'd replaced Mrs. Pezeshk's live-in nurse. Zack had been convinced she was senile. Maybe Nomar had made the pudding himself.

They were both good people, the Pezeshks, and Zack was momentarily ashamed of his earlier remarks. He'd only said what he had to get under Mo's skin. He hadn't really meant them. Or had he? Racism wasn't as black and white an issue as a lot of people liked to believe.

Now he tried to act like the man Jenny had wanted him to be. "Thanks a lot, Nomar. You've both been great neighbors, too. I've got a lot of great memories tied up in this place. It's gonna be really hard to finally say good-bye."

"If you need anything between now and then, don't hesitate to knock on the door," Nomar said. "We're here for you."

"I really appreciate that," Zack said sincerely.

"And," Nomar said, leaning forward and lowering his voice to a conspiratorial tone, "don't worry too much about Ms. Goldcamp over there. After all, what would she do with herself if she didn't find time to pester her neighbors?" A wide smile formed on his face.

Zack chuckled. "All right then, Nomar. You have a great day. Please thank your aunt for me." He closed the door and went to put the pan on the kitchen table. He didn't know when he'd get around to eating the pudding, but he was grateful for the gift.

It was good to know that although a lot of people thought he was a jerk, there were still those who held him in high esteem.

As he sat down and hit the play button he considered his outburst in the corner store earlier. He decided that he hadn't really meant what he'd said. If he had, and America had closed its doors, then he never would have had the pleasure of knowing two such decent people as Mrs. Pezeshk and her nephew Nomar. It was people like that who helped him get through each day.

* * *

"Mr. Hutton, there's someone here to see you," called Morgan Hutton's secretary over the intercom. He checked his appointments. There was none scheduled for this time.

"Well, who is it?" he asked with some trepidation.

"He says his name's Jamar Neil," she said, a note of discomfort hinted at in her voice. "I know he doesn't have an appointment, but he's saying that you should definitely see him now. Should I tell him to come back after he's made an appointment?"

Morgan closed his eyes and clenched his fists. What rotten timing this was. The thought of having to meet with this worthless, do-nothing delinquent made him seethe with anger. "No, it's all right, Tracy. I'll see him. Just send him in." He sat up in his chair, straightening his tie and pushing back the part in his graying brown hair.

When Jamar arrogantly swaggered into the office with his baggy clothing and smug grin, Morgan turned away to look out the window. It galled him to allow this person into his presence, but Morgan had to. It was a serious game they were playing. That didn't change the fact that it humiliated him to be bullied by this delinquent. Morgan leaned over, resting his elbows on his polished walnut desk with his hands folded. Try as he might to use his own impressive physique to exercise control over the conversation, it was a wasted effort. The hoodlum had grown a great deal in his eighteen years. He would not be physically intimidated.

"What's up, Perry Mason?" Jamar called from across the office as if they were long time friends. "How's your day goin'?" He plopped down in a chair near Morgan's desk. "Must've been real busy. Zack ain't heard from you in like a week." Jamar laid it on thick, as if truly sympathetic about Morgan's demanding schedule.

"What do you want?" Morgan asked flatly. He didn't turn to face Jamar.

"For you to stop askin' stupid fuckin' questions and give us those signed papers," Jamar threw back at Morgan. He had gone dead serious in a split second. "You need to quit fuckin' around and hand them over. You think we're bluffin', but we ain't. You've seen the tape. The move's happenin' real soon, and we need to know that everythin's in order. So...?" he trailed of, rolling his right hand to coax the proper response without having to pry it out of Morgan.

"What if I can't?" Morgan said, turning to Jamar with exasperation written all over his face. "It's not like I can do it directly. Not to mention this is all coming out of my pocket."

Jamar could see how desperate Morgan was, but he simply held up a video cassette for Morgan to see. "Then a certain someone's gonna get a private screenin' of our movie," he said, nodding toward the framed picture of Morgan's family on his desk. He stood up, placing a fist on each side of the photo and leaning over. His deep voice lowered. "Don't think for a second that we'll hesitate to expose you, scumbag."

"Please," Morgan said, trying to control his breathing. He massaged his forehead with his fingertips. "Just give me a couple of more days. I'll make it happen."

Jamar took no pity on the man in front of him. He shook his head with amusement. "Sure, hotshot. A coupla more days. Me and Zack, we know what wonders you can work when the money's right. You just make sure that money come's outta your bank account." He turned to leave. "We'll be seein' you, Morgan. Two days." He opened the office door. "Your secretary is one fine piece of ass, by the way."

A small gasp from outside told Morgan that Tracy had heard this. The kid was belittling Morgan, showing him who was in charge of the situation.

When Jamar was gone, Morgan got up and went over to the bar in his office. Reaching into the liquor cabinet, he withdrew a rocks glass and a bottle of Jack Daniels. He dropped ice into the glass and poured himself a drink. His actions were hurried, and he nearly choked on his whiskey as it passed down his throat. He leaned heavily on the cabinet.

Russell had been his best friend in college. Morgan thought of himself as an accomplished attorney and had done everything in his power to help Russell's family at their darkest hour. And yes, it took money to get the system moving along, and it had cost money to help Sally and her kids. But he'd done what he could. He'd done right by them, hadn't he? Is this how he was to be repaid, with Zack's treachery and blackmail?

One question kept going through his mind over and over as he tried to hold down his whiskey: How could my best friend, whom I loved like a brother, have spawned such a wretched and manipulative son?

CHAPTER 6
APRIL 6, 2002

"So am I going to be able to avoid incurring your trademark wrath if I ask you some questions that might make you a little uncomfortable?" Hannah Shearer asked Zack on a Thursday afternoon in her office. School was out for the day, which was just as well since Zack was no longer a student here. He was glad he'd taken the time to come speak with his former guidance counselor, and even happier that it had been she who'd requested this meeting. He hadn't realized he'd grown on her so.

"I think you're one of the few people who probably could avoid it," Zack answered. "Seems like these days everyone wants to talk with me, ask me questions, prod me for answers."

"Don't you think it's because they care?" she asked him.

"Sure. Y'know, contrary to what a lot of people believe, I don't mind talking about it. But people seem to come at me with these preliminary pleasantries. It really drives me crazy, and I don't know why."

"It's not easy to talk about, Zack. It must be emotionally exhausting."

"I just wish everyone knew how to cut through all the bullshit like you do," Zack said.

He looked back across the gray metal desk at her. She had a knowing look on her face. But she didn't really know him. Not completely. Their professional relationship while he'd been in high school had been brief. But he had to hand it to her; she'd shown him she really cared. She cared for all the students she advised, but obviously she recognized that Zack's was a unique case, and she had gone to considerable lengths to reach out to him.

All the boys at school had known Ms. Shearer. She was a petite, twenty-something woman with long golden hair and an olive complexion. She always looked her best—both professional and sexy at the same time. Her hair was done up nicely, her makeup applied perfectly yet sparingly, and her fingernails perfectly manicured.

You could tell *anything* to Ms. Shearer. She never passed judgment and always let you know that you had her support. This was a post-graduation catch-up session, strictly of the record, and it was the first time they'd spoken in person since the tragedy.

She'd broached the subject, and for once he felt at ease about it. He suspected he might even feel a bit relieved.

She tucked a lock of her wavy gold hair behind one ear and leaned back in her chair, crossing her legs as she did this. She was *so* goddamned sexy. Even though her attractiveness sometimes distracted him from focusing his thoughts, he was also convinced that's why he opened up to her as easily as he did.

"So where do we start?" he asked her.

It took her a moment to respond. Apparently she'd given this topic some thought. She chose her words carefully, blinking those thick eye lashes and pursing her lips. "Zack, does your life feel like it has any momentum right now?"

Momentum? "You mean like: Am I college bound? Will I be successful? Do I have hopes for the future?"

"No, not really. I was thinking more along the lines of: Are my wounds healing? Am I depressed? Is life going on?"

Zack didn't get defensive or edgy with her. He responded to her inquiries calmly. "Y'know, someone said to me recently that I should shape up, that I'm not the only one to have lost a loved one that day. True enough. I'll give that one to him. If anything, I feel like I'd been toughened up for the blow.

"Are my wounds healin'? I guess. Am I depressed? Sure. Is life goin' on? Yeah, nothin's gonna change that."

She studied him for a moment. "There's something else," she said. It wasn't a question.

He thought about it. "I feel like everyone's havin' this giant group hug, and I'm standin' just outside the circle, shruggin'."

"And why would that be?"

"Because I don't believe in any of it."

"You don't believe in people supporting one another during painful times?"

"That's not what the group hug is all about."

"Then what's it about?" she asked, narrowing her eyes.

"It's about standin' strong. Unified. America's perseverance."

She looked surprised. "And that's what you don't believe in?" He looked out her office window. He didn't respond right away.

He didn't even answer her question. "Who the hell are these guys? What could we possibly have done to make them do what they did to us? How could the government let this happen?"

She didn't respond. She knew that he was venting, and she let the silence linger. Besides, there weren't really any simple answers to his questions. Then he asked another one.

"Why's it so important to be patriotic?"

"Because this is your country. You live here."

"Just look at our history. What a mess. And here we are. We haven't learned a goddamned thing."

"'Those who fail to learn the lessons of history are doomed to repeat it,'" she quoted.

"Exactly."

"Give me an example."

"Vietnam."

"You think this is like the war in Vietnam?"

"I think this is gonna escalate into somethin' like Vietnam, yeah. It's gonna get ugly. It's *already* gotten ugly. I saw this report on the news the other day; we had rounded up all these guys that we suspected were part of Al-Qaeda. I'm talkin' like hundreds of them. It got me wonderin' how many of them were actually guilty."

"Isn't it only natural that you'd want some kind of justice?" she asked.

"I've come across people who've lost friends and family, people who want to see that whole country nuked. Seriously, I don't consider that rational thinking. What happened to me—to all of us—it reminds me of this time when these lawyers came after my mom for something my dead dad had done."

"So you're saying you've been punished for someone else's crimes?"

"I don't know what went on over there in the eighties. I don't think anyone really does. It's definitely not somethin' we learned in school."

"It was complicated and *very* controversial," she offered.

"If we don't handle this mess responsibly and humanely, we're gonna lose our credibility with the rest of the world."

She tried to steer the topic in another direction. "You mentioned history and Vietnam. What about World War II? That's something you definitely learned about here. Do you have any reservations about how we handled that conflict?"

"Well, all those Nazis can burn in hell for the rest of eternity. You'll get no complaint from me there. But the *Enola Gay*, the internment camps for the Japanese. C'mon, it's not like you chose a shinin' example for me."

"You're right, Zack. War is ugly on both sides. It always is. And it's never simple."

"Especially for us. We're the world's police, right?" he said cynically.

She sighed. "You know, Zack, without passing any judgment on the company you keep, I will say that having observed you over the years and having observed that crowd you run with, you really stood out. And we both know you could have done even better if you'd applied yourself."

"So what are you gettin' at?"

"How many times have I pushed college on you? You've got the smarts, and you've got a big heart. If you don't like the way things work, why not go out there and try to change them?"

"I told you I'm takin' a break to clear my head."

"Zack, don't humor me. We both know your lifestyle is in total contradiction with your potential."

"I'll forget for a second that you just totally trashed my friends. Y'know you're a lot like Jenny was except for one small detail. She knew when to push me and when to give me space."

"I'm sorry you feel that way," she said. "You think I push you too hard?"

"Don't get me wrong. I really appreciate what you're tryin' to do for me. But you know me well enough. I think you already have your answer."

"Just keep it in mind, all right? You're too special a person to waste talent."

God, she really had a way with words. "I don't know why you do this," he said with a smile. "You're talkin' to *me* about wasted talent? You should be out in the city making six figures and saving marriages, prescribin' Lithium and whatnot."

She laughed in that sweet, melodious way that he'd come to love. "Thank you for your vote of confidence, but for now I'd rather be a big fish in a small pond."

He shrugged. "I'm just sayin'..."

"Let's do this again in the near future," she suggested.

"Sounds good to me."

"Two things," she said.

"What's that?"

"First, don't shut people out. You know who I'm talking about. I know that you're confident and set in your ways, but sometimes unwanted advice can be the most beneficial."

Had she spoken with Derek? He decided not to ask, but the question still bothered him. "Okay," he said. He felt as though he was on uneven footing. "What's the other thing?"

"Second, aside from all the academic promise you showed here, I also remember how much hell you raised. When you go out there, try not to be so impulsive. Try to practice some prudence from time to time. I think it would really serve you well."

He stood to leave. Why couldn't he find himself a girl like this? "You've got it," he assured her. "Hope to hear from you soon."

"Please take care of yourself, Zack," she practically pleaded.

After he'd left she convinced herself that she'd been able to help him work through some of his problems. Still though, he worried her. He was young and obstinate. Not a good combination. He was also brash and full of repressed anger. Could she really be the only professional he spoke with?

He would continue life live his way. She was sure of it. The part that bothered her most was that if he were to find himself at the crossroads of a critical dilemma, she wasn't ready to bet on whether he was emotionally mature enough to make the right decision.

CHAPTER 7
APRIL 7, 2002

It was a perfect spring day, and for Zack and his friends it meant that there was basketball to be played. Everyone had come over to Zack's place to hang out in the early afternoon.

Toward the end of high school, Zack had been the only one to have his own apartment. Back then by the time Friday night rolled around it was never a question of where the party was. Some nights there were bigger and better places to party, but Zack's place was always Plan B if nothing turned up. Most of his friends still enjoyed the majority of the freedoms that he did, but Zack had his own place and was therefore the logical choice to host parties and provide a hangout for everyone else.

There were many who had developed fond memories of the apartment and would be unhappy about losing this place once Zack and Jamar moved to Brooklyn. That's why Zack's decision had been a hard one.

It was a great place in its own right. It was spacious by Manhattan's standards, with central air conditioning, modern appliances, hardwood floors, and high ceilings. There was also a small balcony area at the front of each apartment in the building, which was perfect for a day like this one.

Today their attention was divided between the apartment and the basketball court across the street. They'd played countless games on this court. It was well kept by the city and not littered with the broken glass and other refuse that could so often be found on other courts. A lot of people were lured to this particular area. Now that it was starting to get warm again people would be coming more frequently.

After he and two friends made their way across the street, Zack sat on a courtside bench next to Sam. Terence was dribbling behind them, anxious to break in his new Jordan high-tops.

Physically, Zack's teammates were opposites. Sam was a roly-poly Irish kid with pasty freckled skin and a red crew-cut. Terence was a wispy black kid with long black braids and skin the color of mahogany. Sam took advantage of his size when going up against opponents. Terence relied on his speed and agility. With Zack's height and wiry build thrown into the mix, the trio complemented one another well on the court.

There was a two-on-two game going on. Zack didn't know who was playing, but he felt safe in calling it *his* court, not because he'd never been beaten on it, but because he and his friends had been holding it down for years. No one frequented it more than they did.

Zack felt impatient. There were five more people over in the apartment. Jimmy had set up his turntables inside, and Jamar was probably getting everyone else stoned. Zack would call up there whenever they finally got their turn.

Sam got up from the bench and grabbed his skateboard. Zack was glad. Sam had been getting too damned fidgety, and it was starting to annoy him. Sam addressed both him and Terence, "Damn, these guys suck. I'm gonna go screw around for a second. I'll be back if we ever get a turn."

Zack didn't want to be delayed anymore than they already had been. "Don't wander of too far," he said. "You drag your fat ass back here as soon as our turn rolls around." A middle finger from out in the street was the response to Zack's instructions.

Once Sam was gone, Terence stopped dribbling and came around the bench. He sat down next to Zack and said, "All right, now that he's gone, you gotta tell me what you and Jamar got goin' on. I heard you guys are gonna run Marco's operation right out the door here."

Zack was annoyed by Terence's excitement. It was as though he and Terence were conspiring. He could've punched Jamar for running his mouth. Besides, Terence had it all wrong.

Sighing deeply, he moved strands of hair out of his eyes. He sat up straight and said, "C'mon, Terence, think about it. If Jamar and I already take everything to people's doorsteps, then why would we ever start moving it from the pad? Who would come all the way here when it's just a phone call away? Use your damn head."

Terence—now annoyed himself—wanted answers. "Well, then tell me what it is you got goin' on. You two look like a coupla fags whisperin' in each others ears."

"All right!" Zack didn't exactly owe Terence the details of his own affairs. In fact, it was none of his business at all. He would rather have kept the matter private, but he figured it would be wiser to put an end to all their talk and speculation than to play dumb. "I'm gonna tell you what we're doin'. You've heard me talk about my family's lawyer, Morgan. He's the guy who helped out Jenny a lot after my mom died. He helped Jenny win the custody battle for me. The authorities wanted to make me some ward of the state, or some shit like that."

"Yeah," Terence said, "I know about that."

"Well, to level with you, I know I was young and all, but in my gut I always suspected he took us for a ride," Zack conceded. He looked straight ahead, staring at nothing in particular. "Now, we're already talking about a really arrogant prick here. I know he was good friends with my dad a long time ago, but I never felt that he and I ever connected on any significant level. But I really like his family. I guess I just always felt like we were clients to him more than friends."

Terence nodded, not really sure where Zack was going with this, but showing him that he followed.

"After Jenny and Pete died, he called me and told me that there was no way I could possibly keep the apartment. Prices had just skyrocketed in the last year, and apparently even with the life insurance money it wasn't realistic that I should be able to keep the place.

"I tried to argue, but Morgan laid down the law. It wasn't open for debate. Derek wouldn't have anythin' to do with it, and Morgan said his hands were tied.

"Tied my ass. This place is one of the last real things I have in my life, and he's tryin' to snatch it out from under me. The guy could work miracles for Jenny, and then suddenly when it's my turn, he's the judge's bitch. Needless to say, I felt screwed."

Suddenly a grin formed on Zack's face, and Terence wondered what had sparked the sudden change in mood. Zack spit, then said, "You remember that video of us skatin' down at Battery Park? It was that time that Jamar pulled of that sick rail slide."

Terence nodded.

"Well, it just so happened that day Morgan was down there with his mistress, goin' to town on her right in public for everyone to see. Tongue in her ear. Hands on her tits. She was hoisted right up on the railing. I mean this guy really got careless. We zoomed in and got it all. This gave me some serious leverage."

Some of the pieces were starting to fall into place, and Zack could see it dawning on Terence. "I wasn't comfortable at first blackmailin' this guy. I didn't like bullyin' him. But let's face it, I was out of options. Besides, I told you I like his family a lot. I don't want them to find out. As long as I've got this video, I've got him by the balls."

"So, the apartment is the price for your silence?"

"Yeah."

"But who's floating the bill?"

Zack blinked. He'd thought that would be obvious. "He is."

"But you're movin' to Brooklyn," Terence pointed out. "You don't need it anymore."

"I can keep it or I can rent it out. It's all up to me. This is all what I'm tryin' to figure out."

"But it's comin' out of his pocket," Terence stated, as if making sure he had all his facts correct before he formed an opinion.

"That's right," Zack said. He let the following silence hang between them for a minute or two. He was watching some of the younger neighborhood kids play on a jungle gym. He closed his eyes and concentrated on their voices. They reminded him of his own childhood. A cool breeze hit his face and rustled his hair. He wondered where it had come from this deep in the city. For that moment the breeze and the sound of the kids on the playground were the only two things that existed in the universe.

"That's some cold shit," Terence said.

Zack's eyes popped open but he didn't turn his head. His eyes stayed fixed on the kids. "What?"

"Zack, this guy kept you outta foster care. And whether or not you like him, you say you like his family. You could end up hurtin' them, financially and emotionally. I mean, when he first called you to tell you that you couldn't keep the place, I'm sure him payin' for it was never an option.

"Does this guy really deserve what you're doin' to him? Any red blooded guy with a dick might've strayed like he did. How much do you think he'll shell out before he cracks?"

Terence thought he was making a valid argument, and he had no idea how much he was infuriating Zack.

"Hey, I never asked for your goddamned opinion," Zack growled, ignoring the question. "I didn't volunteer the information. You pried it out of me. And now that I have, I gotta listen to your shit?"

Terence put a hand up to silence Zack. "Yo, calm the hell down, man," he said. "I'm gonna say my piece whether you like it or not, not because I wanna argue with you, but because it's what you need to hear.

"First of all, you ain't lookin' out for his family. His wife ain't gonna find out unless he slips, and you already said it would kill her if that happened. So let's not pretend that you're takin their best interests to heart here.

"Second, I think you're disrespectin' your father's memory by goin' after his best friend.

"Third, his hands probably *were* tied until he found out he was going to have to dip into his savings just to shut you up.

"Finally, if all this cloak-and-dagger bullshit is about keepin' the place you call home in your possession, then why is rentin' it out even an option for you? Why, after going to all this trouble, would you move to Brooklyn with Jamar? I mean, it seems like somewhere along the way you lost sight of what this was all about to begin with."

Zack looked flabbergasted. These days, people who knew what a hothead he was knew not to say the wrong thing to him. But Terence had boldly plunged ahead with his assessment of the situation.

Zack didn't have time to respond. Terence gave a wave of his hand, trying to diffuse a potentially disastrous situation before it could occur. "Hey, man, don't get bent out of shape by what I said. I'm not tryin' to act like your father. It's just that you're my boy and I worry about you is all."

Zack wasn't inclined to let it go, but before he could say anything Sam returned. He shook his head and mumbled, "Holy shit, they're not done yet? We should have tryouts for this court." Placing his hands over his mouth he called across the court to its occupants, "Yeah, go ahead. Take all day. We still got next."

"No, sorry, we got next," came a voice from of to the left. All three heads turned in that direction. The speaker was tall and lanky, like Zack, but goofy looking. He had a shaved head and a terrible acne problem. He was easily one of the ugliest persons Zack had ever seen. He continued to address the group. "We took off for a coupla minutes, but now we're back. We're in the middle of a tournament, but we'll be done pretty soon."

Zack only heard half of what was said. His gaze was fixed on the speaker's companion. It was Mo from the corner store. He scowled at Zack when their eyes met. Zack wondered if this new setback was really a coincidence.

Sam began to protest. "Wait a minute! What is this bullshit? We've been waitin' here forever for these guys to wrap it up. We ain't got all day to wait for you."

A hand on Sam's shoulder told him to back off. It was Terence, and into Sam's ear he said, "Easy, man. I ain't in the mood today. Just let 'em have their game."

At the moment Terence didn't have Zack's vote of confidence. "No way, man," Zack said defiantly, pointing toward Mo. "That bastard banned me from the corner store just the other day. Now he thinks he's gonna come onto *my* court and state *his* terms. Fuck that!"

Terence, ever the pacifist, stood his ground. "Yo, our guys are still dickin' around inside. Just give these guys ten minutes."

Zack wanted to submit so that he might calm down. But he just couldn't let it go. He was getting more and more worked up with each passing second. "You know that fucker pretty much threatened to steal my bike?" he said loudly enough for Mo to hear. "Now he's tellin' me when it's my turn to play ball? They don't even play basketball in the desert."

Terence looked pissed, and he wanted to silence Zack now. "Zack, shut your fuckin' mouth! What are you, eight years old? Grow up!"

The game actually ended, and the two losers left the court. Mo and his friend took their places. Zack put his hands on his head and took a deep breath. He walked out into the street and began pacing back and forth.

Right then, as if to remind Zack that at heart he wasn't really a bigoted jerk, Nomar walked out into the street. He had a suitcase and a duffel bag, and was in the process of hailing a taxi. Spotting Zack, he said, "Hey, I'm glad I caught you before I left. I'll be gone for about two weeks. Someone will be coming by once a day to see to my aunt, but I was wondering if you might keep an eye on things while I'm gone."

Zack was still a little distracted. He looked up to the second floor, where Mrs. Pezeshk was sitting on her tiny balcony and smiling. The sight of her actually helped calm Zack down. "Sure, I'd be happy to," he said. "I'll definitely be around." He noted the camera slung around Nomar's neck. "This trip business or pleasure?" he asked.

"It'll only be business if I get paid," said Nomar. "That's the risk you run when you become a freelancer." He opened the cab's trunk and put the luggage inside. "If you need to reach me for any reason while I'm gone, my cell phone number is written down next to the telephone upstairs." He opened the passenger side door. "Thanks again, Zack. I really appreciate it."

"Don't mention it," Zack said.

Zack waved as the cab drove off. The minutes passed as he paced in the street. When he was convinced he'd settled down, he returned to the court. He didn't like what he found when he got there.

Mo and his friend were playing two newcomers. Zack bit his lip and looked to Terence and Sam for answers.

"Said they were playin' a tournament," Sam answered the unasked question. He looked equally annoyed. Terence, of course, didn't look like it particularly bothered him. He just sat there leaning over with his elbows resting on his knees, watching the current game.

For the next few minutes Zack let fly with some snide comments meant to get under Mo's skin. To his disappointment the verbal assaults went ignored.

Zack grew tired of the abuse when he realized how much of his time was being wasted on these assholes who had absolutely no seniority here. He turned around and took hold of the chain-link fence in both hands. He closed his eyes and concentrated on taking deep breaths. Then he went over to his backpack sitting on the ground and took his cell phone out of it.

He counted Mo's crew. There were six of them including Mo. He called Jamar up in the apartment.

"What up?" Jamar asked.

Zack kept his eyes on the game. "The shit's about to go down. Get down here. Bring everyone."

"Alright," Jamar said as casually as if Zack had just asked to borrow his skateboard.

Zack put his phone away and then waited a few moments. A minute ago he'd made comments about how closely the guys on the court were guarding one another. Standing just out of bounds Zack now called out to them, "Hey, you fuckin' queers wanna wrap things up so that those of us who actually belong here might be able to get some court time?"

The game came to a sudden halt. Zack's question had the desired effect. He heard Sam chuckle over his right shoulder and Terence curse over his left.

It was Mo's lanky friend who took the initiative. "Sorry there, little man, I didn't catch that. Care to run that by me again?" He was walking toward the three of them.

Zack tensed up and got ready for what he knew was coming. That was when the five people from the apartment arrived. His crew now numbered eight.

"What's goin' on?" Jamar asked, annoyed at being interrupted by Zack's phone call from whatever it was he'd been doing.

Zack pointed out in front of him. "Apparently these guys are in some kinda tournament."

Jamar had a look on his face that told him only half of the pieces had fallen into place. "Well," he said, "did anyone tell them that we don't hold tournaments on our court?"

Zack shrugged. "I tried," he said. "They don't listen so good."

Jamar, with limited talent for subtlety, could be intimidating when he wanted to be. Now he was facing the players, and when he spoke, he slowly cracked his knuckles. "Real simple solution though: you take your asses over to another court, another neighborhood."

Zack wouldn't have thought it would be Mo who would make the first move, but before he knew it Mo was coming for *him*. In one rapid and fluid motion, Jamar stepped forward and reached out, grabbing Mo's arm and bending it behind his back in a chicken wing.

Mo winced in pain and cried out. None of his friends made a move for fear that Jamar might break his arm.

Jamar spoke into Mo's ear. "All right there, Ali Baba, that's enough. You and your boys are gonna leave right now before I really get pissed, right? Mo grunted something Jamar couldn't hear. "Right?" Jamar repeated. Mo cursed something in another language, but the pain was evident in his voice.

"That'll have to do," Jamar said, a mean grin forming on his face. He let go of Mo and pushed him forward. There were a few laughs as Mo collided with his tall friend and the two nearly fell over.

Zack wasn't laughing at all. He pointed at Mo. "Same deal you gave me," he said. "You're not allowed back. Now take your friends and get the fuck outta here."

No fight broke out. The outnumbered opposition cut their losses and left. Although Zack suspected there would be trouble again with Mo, it was over for now.

Jamar sat down on the bench. "I wasn't lookin' to crack skulls today anyway," he said.

A few people asked Sam questions about what had transpired. When Sam got a couple of laughs out of them, Terence turned to the whole group and said, "Man, this is bullshit! I'm gone." And with that he left, utterly disgusted. Zack noted he didn't return to the apartment.

"What's his problem?" someone asked.

"Forget about him," Zack answered with his back turned. "He's been actin' like a li'l bitch all day."

Jamar dribbled out onto the court and started shooting hoops. "Well, since we're out here, we might as well get this shit started."

Zack looked down at his empty water bottle and grabbed it. "I'll be back in a minute," he said. He walked out into the street and headed back toward his place. Suddenly, he had one of those funny feelings in his gut, and he stopped dead in his tracks halfway there. Looking around he realized something was amiss, but he couldn't put his finger on what it was. He tried to spot what was different. Everything looked the same as it always did, right down to Mrs. Pezeshk on her porch, sitting and smiling.

Zack squinted as he looked up at her. That was it. She wasn't smiling. Not only was she not smiling, but she was looking right at him. The absence of her warm, reassuring smile contributed to the cold Zack felt in the pit of his stomach, the cold he kept buried there.

He couldn't shake the feeling that he'd stripped the smile from her face with his actions.

She was old. She couldn't have heard what had taken place from way over here, could she?

It was troubling to Zack how the absence of that small, almost-unnoticeable smile could change the mood of a scene so drastically.

CHAPTER 8
September 14, 1986

Benazar Rashid looked out the truck's window and stared at the open landscape. The sun was setting, and shadows closed in to mingle with colors along walls of jagged rock and packed sand. How marvelous the beauty was. It was a beauty he could identify for what it was, but could never fully appreciate. True appreciation, to him, would be self-defeating. How could a landscape truly be beautiful when it was forever destined to be the backdrop of warfare? The exquisitely perfect tones of orange and red that painted the miles of rock did nothing to remind him of all that he was fighting for. All he was reminded of was that night was coming and that meant that he and those traveling with him were more susceptible to an ambush.

Moving his eyes to the side view mirror, he observed how much dust was being kicked up and trailed behind the truck as it sped along the gravely road. There was far too much for him to be comfortable. A trail of dust was a sure way of making them visible over great distances, and they could not afford to be identified. What awaited them was far too important for them to be compromised.

He turned to the driver, Timur, and asked, "When are we expected?"

"Sometime in the late evening or early morning," Timur answered. "Why do you ask?"

"Lower your speed until the sun sets," Benazar commanded. "We're leaving a thick trail of dust behind us. We mustn't be seen."

Timur did as he was told. He considered it a pity. It was a great thrill to be driving the truck that he and his comrades had intercepted from the Russians, and he rather enjoyed testing its limits. However, perhaps the fourteen weary men riding in the back would welcome the slower speed. It had already been a long and bumpy journey. The truck had been stolen when he and ten other men had managed to ambush a Russian unit traveling through Shindand. They had been greatly outnumbered when the trap had been sprung, but they had managed to kill every single Red without a single casualty on their side.

The truck he and his fifteen companions now rode in was traveling south over hundreds of miles to reinforce an Afghan force in the making, a force unlike any the Mujaheddin had ever formed before. Timur grew excited every time the thought entered his mind. He was a wiry man of medium height with sharp features, and he had killed more than a few Russians twice his weight over the last seven years. His exploits had earned him a place in the new military. Now he'd have the opportunity to kill countless more, and the thought of him making the enemy atone for their savage crimes compelled him.

He cast a quick glance at his companion next to him. What a strange individual this was. In the brief time the two men had known each other, Timur had learned that Benazar Rashid never agonized over defeat and never celebrated victory. He just kept moving forward at the center of the killing fields, seemingly unfeeling. It was almost like a mercenary's apparent indifference. Only, Benazar was not being paid. He was the one making payments. He had shed blood dozens of times since the conflict with the Red Army had begun. He had been on the front lines of battles all over Afghanistan, but he had never relished a single victory. He had never laughed, nor sung, nor fired his gun in celebration. He merely sought out the next battle and went there.

Timur knew what he, himself, fought for. He wasn't so sure about the man sitting next to him. This Rashid remained a mystery.

Timur decided to seek out some answers. He began by saying, "I want you to know that there's no man that I have more respect for than your brother. All that Mussar has done for us can never be repaid. How is it that the two of you have led such different lives?"

Benazar didn't answer right away. He hadn't yet sized up Timur. He didn't trust him, but Mussar trusted him. Benazar wasn't one to give up information too freely. Anyone could turn a profit from information, and Afghanistan's history of betrayal could be documented in volumes. He gave Timur what inconsequential details he could with the hopes of quieting him. "When this all began, I made the decision to fight on the battlefield rather than squabble with puppet diplomats. In my eyes, they were pretending, nothing more. My father would not stand for my aggression. He had raised Mussar and me with the hope that we might one day serve as advisors or ambassadors. He intended for us to fight our battles behind the scenes as politicians. I didn't share his ideals. It seemed a foolish tactic to me. How does one make a difference as a politician in a country that has no legitimate government? One power rises on the ruins of the one that just fell. I felt it was all a charade. I left him and my brother so that I might find honor and die in combat. I never imagined I'd live this long. When my father perished in the bombing of Herat seven years ago, Mussar and I met to pay our respects. We became reacquainted. It was then that I learned how foolish I'd been. Diplomacy was not as ineffective as I'd thought. He had risked as much as any of us and had gained more for our cause. I realized then that it was something my brother has a natural talent for, something I'll never have. I merely wish to make amends with my dead father for having dishonored him all those years ago." There were no traces of regret in his explanation. He presented pure fact, free of emotional bias.

Timur considered this. He cleared his throat and said, "I hope you don't undermine all that you've done. Your reputation precedes you everywhere you go. That's why I'm glad none of the men in back recognized you. They would have grown excited, and that would not do until we have reached our destination."

"Explain that." It was not a request.

"I knew your name before I ever met you. There've been more than two separate occasions when you were believed dead, yet you returned to us each time. I know that you're on the Russians' most wanted list. The mere mention of your name inspires our men. Some think you're impossible to kill. You've become somewhat of a legend with the populace," Timur said, grinning.

Benazar voiced his contempt. "Ridiculous. I bleed like any other man. I won't put my life in the hands of men who would entertain such notions. We're at war. Have we hand-picked men who would romanticize our situation?"

"Please forgive my choice of words," Timur apologized. "I only meant that your presence here may provide us hope. These men have not experienced the occupation as you have, and they'll surely be able to profit from your experience."

"None of the men in back are part of the inner circle?"

"No, in fact, when we arrive and are briefed, there'll only be ourselves, two others, and this Flanigan. Twenty-one other men will be joining the inner circle in two days. The fourteen in back will complete the hundred we have in reserve. The reserves will be completely subordinate to the inner circle. But the American will explain everything once we arrive. And if you have doubts concerning what I said a moment ago, know this: this American we're about to meet has already been heard saying that he looks forward to meeting you in particular."

Benazar was surprised to hear this. It was somewhat unsettling. He had only just been recruited into this secret organization. He, like dozens of others in the contingent, was currently believed by many to be dead. That would work to his advantage. He'd been put in touch with Timur through Mussar in Shindand. Timur, too, had been declared missing in action. Everything had been done in complete secrecy, yet this American already knew who he was and had become familiar with his background. Curious now, he said, "This American, tell me about him."

Timur appeared pleased to have the opportunity. "He was a highly decorated and distinguished Navy SEAL. Are you familiar with that division of the American military?" When Timur saw Benazar's nod, he continued. "After retiring from the SEALs he spent a brief period commanding an American anti-terrorist task force. For the last ten years he has served as a high-ranking covert agent of their intelligence division. I can assure you that as far as American aid to our war effort goes, he's the best his country has to offer. I tell you, Benazar, I think that what we're doing now with the ISI will bring about great change for our people. I can actually imagine us ending this conflict. I feel victory is near."

Benazar said nothing. He sat in silence for minutes. The only noise was the truck's engine.

Timur eventually grew agitated and tried to lighten the mood.

He asked, "Is it true that you have a son?"

Benazar reached into a backpack sitting on the floorboards. Timur knew he had spoken loudly enough. Was his newly found comrade choosing to ignore him? He pondered this as Benazar took out an object that resembled a camera. "What is that?"

"Soon it'll be dark. Don't turn on the headlights. Put these goggles on. You'll be able to see clearly enough." Benazar pointed toward the lens. "I've already adjusted it. Resume your speed after that."

Benazar leaned his head back into the seat and closed his eyes. Timur did his best to hide his growing excitement over the goggles. Benazar had already made it abundantly clear how seriously he took this conflict. It would not do for Timur to openly show his delight over these goggles the way a boy might over a new toy. Still though, it bode well for them that they were in possession of such technology. After all, if what the Americans promised them was forthcoming, then the weapons and technology that would be at their disposal might actually turn the tide of this war. The thought of victory exhilarated him. So be it if his companion could kill without passion for what he fought for. Their goals were one in the same, and over the months to come they would become the men who are written about in history books, men who would change the destiny of a nation.

Only when Timur glanced to his right did he experience a moment of doubt. Here, next to him, was a fierce warrior, but now he seemed anything but extraordinary. Had he been broken? Perhaps it was not, in fact, a fighting spirit that Benazar Rashid possessed, but rather the shell of a dead man, a body acting on pure reflex. Timur had not been fighting for as long as this Rashid, but he was much younger. Would years of fighting the Reds chip away at Timur the way it had this man? Would he even live as long? He doubted it.

Then perhaps there was yet an undetectable fire within Benazar Rashid that kept him fighting. He certainly was a survivor. Broken men do not tend to live long, especially in times of war. *What drives this man?* He'd find out, one small piece at a time if need be. "I've heard that you have a son." He raised the matter once again, seeming to proceed with caution. "Is it true?"

Benazar's eyes remained closed. The silence hung between them like stale air. Just as Timur began to grit his teeth at having been ignored twice, Benazar spoke with his eyes shut. "Don't ask me any more personal questions."

There was a menace to his command. Timur tried to regard it as more of a casual request than a threat. But he knew he wouldn't be told twice.

He quickly shrugged it off. It was completely irrelevant. The future was what mattered, and the future belonged to them. In just a few short hours, he and his companions would embrace that future. It would be magnificent.

*   *   *

Their destination was a bunker in the pocket of a canyon that ran through the Hindu Kush Mountains. Such places were always ideal for establishing fortresses. The mountain range dominated most of the country, and the treacherous terrain was not easily combed. Those who did not wish to be found could easily disappear into the canyons, assuming they had the means for survival and the ability to escape pursuers. The time and resources that went into such manhunts rarely produced results. Afghan warriors had realized this early on in their history, and had exploited the landscape for many centuries, staging ambush after ambush from the shadowy depths. In recent years, the Mujaheddin had pounced on the Soviets from their stronghold within the maze of canyons.

The truck met the helicopter shortly after midnight. They were ahead of schedule. All sixteen men unloaded the truck and met Abdur Shah, a member of the inner circle and an escort for the group. He was a large man with a leathery face aged by the desert winds. A thick line of scar tissue ran down his face and cut through his thick graying beard. He was accompanied by a young- looking man named Khan, who was to assume control of the truck and reroute it to an undisclosed location. Khan was brief with his introduction and quickly went about his business.

Abdur greeted the newcomers and then turned his attention to Timur and Benazar. "It is a great honor to meet you both. However, you must excuse me if we skip all formalities. I know that you are travel weary, but time's of the essence, and we must be on our way."

With that he turned and headed for the helicopter. The men followed. Benazar looked over their new comrades. They seemed a ragtag bunch, these men. For all outward appearances, they appeared to be no more than a gang of thieves. And perhaps they were. But Benazar knew how deadly they could be. They were unarmed, tired, and hungry, yes, but each one of these men had been handpicked for this military unit because he was an efficient killer. Over time they would perfect that skill.

It was the helicopter that next caught his attention. It was more than a standard issue military transport helicopter. It was a U-60 chopper. He had only seen them in photographs. The United States used them, and this one appeared to have enough firepower to level a village. He could not even guess what it must have cost, much less who had paid for it. He could not believe that the Americans would overextend themselves so with such weaponry.

He noticed Timur to his left, grinning. "You see?" he said, nodding toward the chopper. Benazar ignored him and fell into step with Abdur.

"Was this helicopter captured?" he asked.

"No, my friend, this is a contribution to our war effort."

"How can a nation afford to lend another nation such a weapon? Where does the money come from?"

Abdur turned to Benazar with just the slightest smile on his face. The smile held every indication that Abdur was amused by his ignorance. Benazar wanted to rip the man's lips right off of his face. His education was limited to conventional warfare, nothing more, but he *was* seeking out valuable knowledge. Who was this man to scoff at him?

But Abdur did answer his question. "The money comes from the American people, Benazar. Each citizen pays a tax to the government that provides for such expenses. Their President Reagan has personally approved of the aid that's been sent to us. Don't worry. We have much to learn from one another, and I'm sure that you'll soon find answers to your questions."

Benazar allowed his momentary flash of rage to subside. Yes, his questions would be answered, every one of them. He would find out why they were being befriended. He would find out what the United States' stake in this war was. He would find out if this nation, which he had been taught had a reputation for treachery, could truly be trusted.

*   *   *

So deeply nestled was the newly established compound in the canyon's floor, so completely hidden, that an invader's best chance of locating it would be through the use of heat-seeking surveillance equipment. There was a discreet landing pad for the chopper, watched over by machine gun turrets hidden within crevices along the canyon wall. A door slid open as the chopper touched down, and the men filed out and gathered what little gear they had. They were not ten paces from the chopper before it lifted back up into the air, its rotors pounding, and left the way it had come.

Benazar took notice of how the guns trained on them swiveled, keeping them targeted as they approached. *No one's to be completely trusted,* he mused. This thought had been a fundamental staple of his survival for so many years. It was disturbingly comforting to him that they be regarded as potential threats. It meant that these individuals had their wits about them, and had a familiarity with how the nature of man took its course in these times of violence. The KGB used their money to breed traitors as they might breed dogs.

One person to infiltrate. One bomb smuggled in. That's all it took. Suddenly, an enemy is immobilized. The outcome can be so devastating that the beauty of its simplicity is lost on the combatants. After all, that is what warfare was—an art form. And this was a nation that was quickly running short of all other types of art forms. Warfare was beginning to leave all others in its shadow. What would God have him do if tomorrow the violence ceased? What could he do? He had been irreversibly molded by the war. He was a finely tuned instrument that would become useless in the aftermath of victory. *Better to embrace Shahadat today and die a martyr than live in peace tomorrow, only to have others bear witness to how the bloodshed eventually consumes you.*

As if waking from a dream, he lifted his head and looked to the right of the entrance. The turret had him targeted. He had fallen behind the group, and that instantly aroused suspicion.

He silently stared back at the unseen gunman. Silence filled the air. He stood still and realized that there was a feeling of raw intensity in the air, like an electrical current passing between him and the gunman. One wrong move on his part. One squeeze of the trigger. That was all it took. He resumed his approach, and the current ceased, leaving no trace of its existence. The moment had passed.

Although aware that every moment leaves the previous one in the past, he understood that once he stepped through the door he would be putting an end to an era. Events were in motion that would bring a great change, and he would help bring about this change. This was by far the biggest opportunity he had ever had to prove himself to his people. He did not share

Timur's idealism. He simply desired to make as big a difference as he could, be it accepting the enemy's unconditional surrender or the butchering of every Russian soldier possible until the enemy killed him. The latter was likely. Not far from his mind was the fact that although he'd survived dozens of potentially fatal circumstances, death would find him quickly enough. It was an inevitability that came sooner to men like him.

After stepping through the door, he surveyed the scene around him. The room was much bigger than he could have estimated from the outside. It had obviously been a large cave to begin with, and perhaps it had been cleared out by dynamite to maximize space within. The ground, which was for the most part level, was swept clean of loose rock and debris. In its place was packed sand.

Men moved about in every direction, transporting crates and hardware that served purposes he couldn't even guess at. Overhead was an intersecting set of catwalks with men overseeing the labor, calling out specific instructions. They looked like the foremen of some textile factory. Stack after stack of crates hugged the walls. There were dozens of gun racks adjacent to the crates, filled mostly with the Russian standard issue Kalashnikov AK-47 rifle. He recognized RPG7s, RR82mm rifles, and anti-aircraft guns. Next to those were British blowpipes. The only item he did not see was America's most precious gift to the Mujaheddin, the Stinger missile. Those were far too valuable to be kept here. He took in everything. It was an impressive arsenal, even for that of a nation that was the largest beneficiary of imported weapons in the world.

His eyes wandered to the room's southern wall. He observed men posted at what appeared to be radar screens and communications consoles. Monitoring the safe passage of their transport perhaps? The men tending to the equipment were pale skinned. *Americans.*

Was this all just another gift in the name of good will? It was definitely one of the biggest displays of electronics he'd ever seen in such a controlled area. What appeared to be a giant power transformer within a chain-link cage was humming softly in the corner. He had no real evidence, yet if he were to guess, he would say that although he stood in awe of such an energy source, it was only a minor detail from the Americans' perspective. It might have been deemed obsolete, and would only be of use as a donation to a militia having little to barter with. But again, he had no proof of that. He had little proof of anything.

He felt infantile, standing there astonished by everything around him. There was so much to learn. He would need to be thoroughly trained if he was to be of any use to anyone. He lacked sufficient knowledge about modern technology. Not that he was indifferent to such technology; he embraced science's contributions to modern warfare, and if it meant accepting the aid of foreigners with their checkered past and unclear motives then so be it. As it was, he had already made a personal vow to find out the truth.

As if he were transmitting a signal of skepticism, he was musing on these matters when a voice from behind addressed him, "Benazar Rashid." Benazar turned with a coolness that showed that he was ever alert rather than easily startled. He was now facing what was obviously an American of middle height and build, who appeared boyish in his military fatigues. On his left was Timur, on his right Abdur. The American was the one who had spoken. He spoke again, and Abdur provided an introduction and translation.

"Benazar, this is Colonel Showolter. He is pleased to meet you and requests that you accompany us to the inner bunker, where we might get under way." Benazar remained silent but nodded as he shook hands with the colonel. The four then proceeded to travel deep within the complex.

Their path narrowed into a tunnel that appeared to have undergone a complicated excavation. The tunnel would constantly fork and break of into more dimly lit paths. Abdur knew how to navigate it. Its complexity made perfect sense to Benazar. In the unlikely event of an invasion and penetration of the complex, the intruders would have a labyrinth on their hands. This would provide preparation time to counterattack from within. His assumption was supported when he saw what was literally an inner bunker nestled in a close grouping of jagged rocks at the end of the long tunnel. They waited a few moments before they passed through a heavy iron door. This door had armed American sentries posted on each side. They promptly saluted Showolter and let them pass.

They filed into a room covered wall to wall with maps. There were colorful, detailed maps of all of Afghanistan, Iran, Pakistan, Turkmenistan, Uzbekistan, Tajikistan, China, and India, as well as maps of Afghanistan's largest cities with thumbtacks and red marker highlighting locations of obvious strategic importance. At the center of the room on a large wooden table sat a topographical map of the Hindu Kush mountain range.

Standing at that table, with his back turned to the group, was an American soldier. He could not have been taller than six feet, but even standing there motionless he carried with him a presence that radiated physical power. He looked like a stone statue. His shoulders sloped severely down to his enormous torso, which swelled beneath his green military uniform. His powerful hands were clasped behind his back, and his rolled-up sleeves revealed thick forearms covered in veins and scars alike. Benazar would not want to engage such a man in hand-to-hand combat. He'd heard stories of the many different ways a well-polished American soldier could kill a man. He considered all of this in a mere moment as the foreigner turned to greet the newcomers. The years were evident in the lines on his face and the salt-and-pepper color of his hair. His dark eyes suggested a mix of strength and shrewdness through his intense gaze.

"Hello, it is an honor to meet you all. My name is Stuart Flanigan," he spoke in perfect Farsi. Many Afghanis spoke only Pashto or Dari, but Benazar, Timur, and Abdur, who were all from Herat, spoke Farsi almost exclusively. It was a gesture of goodwill that the American should introduce himself this way. He then turned and looked toward a bony-looking man behind him whom Benazar hadn't noticed previously. The man looked like a rodent both in his facial features and the way he scampered around the table. The American, Flanigan, then said in English, "I do apologize, but from here on Amir here will have to serve as translator for me."

Amir, the bony man, translated the information, but for Benazar it was unnecessary. It was true, his education was limited, but his father, an international trader, had done his best to raise him and his brother to speak in English, Russian, and even some Chinese. Polyglots were rare in Afghanistan, yet understanding several languages was necessary when your livelihood was tied to commerce. Though he understood what was being said, he refrained from volunteering the information for the moment. He listened as Flanigan continued.

"Our meeting at this time of night isn't by chance. I wanted the opportunity to be able to meet with the four of you before the rest of what we're calling 'the inner circle' arrive." Benazar hadn't noticed Showolter retreat to the far side of the room. "And the reason is this: tomorrow afternoon I'll be briefing the entire twenty-five of you on the true nature of our arrangement. Now is not the time for me to get into the details; everything will be made clear tomorrow." He paused so that Amir could catch up. "What is important at this time is that all of you know that although no one's been given any kind of formal rank, the entire inner circle, as well as the hundred in reserve, is completely subordinate to the four of you. We've made each man who has been brought in and processed aware of this fact. When I address the group tomorrow, I'll have the four of you at my side. A distinct chain of command is crucial if we're to be successful.

"It's late. You've all traveled a great distance to be here, and I realize that by now you must be exhausted. The rest can wait until tomorrow. Amir will show you to your quarters. Please get some rest and in the morning we can begin. After the briefing, the six of us will reconvene here and begin to coordinate our plan of attack. I'm truly thankful for your presence. I look forward to working with you all."

He smiled as he gave them an American military salute. He then turned his attention back to the map he'd been studying when they'd entered.

Showolter escorted them out the way they had come. Glancing over his shoulder as he left, Benazar caught Flanigan's gaze out of the corner of his eye. That was fine as far as he was concerned, for he in turn was fascinated by the way this

American carried himself. He didn't know what to make of him. The introduction had not included any formalities that often served as the stepping stones to forming a truly trustworthy alliance. The camaraderie had been assumed from the beginning as if they'd all been brothers in arms for years now. *The hatred between the Americans and the Soviets must run deeper than I ever imagined.*

And yet there'd been no open declaration of war between the two nations. The Cold War was what they were calling it. Benazar could not fathom how such a relationship was possible. *There's so much to learn. I'll learn from this man.*

CHAPTER 9
September 15, 1986

Stuart Flanigan's formal address to the twenty-five members of the inner circle, through the translation of Amir, went as follows:

"Good day to everyone. For those of you who have not met me, I am United States Agent Stuart Flanigan. I represent our country's Central Intelligence Agency. As many of you know, in 1981 the leaders of our nation came together to discuss ways in which we might provide aid to you as communist expansionism threatened to overtake your way of life. The result of these discussions was the funding of an anticommunist campaign that would provide much needed weaponry to your Mujaheddin army. In the interests of disguising American aid, most of the firearms we've provided can be traced to China, Israel, or Egypt. The situation we all find ourselves in is a delicate one.

"It is imperative that you know and understand that the United States is not at war with the Soviet Union. Our involvement in this conflict must remain covert. My presence here, as well as that of the soldiers who have accompanied me, is technically a violation of our original agreement with the ISI. Technically, no American soldier will be directly involved in fighting. Neither will Pakistan have any presence here, despite the fact that it's been our strongest supporter thus far. No one outside these walls need know we even exist.

"I'm going to tell you why I'm here. I'm here because your farms are being burned, your women are being raped, and your culture is being erased. I'm here because when the Russians plowed their way into this great country seven years ago; their bombs claimed over ten thousand lives. This genocide must stop.

"I can truly say that I draw inspiration from the history of your people. Afghanistan's always been the gateway that separates the eastern world from the western one. That's why it holds such strategic value to the Soviets. Your fathers defeated the invading armies of Genghis Khan and the British Empire. For centuries now your land has been invaded, but you have never yielded. You've refused to be beaten, always driving the aggressors out. And it's no different now. You've been holding your ground, and now you find yourselves at the edge of victory. But there's still much work to be done. Thousands have already fled the country, and the rate increases every day. It's our duty to put an end to this exodus and restore your nation's sovereignty."

The reactions in Flanigan's audience of Mujaheddin soldiers varied considerably. Like Benazar, there were men with tired, bearded faces trying to hide skepticism, suspecting embellishment in the translation, and pondering the real nature of the American presence here. Yet, other men, like Timur, were bright-eyed with optimism, listening intently and processing Flanigan's speech with the hope that this meeting might finally be the catalyst for ending the current conflict.

"I'm going to explain to you what the objective of this military unit is. But first I must explain the circumstances that have brought us together. Over the last several years, our government, in cooperation with the ISI, has shared information with the intention of gathering intelligence. We supplemented this effort by specially training an Afghani twelve-man reconnaissance unit. Nine of them were killed during a midnight raid. The Soviets perceived them as nothing more than a tribal suicide squad. They failed to notice that the survivors had returned to us with encrypted messages, which revealed to us a coded network that to this day we are still able to crack.

"Our joint intelligence has uncovered something else as well. Operating within the cities of Kabul, Kandahar, Shindand, and Herat are secret members of a fifth column that offers support to the Red Army. This network is still growing as we speak, and through careful subterfuge we have been able to insert several moles. The treachery of the Reds has come full circle, for we now have precise military locations and transit routes. That brings us all to where we are now.

"We've been provided with reliable intelligence. We're the group that will act on it. What we are is an anti-personnel unit. We're using the information we have to eliminate three of the highest-ranking Soviet military commanders who've been active in this area for many months now. They form a ruling triumvirate among the Russian commandos, and have been personally overseeing the large influx of the weapons that are killing your friends and families. Some of you may fail to see the value in this operation, and feel that your skills are needed elsewhere. Know this: the gun running routes will disintegrate with the deaths of these men. We will be cutting of a major artery of supplies from Russia to the outposts they've established here, and within a year their network will collapse.

"Although it may appear as though we're novices, each of you is already a seasoned veteran of war. Most of you are believed to be dead, which helps us in our need for secrecy. The information will continue to come in. During this time, you will undergo intense training. To my right is Colonel Brian Showolter. Many of you have already met him. Every American soldier stationed here is subordinate to the two of us. You may look to us for instruction and to the rest for guidance. Behind me are four men who will serve as your commanders. We are fortunate to have the combat experience of Timur Hassani, Amir Sarif, Abdur Shah, and Benazar Rashid. Eventually, we'll divide the hundred men we have in reserve into four groups. These men behind me will each assume leadership of one group."

The soldiers in the audience sized up the four men, some wondering which one he would have to serve under. Others were already familiar with some of the commanders, having served with them on different fronts. These men already knew whom they'd prefer if given a choice.

"The tactical decision-making process will take place in the main bunker, which will serve as our war room. These four men, Colonel Showolter, and I will be involved in this process. When we have developed concrete strategies, we'll then provide all of you with individual orders as well as any intel and arms you may need to carry them out.

"Most of you will see no action over the next few months. As our flow of intelligence continues to be processed and analyzed, you'll be training. Under Colonel Showolter and me you will receive instruction in the use of weapons we have provided as well as dozens of methods of conventional tactics that are practiced by the United States military. With time and discipline, we'll hone the skills each one of you already possess so that you're the most elite, professionally trained soldiers of the Mujaheddin. You'll become the pride of your people.

"Make no mistake: the road ahead of us all is a dangerous one. We have no guarantee that we'll succeed, and you can expect many of us to die before this is over. But I know that every man here has been ready to die for this cause since the beginning.

"We'll stand firm in our objective. We'll neutralize these three targets and then watch as the communist regime unravels at the seams. Here we begin the first steps toward rebuilding your great nation. Everything changes from here on out. Tonight you may rest and gather your strength. Tomorrow we will begin. Feel free to approach either Colonel Showolter or me with any questions or concerns you may have. That's all for now."

CHAPTER 10
DECEMBER 2, 1986

"What is his name again?"

"Shachmeva. Drazen Shachmeva."

"And he is?"

"A colonel. He's one of Morodov's most celebrated interrogators. He's brilliant at the art of torture, and he's Morodov's lapdog."

"All the better." The soldier released a chuckle and cradled his bazooka closer to his chest. He frowned when he saw Benazar crawling toward the two of them. If Abdur was their commander, then why had Benazar escorted them on this mission?

When Benazar spoke, his voice was low and had an edge to it. "The reason you didn't know his name is because you weren't listening when you were briefed. The rest of the information you shouldn't even be privy to. Tend to your bazooka." He leaned closer. "When the order comes, you'd better be ready."

The younger man slowly crawled back to his position, keeping close to the ground, and Benazar returned his attention to Abdur. He was glad they were both here. Abdur's mind was racing with the task at hand, so Benazar kept close watch over the men. Perhaps Abdur could have handled his command on his own, but he was the group's best sniper, and his skills were presently required. He held the radio's receiver to his head. His hand came up in front of him to keep Benazar from speaking as his ever-calculating eyes kept moving over the ground. His voice was barely audible.

"Copy that. Out." To Benazar he said, "That's the word. They'll be along in just a few minutes." He let out a brief, low whistle, and all three pairs of eyes fell on him as he made the hand signal to assume attack position. The demolition men kept their heads to the ground while Abdur and Benazar slowly peered over the edge of the cliff. Abdur looked through his binoculars. Nothing yet. Without taking his eyes off of the road below, he spoke, "Once I've lined up a shot, this becomes your show. Are you ready?"

Benazar squinted and through naked eyes saw the first truck on the road half a mile away. He sheathed the knife he'd been sharpening and reached for his rifle. "Just make sure you're ready."

Drazen Shachmeva frequented various outposts scattered throughout the immediate area. The captured and wounded Mujaheddin soldiers were quickly spirited away from the battlefields to these outposts so that Shachmeva might "visit" with them. Many were dead before these visits were over, and those imprisoned after having information extracted from them didn't live long. He was an invaluable asset to the communist invaders, yet his priorities as an officer put management of the outposts under his command before interrogation. He personally oversaw the procession of Russian supply lines for hundreds of miles, and through fear he ensured that the daily progress reports he received for every base were exemplary. Commanders who showed even a hint of incompetence in their duties were swiftly made an example of.

It was only natural that when an entire Russian platoon went missing in action and reports of their remains surface shortly thereafter, it was the responsibility of the commanding officer of that territory to assess the validity of those reports. This was how Flanigan had devised a plan of attack against Shachmeva.

"Once you detect even the slightest bond between two of your enemies, you exploit that weakness as quickly as you can,"

Flanigan had said. "In this instance, we have custody of the target's brother, the leader of the captured platoon." The platoon Flanigan referred to was now only one-third of its original number, a fact that mattered little in light of the fact that they now had Shachmeva's brother in their custody. "Prisoners of war are usually of more value than dead men, as they can be used like currency. But for now it'll be better suited to our purposes that Shachmeva believes that his brother is dead."

The long silence was broken by the distant whine of a powerful engine. A tank. The convoy had arrived. Benazar tensed as he saw the first armored truck come around the curving cliff face that hugged the gravel road. The Russian group was made up of an armored Datsun truck that led the way, a fully armored tank, and another Datsun that brought up the rear. The massive tank appeared impregnable. As Abdur took in the trucks, each equipped with a machine gun turret, he counted four men to a truck. There was no telling how many were concealed in the tank, but it mattered little. Their information had been exact down to the last man, and they would now waylay the Russians as they had planned out to the finest details.

"Everyone, stay down," Abdur ordered. "Hamid, Haide, move forward." As Benazar watched the three men inch their way to the cliff's face on their bellies, he noticed for the first time the military precision their communications and movements had taken on. It was the kind of discipline he'd been searching for. There was much to be said about this new way of fighting. Their actions were dictated by solid intelligence and split-second timing. The weapons provided had finally allowed them to level some of the playing field with the Soviets.

The sniper and his two demolition men were in place. They waited. A few feet away Benazar heard a soft voice followed by brief static. "We'll await your signal, Benazar." Benazar gritted his teeth. The convoy below could not possibly have heard it, unless they were listening in on the channel, which is why Timur's incompetence enraged Benazar. Flanigan's plan had called for radio silence after Abdur received word of the convoy's impending arrival. Benazar took a deep breath. The whine of the tank persisted. Safe for now. He didn't dare respond. If they survived this day, Timur would be dealt with.

The convoy halted at the sight of an overturned truck. It too was an armored Datsun, and it had belonged to the captured Russian platoon. It was charred black from the attack that had stopped it in its tracks, and the roof had nearly caved in. It was just off the road, and it appeared that it had been there for quite some time. In actuality, it had been placed there just days before under Flanigan's orders. The truck was a ruse, and the real trap lay within. As the engine of the lead truck shut off, one soldier jumped off the back and another exited from the passenger side door. After a brief consultation with the driver and a military hand signal to the tank, the two men proceeded with caution to the wrecked vehicle. High atop the cliffs, Abdur surveyed the entire scene through the scope of his rifle, which protruded from underneath the sandstone covered net which concealed him. He waited patiently.

The two Russian scouts finished their investigation. Abdur smiled at the look of dismay on their faces. Two days ago Shachmeva's current outpost had received a garbled message indicating that a small tribal village, about one hundred kilometers to the west, was sheltering Major Oleg Shachmeva and the surviving members of his platoon. The message requested immediate assistance and indicated that Afghan rebels were advancing from the north. This, of course, had been a clever fabrication conceived of by Flanigan, and was given validity by the secret codes Colonel Showolter had coerced from Oleg. What happened from that point on had been a result of Flanigan's pure intuition.

The American had reasoned that Colonel Shachmeva's first move would be to take a convoy west to the next outpost that lay between him and the village. From there, he would assemble a force big enough to counter a Mujaheddin attack. Flanigan was moving the reserves south toward the village to give the appearance of impending danger to any air patrols that should investigate. The reserves were well equipped with Stinger missiles to repel the helicopters, but it would never come to that. Shachmeva would never reach the next outpost to regroup.

Abdur watched as one Russian soldier made his report to the truck driver, who in turn spoke into his radio. Several long minutes passed. The two scouts avoided eye contact with one another. The wind howled as it whipped across the cliffs. The sun was low in the west. Abdur waited.

Eventually, the tank's hatch opened. The first scout returned to the ruined truck to do a follow-up search as the second walked back to the tank. The man who appeared out of the tank's hatch wore a grim expression. Abdur could not hear what was being said, but he could imagine the dialogue. The scout was reporting to the colonel face-to-face that one of the blackened corpses found in the truck belonged to his brother Oleg. Abdur saw the Russian's jaw muscles tighten as he received the news, and that was the moment Abdur's black cross-hairs lined up with his forehead. The man in the scope fit the description: middle-aged, sharp facial features, wide shoulders. As if to help Abdur with his aim, the Russian removed his military hat to reveal a balding head with dark gray hair on the side.

Abdur heard two words. "It's him."

Abdur squeezed the trigger on his rifle. The shot echoed across the desert as Drazen Shachmeva's face caved in. The exit wound at the back of his skull sprayed blood and brains into the air and across the tank. His dead body slumped over the edge of the hole, obstructing the hatch. Abdur loaded his next shot.

"Primary objective complete. Commence cleanup." Abdur took aim at the shocked scout, who had not moved an inch in the few seconds he'd been granted. Abdur dropped him just as Hamid and Haide each lined up a truck with their bazookas and fired. The ground-quaking explosions that showered the ground below sent up a giant dust cloud that engulfed the entire convoy. For a moment there was more waiting.

"Much of your land is basically ideal for trench warfare," Flanigan had pointed out over the topographical map during their briefing. "This is how a man like Shachmeva expects to engage you. Unless you're forced to fight in the canyons and the caves, guerilla warfare just isn't practical. This assassination is being staged where the desert meets the mountains, so in this instance we can take advantage of both."

The cliff face was on the south side of the road. Waiting for the dust to clear, Benazar lifted his binoculars. Peering through them just as visibility was returning, he surveyed the scene. The lead truck must have taken a direct hit to the fuel tank, for it was completely ablaze and neither the driver nor the gunman with him could be seen. Also missing in action was the first scout. Benazar turned his eyes toward the other truck. Not nearly as much damage. The truck was smoking heavily from the engine, and those inside were either unconscious or dead. One of the men in back had been blown a full ten feet from the truck. He was screaming in agony and writhing on his back. Benazar saw that he'd lost a leg. He next saw a smoking pile of Russian fatigues, presumably the body of the other soldier in the back of the truck. No movement there.

Benazar got on the radio. To Timur he said, "Move in now." Most of the sand that had helped to conceal the two hidden trenches on the north side of the road had been swept away with the simultaneous explosions. Timur and his five men slid back the thin boards above their heads and emerged from their hiding places. Running at full speed, they charged what remained of the convoy. Two of Timur's men in the west trench approached the wreckage of the first truck and ensured that the area had been cleared. Two more from the east trench did the same with the tail truck. Two quick shots to the head silenced the screaming Russian soldier.

Timur ran at the tank from the east trench as another joined him from the west one. Together, they scrambled on top of the tank. They got to the hatch just as one of Shachmeva's men was trying to pull the colonel's body back inside. The two Afghanis unloaded the magazines of their AK-47s into the man, and his head bobbed forward as he disappeared back down the hole, taking Shachmeva's slack body with him. Timur heard more movement inside the tank, but he had already pulled the pins on both of his grenades. He thought about how remarkably the plan had been executed up until this point as he dropped his grenades into the tank and jumped clear.

During all this action, the Mujaheddin high on the cliffs had ceased fire. They risked hitting their own men if they supplied cover fire. Besides, the Russian force had been crippled in the first few seconds. The rest was a mopping up exercise.

Just as Benazar formed his first thoughts of a victory, a shot rang out. He quickly scanned the ground below, and saw one of Timur's men from the west trench go down. He was holding his right leg, which was spurting blood from the thigh. *There.* The first Russian scout was hunkering behind the overturned decoy truck. That he had survived at all was incredible, but they weren't about to let him live. From down below, he heard Timur cry, "Cover fire now!"

The men from the trenches overwhelmed the truck with bullets as Timur grabbed his fallen comrade by the collar and dragged him back to the trenches. His men retreated slowly behind him, firing all the while. When they were safely under cover again, Timur inquired of Benazar, "Could you provide some assistance?"

Benazar was still receiving the unnecessary request when Hamid aimed his reloaded bazooka diagonally down at the mangled truck. He called over to Hamid. "Wait. We don't need to waste those."

Abdur, in plain sight now, came to the west edge and took aim through the windshield of the upside down Datsun. He could make out the *Roussi's* knee. He fired.

The Russian soldier fell forward on his stomach and lost his cover. He let out an unnerving scream and rolled over onto his back. In that time Abdur had loaded another bullet into the rifle's chamber and placed a precision headshot that extinguished the last of the enemy threat.

Benazar met eyes with Abdur. "Excellent shooting."

"Thank you. Now let's see what we can salvage from this mess."

CHAPTER 11
December 3, 1986

The table the four men sat at had been designed for card games but was presently being used for a review of the previous day's mission. Showolter stood a few feet away with his arms crossed over his massive chest. He had a menacing appearance while in the shadows that accompanied the cave cabin's pale fluorescent light. Timur was glancing in his direction frequently with apprehension written on his face, as if he feared that the man might lunge at him and rip his head off of his shoulders if his report should displease Agent Flanigan. Benazar might have applauded the man had he done so. Timur had acted rashly yesterday, and Flanigan would make him answer for it.

Over the last few months Benazar had developed quite an admiration for the man. He was a military genius. His battle plans were simple and straightforward, a direct result of his ability to manipulate intelligence. What had transpired yesterday had the makings of psychological warfare, with the falsified corpse of a target's brother carefully placed as bait. The convoy had been caught completely unaware because it had been unfocused.

The two-sided attack had been brilliant. Stealthy ambushes were, like psychological warfare, something entirely new to Benazar. He was now even more convinced that his survival was a strange fate. Until he had placed himself in the hands of the Americans, he'd been throwing himself at the flying bullets. How many times had he rushed his enemies within their bunkers with no second thought? And now he was being trained to fight with a certain finesse that not only increased his chances for survival, but also hurt the Soviets two-fold. It was like the fine-tuning of an instrument, all to one day serve a greater purpose than petty vengeance.

He relished the thought, but betrayed nothing on his face. For him even a grin would be a display of personal weakness and lack of discipline. Timur, this silly man sitting across the table from him, was the polar opposite. He was ruled by his passions. In just a moment, he would have nothing to be happy about.

Flanigan rubbed his eyes with his right hand as he ashed his cigarette with his left. He'd become more at ease around the men in the last few weeks, today even more so. Perhaps this was because of yesterday's success. When he brought his hand away from his face, Benazar imagined that each line that clung to the corners of his eyes represented a different conflict the American had participated in, much the way each medal on an American soldier's dress uniform represents a different accomplishment. After a moment, he said, "The attack was executed with great effectiveness. Abdur, from what I understand your marksmanship is exceptional. I'm going to be frank; I wasn't expecting all of you to return from this. This was our first contact after a short period of preparation. But other than the shot Raheem took to the leg, everything went perfectly. In short, you've impressed us all with what you've accomplished. I see now that we have even more possibilities available to us than I had realized."

He paused for a moment, looking thoughtful. He continued, "Enjoy this first victory, but know that we have much to do in the next two days. And two days, at the most, is all we're afforded." He placed a manila folder on the table and opened it, revealing two black and white photographs. The circle tightened as the men peered in to see two photographs of the same man. One was a military portrait, the other a surveillance photo taken from a distance. Other than his large size, there were no particularly distinguishing features about him. To Benazar he was just another middle-aged Russian thug, a leg breaker for the few real thinkers for the communist ideology.

"Major Roman Minshki," Flanigan identified the Russian after releasing smoke. "He will be assuming command of the territory now that Shachmeva is out of the way. We've managed to disappear without a trace, which is fortunate since the Russians are sweeping every inch of ground within a fifty mile radius of the kill zone. This also buys us some time, since the major won't approach until he thinks the area's been cleared of threats. Congratulations, men; you've been made their number-one priority."

Flanigan reached back over his right shoulder, and Showolter handed him some printed documents. He took another drag as he momentarily reviewed the content. "Here's what we know," he continued. "We've managed to spook them. They'll be more cautious, but we can use that to our advantage. This is where we utilize our inside sources. Don't forget, our ability to identify transit routes is what presents these opportunities to us.

"The major will be coming, and he'll be coming soon. He won't be arriving by plane, but by helicopter, and he won't be coming in along his normal route. He's tied up for a few days, but we'll receive word as soon as he moves, and when he does, you'll all be waiting patiently to shoot him out of the sky."

He extinguished the cigarette in the ash tray. "So, that's all for now. I want you men to get some sleep. We'll begin coordinating our attack in the morning, and I want you all well rested." He began gathering the papers and photos into a pile, his attention now elsewhere.

Benazar watched his companions rise, and he locked eyes with Timur, whose expression bluntly read, *back off.* But he wouldn't let it drop. This war had turned the Afghan people into whisperers and backstabbers. A woman could make the wrong remark at a dinner table only to have her son report her to the Russians and have her whisked of in the middle of the night. For Benazar to inform Flanigan of Timur's folly would be a blemish on his honor, especially to bring a foreigner in between him and his fellow countryman. But he now believed in what American aid could do for them, believed in it even more than Timur did, more than the rest of these men. And orders *needed* to be followed.

Clearing his throat, he said, "Tell him, Timur."

Timur seethed, but he said nothing. Flanigan shot Benazar a quick glance that suggested he knew what he was getting at. He then looked over the men. "Yes. Which brings me to another issue that'll also be discussed tomorrow: how to execute a mission *exactly* as planned down to the finest details. There were some mistakes made with Shachmeva, ones we don't wish to repeat. We just have a few loose ends to tie up. But again, this can wait until tomorrow." They filed out of the cabin one by one. Before Benazar could exit, Flanigan said, "Benazar, stay a minute. I need a word with you."

CHAPTER 12
DECEMBER 6, 1986

During times when tension was in the air, especially in those few moments before the killing began, Benazar would sharpen his knife. Though he ran the blade over the stone slowly and with intent, it was a nervous habit born not out of fear but of anticipation of the engagement. *If they come this way...* It was wise to keep oneself a bit on edge when there was the possibility of danger. He had no way of knowing if the helicopter would be passing through his particular line of fire, but he would be ready for it if it came.

Sparks flew off of the steel and disappeared like melted snow. The scratching sound of hard surfaces grinding against one another tended to unnerve some of those around him, as was the case now with his partner for the mission. *Good.* He liked to think that his habit inspired a feeling of unease in his brothers in arms. *Everyone* needed to be ready.

Minutes passed slowly. Apprehension grew with the waiting. The raking of the knife on the stone grew louder. Khaled was silently waiting over a tripod-mounted M60 machine gun, and Benazar saw that gooseflesh had formed on his partner's forearm.

"Benazar, please. I promise you, you won't need that today."

It was true enough. There was no opportunity for a melee; not today. But keeping the blade from dulling was symbolic of his will to keep from losing his focus. Some men attributed his prowess to his ferocity and brute strength. Those who knew him better knew that it was his undivided attention to the task at hand that had kept him alive for so long.

More waiting. They had been lying in wait for almost three hours now. Just when Benazar thought that perhaps their information had been faulty, he heard something in the distance. He stood up in the wind and listened carefully. What might be mistaken by some for thunder was what he knew all too well to be distant gunfire. It was a barely audible cracking that bounced back and forth over the rock walls, and was then carried through the canyon.

In his headset he heard, "The target has fled the minefield." What was being referred to as a minefield was in fact airspace. Spread out over an area of about five thousand square meters were dozens of strategically placed Mujaheddin soldiers, the reserves, concealed within foxholes and armed with stinger missiles, anti-aircraft guns, and British blow pipes. If events were playing themselves out as planned, then the Russian helicopter carrying their target would have just appeared over the ridge. The initial bombardment of missiles was meant to bring the chopper down. Benazar and Khaled were merely part of a contingency plan should the chopper be able to flee the ambush intact.

With the minefield spread out over such a great distance, the missiles were fired one by one in rapid succession. Flanigan had reasoned that those aboard Minshki's transport would have no way of knowing how great a force they faced, and seemed certain that after a threat assessment was made, the chopper would choose evasive action over engagement. It was never meant to come to that. Having heard those words in his earpiece, however, he now knew that he, Khaled, and his team of a dozen men were perhaps their only hope of success.

Into the speaker of his headset, Benazar said, "Everyone be ready; this could be it." If the helicopter had indeed escaped unscathed, then it would have gone low to the ground and been flushed into the canyon. At least, Flanigan seemed to think so, and it had been his uncanny ability to anticipate such moves that had made their first mission such a success. And he was sure of himself now in his deduction that the chopper would seek safe passage through the canyon if the rebels failed to destroy it.

Flanigan had mapped out the canyons and ascertained three possible escape routes, all forking off of the canyon that served as the entrance. Benazar's team was dispersed across the walls of the middle passage, with lines of fire being drawn in a zigzag pattern to avoid catching one another in a cross fire. It was the same in the other two branch canyons, with Amir and Abdur each leading a team. The chopper would have to choose one of the routes, and no matter which one it took, it would find itself overwhelmed by projectiles.

The waiting continued until a new sound reached Benazar's ears. Kneeling down, he placed the palm of his hand to the limestone, and then pressed his right cheek against the rough surface. He looked up at Kaled, determination written on his furrowed brow.

"It's coming this way." Within a minute, a powerful wind tore through the canyon, whipping his clothing, hair, and beard against his skin and lifting the bearskin hat from his head. The chopper emerged from around a sharp bend at astonishing speed, a hulking steel body looking more intimidating than the ones the Americans possessed and heavily armed. This was it.

"Open fire."

Bullets and rockets streaked toward the helicopter from all directions. The chopper was agile enough to evade the slower moving rockets, but the bullets found their mark, effectively pinning the chopper in place. The pilot must have panicked when he realized that he couldn't go to a higher altitude, for he spun the chopper into wild rotations, machine guns blazing. It was like a wild animal trying to fend of predators slowly circling in for the kill. The defense kept Benazar's men momentarily pinned in place.

In addition to leading this part of the mission, it was Benazar's job to make sure Khaled's M-60 had a steady stream of ammunition. As he made sure the bullets were being properly fed into the chamber, he observed Khaled's line of fire. Crouching behind Khaled, he got a better view.

"You're aiming for the pilot. I told you to take out the trail rotor." As soon as the words came out, a rocket from the far side of the canyon and beneath them found the underbelly of the chopper. There was an explosion, but to the Muhjaheddin's shock the chopper remained airborne. Black smoke poured from the ruined segment of its hull. In retribution, it rained down a shower of fire on its attackers, cutting them down.

All the while, Khaled unleashed hundreds of rounds at the chopper's nose. Benazar had to cover his ears from the deafening sound, but he could see that his subordinate was persisting in a futile gesture.

The chopper was out of control, spinning wildly back and forth across the canyon, but never meeting the rock. It continued to lay down fire in all directions, if only merely to repel further onslaught. Then suddenly the pilot appeared to regain control of the riddled craft, for it began to rise up and out. Benazar's men were about to fail in their objective.

"Idiot!" he spat, "Follow orders!" He raised his foot high and brought it down in a drop-kick to the right side of Khaled's face. Khaled rolled over onto his side, either stunned or unconscious. Benazar shoved him aside. Getting down on his stomach, he manned the machine gun and took aim at the chopper's main weakness, its trail rotor. He squeezed the trigger and did not let go for a long while.

As it usually did, time seemed to slow down for him as he set to his new task. He was able to clear his head of all extraneous thoughts, calming himself and focusing solely on the seemingly insignificant propeller at the end of his gun sight. There were only the banging sounds of the bullets exploding from their chamber and the metal pings of hundreds of shells being emptied onto stone.

It was Benazar who saved the mission. The chopper, wounded as it was, might have escaped had not his relentlessness resulted in the disintegration of its tail end. The helicopter spiraled a few hundred feet before its rotors smacked into the canyon wall, chopping at it and sending flying slag in all directions. What remained of the blackened metal skeleton disappeared from sight as it plummeted to the dark depths of the canyon.

Benazar let out a breath he didn't know he'd been holding. A cold sweat soaked his brow, and he wiped it away with his right sleeve. Already he could hear cheering from all corners of the canyon. Celebratory gunfire followed, an undisciplined and wasteful display the Americans would have frowned upon.

Glancing to his left he saw Khaled massaging his jaw, nursing wounds to both his head and his pride. And he had well deserved them. It was arrogance for Khaled to assume he knew better than those who saw fit to provide him with the needed information in the first place.

Benazar leaned over the edge of his perch and peered down into the rocky chasm. He heard the rising echo of grinding metal and then silence. It was such a bi-polar pattern they were developing: silence followed by chaos followed by silence.

Two assaults. Two victories. Battles were being fought on dozens of fronts all over Afghanistan, but from now on the communists would know where to concentrate their fire. And so the stakes were higher. Very well. *Let's see this through to the end.*

CHAPTER 13
December 8, 1986

Flanigan didn't tend to smile. Some days, the right side of his mouth would twitch ever so slightly. This might have passed for a grin. But most of the time he wore a deep, thoughtful frown.

Nevertheless, all the sons of Afghanistan who had come to learn from him had developed a deep respect for the man's intelligence and cunning. He had earned it with his flawless strategies. The men didn't really ever need to see a warm side to Flanigan. Two major victories and high morale would suffice. But when Flanigan's rarely seen smirk formed on his face during the review of the second attack, Benazar realized something: *We're exceeding his expectations.*

Benazar had known from the beginning that this operation was risky business for the Americans. It was a delicate experiment, where unforeseen developments could lead to disaster. He also knew that this was not the only collaboration between the Mujaheddin and the CIA. Training camps similar to theirs were established all over the country. *We're simply the most effective.*

Benazar never smiled. It just wasn't his way. It was enough simply to imagine that maybe, one day, one of his own could feel some small measure of peace that he'd never known and probably never would.

"Excellent," Flanigan said with a nod. "This is all going extremely well." He took a drag on his cigarette, and then exhaled. "I want you all to know what I've seen since this was all conceived, something the Reds failed to see. You men have resolve. And the Russians, in their attempts to outgun you, have been ignorant of this." He got up from his seat and went to the wall where a map of the region hung. Studying it intently, he ran his hand over the stubble on his jaw. He took a drag and exhaled.

Turning to face the men he said, "You've opened us up to many more possibilities. There's much to discuss. We'll meet again here in two days time. Amir and his men will be embarking on a reconnaissance mission to investigate the activity down at the Helmand River. But before that I want to meet with all of you so that we might start planning our next assault. Of course, whatever Amir is able to find may dictate our next move, but we have important decisions to make, and I would like to hear your thoughts when we meet.

"Good work, men. That's all. Colonel Showolter will contact you when we need you."

Once again the men filed out of the room, and as before Flanigan asked Benazar to stay. Pulling his chair back, Flanigan resumed sitting. "Colonel, please see to our inventory. And tell the men in the hall to enter on your way out."

"Yes, sir."

After extinguishing his cigarette, Flanigan lifted his head, and his eyes met Benazar's. "So it was you."

"That's correct," Benazar replied in accented English that showed not a hint of pride.

"Helicopters can be effective weapons, but it's amazing how vulnerable they are when you get them within range."

"As I've now seen."

Flanigan's eyes went to the heavy metal door as Showolter held it for two newcomers. "It went almost perfectly," he said.

Benazar thought that he might have more to say. Then he saw the two men who entered and sat down at the table. One he recognized as one of the reserves under his command, whose name eluded him for the moment. The other was Khaled, who wore the imprint of a boot heel on his swollen and bruised face. No one doubted that the mark was Benazar's handiwork.

The first time Flanigan had asked Benazar to remain was only days before.

"Benazar, stay a minute. I need a word with you," he had said. He had then gone on to tell Benazar that their entire relationship was a delicate one, and that fast and presumptuous action was the way toward problems.

"We're not here to lead you, Benazar; we're here to aid you," he had said. "I know what you're feeling. The orders called for com silence, and Timur disregarded them and almost compromised the entire mission. Your life is tied to this man's, and he cannot follow the orders that are there for your own safety.

"But you must work this out amongst yourselves. I can't presume to take disciplinary action against Timur. You're all here of your own free will, and I'm in no way empowered to take such action. Believe me, if I had it my way, I would have every one of you standing like a row of statues, obediently acknowledging my status as your commanding officer and weeding out the weak. But that's just not possible. It's not in the nature of our alliance.

"I recognize that I've set up a chain of command for you four and the rest in reserve, but that only encompasses all of you, and you and Timur are of the same rank. You must understand how important it is that we Americans remain in the shadows during all of this."

At the time, Benazar wasn't at all sure that he *did* understand it, but he did have a retort.

"No, Agent Flanigan, I don't see how I can expect that. With the weaponry you've brought us and the insight you've shown us, we can accept this gift for what it is and embrace it, or we can waste it. But I see no way where we can meet on some middle ground where the men who are fortunate enough to receive this training are allowed to act on their own. It's all or nothing. If we can serve with you, then we can serve under you. We've been given a chance to make great change, and we must respect the terms of that change.

"Believe me, no one had more reservations about these dealings than I, but as soon as I saw Shachmeva dead, I knew that we were on the right path. I believe in the direction we're moving. And if that means adopting your western fighting style, then so be it."

Flanigan had listened with deep concentration. After an awkward silence, he told Benazar that he'd given him much to consider, and that perhaps certain revisions in the structuring of their agreement were in order.

* * *

A few days later, Colonel Showolter informed the men that he was assuming tactical command of the entire unit. Interaction between the two groups would remain the same, but further disobedience of commands might result in demotion or even dismissal.

Sitting there now, with Khaled's battered face avoiding his stare from across the card table, Benazar would see the irony in finally getting what he wished for. *He* was about to be disciplined.

"Benazar, I'm taking you off of all reconnaissance until further notice," Flanigan stated bluntly. "One of the first lessons you learned during those first few days was that you're never to lay a hand on one of the men under your command."

Benazar sat expressionless. *And so what now? A court-martial?* He kept silent.

Flanigan leaned closer, his voice lowered and lost a bit of its edge. "Look, my friend, this alliance is fragile enough as it is. I know how many of your countrymen disapprove of it. We have representation from all seven parties of the Mujaheddin. If you men are allowed to lay your hands on one another, if violence breaks out within, we risk the formation of a schism. We can't allow that. We've got to stay focused on our common enemy."

Things suddenly began to make more sense. Whereas Benazar earlier had been disgusted by the lack of discipline in those he fought alongside, he himself was guilty of the same animal instincts. He often wondered why God had cursed him with such raw impulses.

"You must understand, Benazar, this is the way my team operates. This is what you yourself wanted."

Having witnessed yet another display of the American's wisdom, Benazar asked, "Will that be all for now, Agent Flanigan?"

"Yes, that'll be all. I'm still going to need your input when Amir returns, so I'll send for you when that happens. Until then, rejoin your men and get some rest. You're dismissed."

Benazar rose and turned to leave. He could feel the American's gaze behind him. A moment before there had been a wave of shame, one he had not felt since the days of his youth. But he had quickly overcome it. He had quickly learned from it.

CHAPTER 14
December 15, 1986

"I think that we may be in over our heads."

"Don't think I haven't considered it. This whole operation reminds me of those old bomb-diffusing training sessions."

"When you told them that they have resolve, well, I've seen it too. And it saddens me to see what the ISI is doing to these men."

"Meaning what?"

"Sir, they've got them by the balls. They're using them for their own agenda. The seven parties are trigger happy right now. I see this ending badly."

"Using them? Colonel, where exactly do you think Uncle Sam fits into all of this. Do you really think he's here to save a nation. Don't get me wrong, I meant every word I said to those men that day, but let's look at the larger picture here."

"The larger picture?"

"Yes, Colonel. Forgive me for saying this, because I've always felt that you're wise beyond your years, but you weren't in 'Nam. You were too young. It's something you might not be able to understand. There are always hidden agendas."

"All right. I can accept that."

"You know me. You know I always want to have a plan, as well as a back-up plan, as well as a back-up for the back-up plan. Well, if the Soviet Union withdraws within the next year or two, we've got a whole new problem on our hands, because in that event, try as I might to form Plan A, it eludes me. I've already spoken with the general and the men back in Langley, and just between you and me, they've got nothing. They equivocate; they dodge important issues. What they don't do is share with me any kind of post-war plan. Sometimes I think we're completely on our own out here."

"So, where do we stand?"

"I've asked myself that. There's not much we can do. The ISI has held up their end of the bargain, and all of their information has been precise."

"We need more guns and ammunition and—"

"I assure you, Colonel, this is one of the few places on earth where we don't have to worry about running out of guns or ammo."

"And other miscellaneous supplies. And warmer clothes. These space heaters are failing us. It's the dead of winter and the men are freezing in these caves."

"Don't forget that they were occupying these caverns long before we powered them up. We don't want them going soft on us now."

"No, there's no chance of that. These men … it's like war is all some of them have ever known. They walk around with haunted looks on their faces, especially Benazar Rashid. I look into his eyes and I see two black holes."

"I agree. You can tell that man's had his share of horror. He's unpredictable. He could turn out to be our greatest ally or our loosest cannon. I guess time will tell. But we do need him."

"Do you really think we can take out Morodov?"

"Where's your optimism? Look at what we've already accomplished."

"That's what scares me. I think it's only a matter of time before a shit-storm rains down on us."

"Let's wait until recon returns. We don't know yet if he'll come to us. I'm thinking he has to though. He's losing face back in Russia. He'll need to flush us out. Time's on our side."

CHAPTER 15
DECEMBER 25, 1986

"I've gathered you all here this morning because I have important news," Flanigan began as he once again had the attention of the entire group. "Whether the news is good depends entirely on how we respond to it." He paused thoughtfully, allowing the translation to catch up to him. "I know many of you are on edge. Lately there's been a lot of training and preparation and a lot less real action. I know many of you want to get out of this cave and return to the front lines. I ask that you all remain patient just a little while longer. We'll have battles to fight soon enough. In the meantime, I have something to show all of you. This will illustrate our present state of affairs far better than any explanation I could give."

He gave a slight hand gesture to someone behind the men seated at the back of the miniature auditorium, and the space went dim. Then a film projector sent a beam of colored light at the white screen hanging on the wall behind Flanigan.

As the pictures in the slide show came into focus, Flanigan resumed speaking. "These pictures were taken by Amir Sarif's team during a two-week information gathering expedition. I'm going to be short and to the point here. What you're seeing is a Soviet withdrawal from the immediate area."

When Benazar squinted he could see greater detail on the brightly lit shapes being projected. Taken from a distance, the photos were difficult to process, but after a few moments he saw what Flanigan meant. There were pictures of crates being loaded onto trucks, jeeps being refueled, airfields being evacuated, gun emplacements being broken down. Others showed giant dust clouds trailing whole caravans as they deserted their camps.

"These were taken at no fewer than three locations running along the Helmand River," Flanigan continued. "The fact that this is taking place only to the south of us indicates that they still have no idea where we are."

The pictures continued, showing large, green army rafts ferrying supplies down the river. Benazar took it all in and wondered what this turn of events meant for them. Flanigan addressed his unspoken concerns. "I'm sorry to say that we can't really know the nature of the retreat. It could be that this area has been deemed a hostile zone, and they had no choice but to give ground. But I don't think that's likely."

The translation caught up with his words. "It could also be a ploy, an attempt to get us to expose ourselves. We know through numerous reports from our inside men that they have no idea how large a force we have. They may need time to gather intel of their own.

"The third possibility, the one I'm inclined to believe, is that this is a regrouping. I feel confident that Morodov is going to amass a force large enough to return here in an attempt to wipe us out. This is a scenario we've anticipated and can be ready to counter. But once again, there is much to be learned before we can act, and the situation requires patience if we're to respond appropriately."

He paused, lowering his eyes. "But I'm not here to be negative. Congratulations, men. We've accomplished more than we'd imagined in far less time than we'd planned. There may yet be dark times ahead, but not today. Today we celebrate."

* * *

The mountain air at night was so cold that the wool blanket Benazar had wrapped around him could do little to retain the heat within. It was so cold he imagined that the small clouds of breath forming in front of his face might crystallize and shatter into an icy pile at his feet. He looked up at the cloudless sky. The moon could have been the biggest he'd ever seen it. Its light spread across the entire snow-capped mountain range, casting a luminescent beauty everywhere.

Maybe one day we'll return to the times when such sights could move a man, he thought, as they had the day he had traveled to this solitude. Nature's beauty called out to him, only this time it was lunar, not solar. And like that day, Benazar had refused the call. He could not afford sentiment. Besides, he had not come out here to gaze at the stars. Now was a time for reflection.

"Salaam, Benazar, I would have thought you'd be celebrating with the others," Flanigan said as he took him by surprise. They were not at the iron-gated entrance, but at an elevated balcony formed from blasted rock. The holes in the cave wall had been opened along the cracks to make openings for heavy armament.

Benazar had come here to be alone, but he didn't feel that Flanigan had infringed upon his privacy. Here was probably the only individual in the entire cave whom he'd have welcomed at the moment. His one-time mentor had bestowed upon him an insight that gave him an advantage over the Russians and his countrymen alike. "No, Agent Flanigan, not tonight." Benazar said as his head turned back to the landscape.

"I'm sorry. I didn't mean to interfere," Flanigan offered.

Benazar said over his shoulder, "You haven't. With all respect, sir, it simply isn't appropriate for the men to be drinking and acting like fools today." Benazar had explained himself only so that Flanigan would not think he was in any way sulking over his demotion. He knew the American had trouble reading him. Only now he was in a situation where he should elaborate. Before he could, Flanigan beat him to it. "Ah, I see. It's inappropriate to throw parties on the anniversary of the invasion. Now's the time for remembrance, am I right?"

Perhaps Flanigan could read him after all. Benazar credited him for his perception. "Yes, you're right. Today was the day everything changed. I'm here trying to remember what we once were and to imagine what we might one day become again. But I'm also here to remember those we've lost."

"Shall I leave you?"

"No, please stay." He turned to face Flanigan. "And what brings you out here?"

"I also wanted to be alone. I'm missing my family this Christmas day."

Benazar thought he saw a twitch underneath Flanigan's right eye, as if he was concentrating on not letting the longing show on his face. "It must be difficult for you."

"It is," Flanigan said. "But this is the life I've chosen. I will say, though, that this is the hardest day of the year to be separated from them."

There was a long silence. Not an awkward one, but one that the moment called for. After a few minutes, Benazar's curiosity got the better of him. "Tell me, Agent Flanigan, are you a practicing Christian?"

"Yes, I am."

"There is civil strife within our circles," Benazar said, moving toward his main question. "Many object to the partnership we've made because these men believe this invasion is an assault on Islam itself. You'll notice most of the men inside *aren't* drinking. This is a jihad; this is a holy war to them, and there's no room in this war for unbelievers. Others believe that you have a hidden agenda. Why this concern for us? And therein lies the problem. If you don't fight for Islam, what do you fight for?"

Flanigan apparently didn't need long to think of a response. "I don't know what you know about where I come from, but the United States separates matters of religion and matters of state. We're what you might call interdenominational. That's why our government has worked so well. Our history has shown us that any conflict born out of religion is destructive to the order of societies. Our nation is made up of all sorts of religious doctrines. And there are many thousands of practicing Muslims within our borders."

Benazar had once heard of what the American spoke of. *The free world*, it was called. Benazar had heard much about the western world. He had seen movies and photos. He had never met anyone who'd been there. Those who went there ended up staying there. He had never really concerned himself with a nation a world away. There had been plenty to do here in Afghanistan.

Now his father's words came to mind. "Benazar, I'm going to tell you everything you ever need to know about the United States. They try to set a shining example for the rest of the world to follow, but their history is written in blood just like any other nation's. The people of that country are the spawn of Europe— the British, the Spanish, all of them. They invaded that land the same way we we've been repeatedly invaded. Not only did they nearly wipe out the native peoples of the land with bloodshed and disease, they enslaved whole tribes from Africa, shipping them to America under inhuman conditions that would make you want to vomit. Always remember this, Benazar, and you'll need not trouble yourself with that nation."

Now Benazar wasn't so sure. He knew the tension between America and Russia was based on a difference of ideologies, capitalism versus communism. But when that tension grew into a nuclear arms race that one such as he could not even begin to fathom, why would the Americans make a play that just might tip the balance? It was a risk that offered little reward. This could lead Benazar to only one conclusion: the American cause was genuine.

He found himself conflicted, something that never happened to him. He had always been told to be wary of Americans. Indeed, there were those who would see him murdered if they knew he was involved in this force. Ironically, it was fortunate for him that he was widely believed to be dead. But the conflict remained.

And now Flanigan needed answers. "So then, where do you fit into all of this?" He was one to speak his mind. "How do you feel about accepting the help of an unbeliever?" There was no challenge or mockery in his inquiry; he was merely playing the hand he'd been dealt.

Benazar took no offense. "I don't know if we are or ever will be ready to embrace the democracy you hold so dear. But I too think such a separation between religion and government is necessary for our people. However, that's not Islam, and I feel that those who interpret the Koran as they see fit are eating away at our way of life from within. Many are fanatics, and fanatics are rash and unpredictable. Islam is peaceful at its core; it's misguided men who deface it.

"When I came here I was doing some reconnaissance of my own. If, when I arrived, I had suspected foul play, I was open to the possibility of killing you and every one of your men until I was cut down. But now, after a short time under your leadership, I can truly think of you as a comrade."

The impact of the words hung in the air for a moment. Benazar felt the exchange had been sufficient, and he began to head inside. "I'll let you be alone with thoughts of your family." Not one to express sentiment, he surprised himself with his next question, "How old are your children?"

Something like gentleness was evident in Flanigan's voice. "My son is sixteen and my daughter is fourteen. And how old is your son?"

Benazar's body stiffened. He was not as surprised by the question itself as he was that the American had concerned himself with obtaining this seemingly irrelevant information. *There's little these information gatherers don't concern themselves with,* he reminded himself.

"My son is nine years old," he answered. He felt the need to explain *his* separation from his family. "The invasion happened right after he was born. Since then my brother, Mussar, has sought a peaceful resolution to this conflict. I am a wanted war criminal and can only put my son in danger. He's much safer in my brother's care."

Flanigan offered a gentle nod of understanding. Benazar resumed his departure. Just before he stepped through the doorway, he heard at his back, "You're going to win this war, Benazar Rashid. You'll be seeing your son soon."

Benazar would not have thought it possible for him to ever embrace words of hope so wholeheartedly, but he did.

CHAPTER 16
JANUARY 6, 1987

Flanigan had moved his slide projector from the main hall into the war-room bunker. The usual six men were present. Flanigan wore a grim expression. He was to be the bearer of bad news. Not one for flowery preambles, he got right to it. "It's as we feared. Morodov has returned in force and he's blazing a path back to us, razing every local village on the way."

Benazar felt the pit of his stomach tighten. Flanigan hit a button from the cord connected to the projector, and a vivid picture came into focus on the screen. The men gasped. It showed a tribal village in ruins, smoke pouring from crumbled buildings. The next was of wailing women, some holding infants to their breasts as they were herded into Russian trucks. The third showed a row of five men on their knees awaiting execution, staring in horror at one of their own who lay on his belly in a pool of his own blood.

The slides continued one by one, each one sickening. Benazar clenched his teeth and unsheathed his knife. He began cutting tips of hair off his beard.

"These pictures were taken three days ago," Flanigan explained. "Morodov is frantic. He may have concluded that these poor people have been harboring us and supplying us. He's hurting them to get at us. Or he may be aware that the villagers know nothing about us and is using this cruel tactic to draw us out."

Timur shot up. "We must do something now. What good are we to anyone buried under all this rock?"

Flanigan had not understood Timur's words, but he raised his voice instantly in response. "Timur, sit down! Now!"

Timur sat back down. Flanigan's voice softened a bit. "I have more to show you." He clicked to the next slide. This one was of yet another Russian outpost under construction. "Morodov has established a defensive position similar to our own. He's cradled himself into these rock formations."

Benazar was not sure exactly where these photos might have been taken, but he was fairly certain it was nearby. He wondered how long it might take to get there if and when Flanigan decided to attack.

"Now here is some welcome news," Flanigan continued. "While they were manning their trenches, they were taken by surprise and overrun by a small force dispatched by General Gul."

Benazar suppressed a grin. If any one man embodied the spirit of the Mujaheddin, it was General Gul. It was a comforting thought to know he had responded in kind, yet at the same time it was troubling that Flanigan had until now been unaware of this turn of events.

The next slide showed a row of three defensive trenches stretching across the entire frontal perimeter. There was no way to enter the defense post without crossing them. What were once dug to ward of hostiles were now being used by Gul's forces to stage an assault on the fortress.

"What we have now is a standoff," Flanigan resumed. "But it won't last long. Russian air support is due to arrive at any hour now. Gentleman, I don't see any alternative but to join General Gul on the front lines and prepare for a full frontal assault. This may be the only chance we have for this, and I can guarantee we won't have the chance to utilize the help of General Gul again."

Timur and Amir nodded in approval. Abdur did nothing to hide his look of skepticism. Benazar remained still, his face blank. So this is what it came down to. After months of careful planning and deliberate action, they were going to throw everything they had at an uncertainty. There was no time to plan or prepare, at least not in the efficient and calculated manner to which they'd grown accustomed.

"We have the reserves armed and ready for action. We're gathering together as many trucks, motorbikes, and horses we can muster even as we speak. You'll be flown to the drop zone in small groups. I want you all to go now to tell your battalions what's happening. Make them ready. I'll be by shortly to brief you all."

The four battalion leaders began to leave. Flanigan called out, "Benazar, I need to speak with you."

Benazar couldn't believe his ears. Could it be that now, at possibly their most desperate hour, his demotion stood? He'd wait and hear what Flanigan had to say before jumping to conclusions.

"I have a special task for you," Flanigan told him. "Let me show you something." He unfolded a large map on the table. "You know that the Soviets have been destroying your irrigation channels since they've arrived."

He put his finger along an inked line representing the edge of a rock. "They've done the same to this village. Right here where this line is drawn is a narrow crack in the cliff's face. This is where the Russians blasted away the rock with dynamite to destroy one of the village's main water veins. What I'm sure they don't know is that there's a cave opening on the other side."

Benazar began to see where Flanigan was going with this. If what he suspected was true, then they had been presented with yet another great opportunity.

"The opening they've blown in this pipeline is just large enough for a man to crawl through," Flanigan said, raising both eyebrows.

"Or twenty-six men."

"To what end?" Benazar asked.

"If you were to crawl through the pipeline and emerge on the village side you will have taken them completely unaware."

"You want us to flank them," Benazar said.

"It's more complex than that," Flanigan explained. He continued the slide show that Benazar thought he'd concluded. "These pictures were taken from far away, but you can see that observation tower there, can't you?"

Benazar could see. It was a tall tower standing adjacent to the spot in the cliff face that Flanigan suggested he and his men emerge from.

Flanigan had his own nervous habits much like Benazar's fixation on his knife. He took out a cigarette and lit it. He took a deep drag and exhaled. "Benazar, I can't stress how important this is. Even if our front lines fall, you still have a chance to win this. Not only are you capable of taking out the machine gun emplacements from your hidden position, but you can take out Morodov as well. He's turned this into his observation tower."

Full awareness washed over Benazar. Flanigan wasn't desperate. He still had tricks up his sleeve. "You're saying if all goes according to plan, I'll have the chance to assassinate the Russian colonel?"

"That's exactly what I'm telling you."

"But why not Abdur? He's easily our best sniper."

"Because," Flanigan explained, "I'll need him in the trenches. He's a natural leader. I'm sending Yussef from his battalion to join you. He's second best to Abdur but more than capable of making a shot at that range."

"Then why send my entire battalion? If stealth is required, such a large force might expose us."

"Because if you fail to confirm the kill and Morodov escapes, then you're to shower the entire encampment with rockets. They won't be able to withstand a two-pronged attack, not when one comes as a complete surprise."

Benazar ran his hand over his beard as he stared at the latest slide. This would be their riskiest mission. Still young, the men were going to use all of their resources on a suicide run meant to take out a single man. It was either brilliant or foolish. They'd know soon enough.

"I'll ready my men," Benazar said.

*   *   *

Flanigan addressed the entire detachment, giving words of encouragement to men about to give up their lives to defend the land they held dear. "I'm not going to waste precious time to delude you. This is the decisive battle we all knew was imminent. We're all surprised that it found us so soon, but it did. Regardless, every single one of you is ready for this. In the short time we've known each other, you've shown me you're capable of taking your land back. Those of you that die today can rest knowing that as a representative of the United States of America I promise that we shall continue to do whatever we can to end this threat. Go now, and make your people proud."

*   *   *

"I hope we've done the right thing, Flanigan."
"So do I, Colonel. So do I."

CHAPTER 17
JANUARY 7, 1987

In a period of about two hours, three groups of six and one group of seven were flown to the drop zone. Benazar had lost two men during the attack on Major Minshki, but he had been lent Abdur's best sniper for the mission. Including him, the group numbered twenty-five. Unlike Benazar, who almost always donned his bearskin cap, most of the men had resumed wearing turbans for the battle to come.

They wasted no time, covering ground on the run. The map Benazar had was crude, but it would get them to where they needed to be. Switching on flashlights, they plunged into the dark cave that was on the mountain's eastern face. On the western face the battle already raged.

They found the pipeline quickly. It had been blown. The space it provided would not make entrance easy for the men, especially with all their gear, and if his map was correct, then they were looking at about a quarter of a mile to cover on their bellies.

"Quickly now," Benazar's voice boomed. "I'll go first. Yussef, you bring up the rear. No crowding, no pushing. It's going to be tight in there."

And with that he lowered himself into the exposed pipeline, the vessel for precious water that the Red Army had emptied.

He moved steadily, leading the way with a mining light strapped to his head. It was a last-minute gift from his American ally. His breathing grew heavy, and sweat began to bead on his brow. He maintained a moderate pace.

After a few minutes of crawling, some of the men were seized by claustrophobia. It affected Benazar as well, but he resolved to overcome it. He picked up his pace to avoid jamming up the confines of the piping, but behind him some men were beginning to panic.

"Move faster!"

"I can hardly breathe."

"Stop pushing me!"

"This tunnel's going to collapse, I know it."

"I can't see."

"What if we can't get out on the other side?"

"Look out! I'm turning back."

Benazar had heard enough. He stopped, flipping onto his back as he turned to face the line behind him. "If any of you tries to turn back, I'll see you dead," he shouted. Flanigan had forbidden him from taking physical action against the men, but a mutiny he would not abide. "Get a hold of yourselves! We'll be out of this soon enough."

Flanigan had referred to Abdur as a natural leader. Benazar was anything but. True, he could get men to follow him through fear. The men who whispered about him knew he could be ruthless, and he never bluffed. But in the last few months that was not the kind of leadership he'd been taught to exhibit. He merely did it out of old instincts because he feared a loss of focus. And now was a time where focus mattered the most.

Wiping his brow with his sleeve, he twisted back onto his stomach and continued the long crawl to open air. His words had the desired effect, the men were now moving quickly and silently. Perhaps they'd been ashamed of themselves, these men who'd been hand-picked and trained to overcome the severest of hardships.

Left elbow, right elbow, left, right, left, right ... Deep breath in, then out. In, out. In, out. Getting hotter. Light not that strong. Nothing ahead but darkness. More darkness. Kick hard off the walls! Push! Keep counting, it can't be that much farther. So hot! Curse this heat! I need to stand up. How much farther?

Benazar could not even guess how much time might have passed, but suddenly there was space, lots and lots of space. He shot out and took a quick look around. The first person to follow him out was Khaled. Benazar stopped him, putting a hand to Khaled's chest, and then his index finger to his lips. He nodded to the piping. *Time for silence.* Khaled took his meaning and stayed behind to give the word to the men as they emerged.

Behind him, Benazar heard the familiar sounds of battle echoing off of the cave walls. He rushed ahead, rifle in arms, ready for anything. A bright light hit his face as he rounded a corner of rock. He'd found the cave's entrance. He peered back around the corner and whispered to Khaled. He signaled for silence and a stealthy approach. He crouched down and moved toward the narrow crevice. He took a moment to take his pack off, and then removed his hooded camouflage tarp from it and threw it over his head. He got back down on his belly and crawled through the small opening.

The sun reflected brightly off of the desert terrain, and Benazar moved slowly over the rocky ground to avoid detection. After ten feet of steady progress, he came to a steep drop. He was now overlooking the battle zone. It was about another fifty feet to ground level, and that's where the Russian defense post was. Taking out a pair of binoculars, he surveyed the scene, making a search for his priority target. There was little to suggest that the structure in front of him had once been a part of a peaceful village. A giant stone slab resting on concrete columns protected the Soviets, and atop it were machine guns. The outpost looked impregnable.

He next looked to the battlefield. Halfway from the outer wall to the defense trenches was a flaming Russian tank that had been smashed by a rocket. The Mujaheddin were holding their own.

They had indeed turned the defensive trenches into their forward attack position, occupying all three rows that ran across the northern perimeter. Benazar could see that they had dug themselves in deep. There was no sign yet of Russian air support, the famed MIG 17s, but it was a good possibility that the Mujaheddin possessed enough anti-aircraft firepower to repel an attack from the sky. Apparently it was still a standoff.

Time to wait out the chaos. They weren't here to support the frontal assault. They were here for an assassination.

He had a clear view of the observation tower. It was the structure closest to him and the men. From here the shot would be fairly easy. But now he saw that the Russians had erected a spacious command tower, standing taller than the observation tower and farther away. This complicated matters.

He turned his head and watched his men approach. *Good.* They were still in single file, approaching on their stomachs and concealed under tarps the color of sandstone. They had done it. It seemed that the invaders had no idea that he and his men were close at hand. His group could wait for the right time to attack.

His eyes sought out Yussef. Their sniper located Benazar and crawled up beside him. "If he goes anywhere, it'll be there," Benazar said pointing to the open windowed shack on stilts. Yussef nodded and began to calibrate the scope on his rifle.

"He's not in there now," Yussef said a moment later, while looking through Benazar's binoculars. "I count five, but none of them are him."

Benazar and Yussef had examined every single photograph of Ivan Morodov from the Americans' files. They had burned his image into their memories. His most identifiable feature was the thick brow that loomed over the rest of his face, casting his eyes in shadow in every single picture they'd seen. Bearded, aged, scarred, or burned, they would not mistake him if he showed himself.

Benazar kept his binoculars fixed on the tower as Yussef brought his rifle to bear. Peering through the scope, he made a few final adjustments, and then went still. Benazar turned to the men behind him.

He addressed them in a low voice. "I need you all to remain silent. You'll know when it's time to act. Until then, no one moves without my word."

The men settled in. For now, all they could do was wait and watch the battle in front of them play itself out. Benazar's eyes remained locked on the command tower. It was shortly before dusk, and the battle had worn the Mujaheddin thin. There had been several failed attempts to penetrate the fortress. There were bodies scattered about the ground between the trenches and the front wall. Some men still lived, screaming to God, begging for mercy. Other men had been turned into blackened and bloody corpses. All of this unfolded in front of Benazar and his men, and it was devastating for them.

"What are we waiting for?" one man hissed between clenched teeth. "We could have ended this hours ago. Benazar, please, let's hit them now while we still can."

"Silence!" Benazar demanded. He too was conflicted. If they had unleashed their explosives on the outpost earlier, chances were they would have taken out Morodov in the inferno that followed. But they had their orders, and those orders specifically forbad a premature assault.

"Why do we hesitate?" the man persisted. "Because some *kofr* American tells us to. Where is he now? Not here. Look out there, Benazar; our army's been decimated. We've passed up our only chance for success. I tell you, we must—"

Benazar unsheathed his knife and held it to his subordinate's throat. Their tarps came of, exposing them both. The man's eyes went wide with sudden terror, and he began inching backwards. Benazar held the blade in place for a moment, and then waved it around for the entire group to see.

"Apparently you didn't take me seriously in the tunnel. If *any* of you endangers this mission again, I'll gut you here and leave your carcass as an example as to what happens to traitors."

Intimidation. It had always been one of his greatest assets, his most instinctual reaction to perceived threats. And it always got results, as it did now. He had put down a second mutiny before it had a chance to begin.

But now there was more waiting, as always, and the men had to watch their brothers in arms die right in front of their eyes. Benazar suspected that if Morodov didn't show himself soon, the men might overpower him and take matters into their own hands. It never came to that.

"Benazar, look!" Yussef said, pointing to the narrow staircase that led into the command tower. There were two shadowy figures ascending, and one of them appeared big enough to be their target. Benazar pulled his binoculars to his eyes as the first man reached the landing. He was short, stocky, and definitely not the colonel. He tried to zero in on the other man, but he was angled the wrong way, and his view was obstructed. Yussef, however, was lining up his shot.

"Can you confirm it? Is it him?" Benazar asked, betraying a show of eagerness that was uncharacteristic of him. He couldn't help it. Everything they'd fought for, everything warriors had died for came down to this moment. They were about to remove a key player from the game, a KGB colonel who commanded thousands. It was a moment to savor. He'd *earned* this.

"Do you have a shot yet?" he asked quickly.

"Almost," Yussef replied. "If he'd just turn a bit to the..."

"What?"

"Oh, no," Yussef whispered, tremors creeping into his voice.

"What is it? Is it him?" Benazar saw that Yussef was startled. His finger jerked away from the rifle's trigger.

"It's him. He's looking right at us."

Benazar saw a figure come to the window, and he raised his binoculars to his eyes. He felt his stomach tighten when he saw Ivan Morodov, also with binoculars, staring right back at them.

"Take the shot!" Benazar screamed. "Take it now!"

"Incoming!" someone yelled.

Benazar heard an ungodly sound in the sky, a deafening shriek speeding towards them. A rocket shattered in the center of the group, sending bodies flying. Benazar was up and moving when the rocket hit, but the force of the blast sent him flying over the edge of the cliff. He fell ten feet before he collided with the steep slope, and then he tumbled end over end, until his battered body skidded to a halt near the edge of the outpost. A giant cloud of dust engulfed him. Lying on his back, he suffered a coughing fit before he tried to lift his head. The sudden motion proved to be too much for him, and he lost consciousness. When he came to, he had no idea how much time had elapsed since he had blacked out. There was a high pitched ringing in his ears, and when he put his hand to his right earlobe and took it away, he found blood on his fingertips. He looked around but could see nothing; clouds of dust still enveloped him. He tried to move his left arm and almost passed out for the second time from the sharp wave of pain that jolted him. He grunted heavily, stifling a scream. His left arm was broken and useless. Helpless, unable even to crawl, he began to take in deep breaths.

Think! Not much time. He rolled onto his right side, and using his knees, right shoulder, and the right side of his face he managed to raise himself into a kneeling position. When he turned to look back up the hill, he could begin to make out the men. They were strewn about everywhere, wailing, mumbling incoherently, or dead. But about five of them had managed to pull themselves together and regroup, and they began targeting rocket launchers, grenade launchers, and bazookas at the compound.

Benazar accepted the fact that he was now about to die in a cross fire. The first part of the mission had been a failure, and now the only course of action available to them was to salvage the situation any way they could. As he closed his eyes and prepared himself for death, he heard another projectile.

He opened his eyes and his jaw fell slack as he witnessed another rocket detonate and engulf the men in shrapnel and smoke.

Everyone was dead.

Benazar let out a cry of rage and tried to stand up. Just as he got to his feet, something moved in the corner of his vision. The ringing in his ears had prevented him from hearing the approaching Russsian soldiers. He reached for the pistol on his thigh and staggered behind an outcropping of sun-parched rock for cover.

The *Roussis* opened fire. Benazar waited out the bullets, knowing it was only a matter of time before someone tossed a grenade his way. He was still deaf, but the vibrations from the rocks being hammered suddenly ceased. He peered around the edge of rock to see two of the soldiers reloading. He took careful aim with his pistol, but one of the Reds hadn't spent his AK47's magazine and let of a heavy stream of rapid fire. The shots missed him, but hit the rock near his face, sending splinters of stone flying at his head, cutting through the flesh on his face. A heavy flow of blood ran over his eyes, and he fell back down to his knees.

The Russians swiftly moved around and past him, heading up the steep slope to where the rest of his men lay. They left one soldier behind to collect him. The blond soldier regarded him like one might a wounded animal. He moved in slowly, utterly amused with his blinded prey.

Benazar couldn't see the youthful Russian scout, nor could he see the sneer on his face. All he really could see was a dark blur in front of him, getting larger as it moved close to him. Reaching across his body to his left thigh, he unsheathed his knife and lunged at the approaching enemy, bringing the knife across and away from him in a wide horizontal arc meant to cut the man's throat. Nothing. He'd misjudged, and his swing fell short of the cursed *Roussi,* who was just out of range.

Benazar fell over forwards. As he propped himself up on his knees once again, his attacker smashed the butt of his rifle into Benazar's forehead right between the eyes. Everything went black.

CHAPTER 18
February 3, 1989

The incarceration lasted just over two years. Benazar was kept in complete isolation the entire time. In those first few days of darkness, darkness both within and without, he drifted back and forth between vague conscious thought and vivid nightmares that encompassed his past, present, and future. His concussion made the two states of mind merge in a hellish blur. Eventually, his body mended itself without medical aid. His body craved the slop his palate rejected, craved its healing nutrients, and he found himself consuming it heartily. When finally he was able to re-establish some semblance of coherent thought, one question kept repeating itself: *Why am I still alive?*

Originally, the question stemmed from curiosity about why he had not just been executed outright. But when he put a hand to his forehead and felt the many stitches that were tracked across it, he knew they'd tended to his wounds for a reason. He got his answer soon enough. He had only regained about half of his usual strength before he was whisked out of his cell and strapped down to the rough planks of a crude table. He would eventually lose count of the times his body was used for the blood transfusions that helped save the Russians' wounded.

There was to be treatment far worse than the regular transfusions, however. When the Russians finished sorting everything out in the aftermath of the battle, Benazar was soon identified as the leader of the flanking force. He was promptly put before a Russian inquisitor and his Pakistani translator. Benazar was surprised by how much intelligence the inquisitor had gathered on him and his men, as well as their activities as hit-and-run assassins.

During his first interrogation, a dull black-and-white photograph was placed on the table right in front of his face. It was a picture of Stuart Flanigan, dressed in his military fatigues and looking younger than Benazar remembered him. The inquisitor fired of a long string of questions in rapid succession. Benazar would never ascertain how much the inquisitor actually knew about the American, and he gave the Russian nothing. The inquisitor was seeking confirmation of either his information or his speculations. Benazar gave him nothing.

When it became apparent that Benazar was not going to cooperate, he was tortured. The Russians began by stripping him naked and whipping him with leather straps. A new series of questions ensued. Benazar remained silent. The Russians beat him with boots and fists. The questions resumed and achieved the same response as before. They burned him with cigarettes. More questions. Nothing.

Benazar's captors allowed him to regain some of his strength before he was strung up by his wrists. Then they inflicted a lengthy session of electric shocks. It would have been hard for anyone to identify the sounds that escaped his mouth as actual screams, but they were able to chill the blood of some of his tormentors. They continued to electrocute his ears, nose, teeth, and genitals.

When they finally cut him down, he collapsed into a twitching heap on the floor. The inquisitor gazed with disgust at the broken man in front of him. He knew a lost cause when he saw one. He accepted this small defeat and ordered his men to immediately remove the Afghan filth from his sight. They shoved Benazar into his pitch-black cell and left him. When weeks later he had recovered, the blood transfusions resumed.

*　*　*

Benazar's eyes were nearly swollen shut, and all he could make out was the harsh, bright light that shone outside his cell. An officer was snarling and cursing in a dialect that Benazar understood. This was a higher-ranking officer than the inquisitor. This man was paying Benazar a special visit.

"Your insurrection has failed," he said. "Did you really think us so careless that we would forget the very water mains that we ourselves destroyed? We were aware of your foolish assassin mission before you even embarked on it."

Benazar clenched his bound fists. *We were betrayed.*

The Russian pushed on. "Your own countrymen were suing for peace. This all could have been over by now. But men like you always complicate matters. My superiors need to gather harder evidence of your western friends' involvement. Tell me something of value that I can relay to them and I can use my power to see you pardoned. Persist in this obstinacy, and you'll be executed."

Benazar's neck lacked the strength to hold his head up. The Russian took a handful of his hair and yanked his head back. He held a photograph up in front of Benazar's face, a photograph Benazar couldn't make out.

"Tell me about the American!" shouted the *Roussi*. "My patience wears thin. You think you owe an allegiance to this man? You are absurd. I'm sure you were promised a way out. I'm sure there were plenty of empty promises." He moved his mouth closer to Benazar's ear and lowered his voice. "This is my promise to you. Right now the American ally you remain so loyal to is enjoying a nice leisurely breakfast with his family, his mind on problems that pale in comparison to yours. Do you think he knows you're alive? Do you think he'd even care if he knew?"

Something cold and hard knotted itself in the depths of Benazar's stomach, something that perhaps only his subconscious acknowledged. He would hold true. He had faith in something worth his struggles and suffering; *no one* was going to take that away from him.

The commander's voice lowered even further. "One last chance. Tell me what I want to know. Tell me about the American."

He let go of Benazar's hair and let him decide. Benazar focused his blurred vision on the shadowy figure in front him who obstructed the blinding light. Benazar had no saliva, but he opened his mouth to speak. The Russian waited.

"The American...," Benazar began, the only words he would speak in the entire two years, "The American was a guest in our country."

* * *

The Russians' perception of Benazar as a threat slowly ebbed. He had, after all, died inside. To them, all that remained was a shell. There was no outward evidence that his mind still worked, except for the most basic motor functions such as eating or urinating. Then, one blistering summer day, his jailers decided it better for him to sweat out the heat in an outdoor shed than to remain shaded in his dark cell. His escort didn't seem pleased with the lazy pace Benazar had set for himself and used the butt of his rifle to prod his prisoner forward. Benazar surprised everyone that day as he whirled on the man behind him, choking him with the chains that bound his wrists before swiftly cracking his neck.

Benazar was almost shot by a prison yard sniper, but another guard closer by quickly overpowered Benazar and beat him unmercifully until someone took the initiative to intervene.

"You told me not to expect anything from this one," one man shouted.

"That's the most he's moved in the past year," another insisted.

"Get him back to his cell!" ordered the first man. "I'm going seek permission to execute him."

The execution never came.

* * *

Benazar dreamed of his son's mother. He dreamt of her soft, perfumed chestnut hair that sloped down her slender neck and draped her shoulders, ending just short of her full breasts. The dream turned sour, as it always did, as her image turned its back on him and faded to black. Suddenly, he was wrenched back into consciousness as his cell door burst open.

Benazar had trouble adjusting his eyes to the light from the hallway, but when they finally focused he read nothing but contempt and fury on the face of the man staring at him.

His prison guard shouted a Russian curse, and then spit on Benazar. The fire in the man's eyes suggested that he knew something that Benazar did not. He began speaking, "My friend will never move again because of you. He's paralyzed. And although you may think your Allah has blessed you, tomorrow when you depart, I'll make sure that you don't make it even one kilometer from here."

Stepping back into the brightly lit hallway the guard reached at the wall for something. He returned with a shovel in both hands. He approached Benazar and raised it over his head. Benazar struggled weakly against his chains as the man brought the shovel down hard onto Benazar's right shin. Benazar let out a terrible shriek as a feeling like fire overwhelmed the nerves in his right leg.

Breathing heavily, he sagged back against the stone wall and waited for the next blow. He didn't even attempt to avoid it as the flat head of the shovel caught him full in the forehead, sending him back into unconsciousness.

*　　*　　*

A day two years after Benazar Rashid's capture marked the release of three comrades, men who'd had absolutely no contact with Benazar whatsoever over the last two years and who knew as little about his fate as he knew about theirs. They were released at the same time as Benazar. When they were ushered into the prison yard toward the main gates, they found him already there, lying on his back and breathing frost up into the afternoon's cold winter air.

Abdur was the first to identify him. "Benazar!" he shouted and dropped down to his knees. The sight of Benazar shocked

Abdur. With a huge mane of dirty, unkempt hair and a long graying beard, he looked like an island castaway, as they all did, but he was by far the worst to behold. He looked frail, as if the muscles on his body had melted right of his bones. What patches of skin on his body that weren't covered by the grimy, tattered rags he wore were scarred by lacerations or burns. His face was the most scarred, with one line running deep and jagged diagonally across his cheek. There were patches of beard missing from places on his face where hair would no longer grow. When Abdur looked at his friend's cracked lips, he could see that his two top front teeth were missing.

Before Abdur could even consider what to say, the huge iron doors of the front gate began to grind inwardly open. The four men were herded together, and then the Russians backed away with their rifles still trained on them. Snipers took careful aim at the prisoners. Abdur half expected a flat bed to be backed up through the gate to receive their executed corpses, but instead he heard a single voice speaking in Dari.

"You will collect your comrade and slowly move out the gate with your backs to us," the voice boomed. "If you turn around, you will be shot. If you try to run, you will be shot. Do not make any sudden movements."

Abdur could hear the conflict in the voice, a conflict born of discipline, as if the man longed to order his subordinates to unload their ammunition on the prisoners but was under orders not to. Abdur wasted no time, placing Benazar's arm around his shoulder and grabbing his belt at the small of his back.

"Timur, help me, quickly," he commanded. Timur hesitated, and then quickly lowered himself to assist Abdur. Together they pulled Benazar into an upright position. "Now let's go," Abdur continued. If this was some sort of ruse, they'd find out soon enough. They hoisted up Benazar's sagging body and slowly moved for the front gate.

They could feel the guns at their backs as they struggled past the gate, past the outer perimeter, and away from the prison.

"We're heading east," Timur muttered. "The sun's at our backs."

"Whatever you do, don't turn around," Abdur pleaded.

Having no idea where they might be headed, the four men labored toward the horizon, not daring to risk a glance behind at the place that served as their personal hell for the last two years. They had no idea why they'd been set free, but they knew that if they lived out the next hour or so, they would have plenty of time to think about it.

CHAPTER 19
February 4, 1989

"We need to keep pushing north," Abdur said, surveying the landscape from atop a boulder. "As soon as Mosa returns we should head for the mountains and then cut west."

Timur looked up at him from the ground where he was tending to Benazar's wounds. "Absolutely not. We've been out of contact with the world for two years. We have no idea what's transpired in that time. We need to make a push for Pakistan."

"And head right back into the hands of our captors?" Abdur asked. "We'll be shot on sight."

"If they'd wanted to shoot us, they'd have done it already and not set us free," Timur retorted.

"What can you hope to accomplish, Timur? We're soldiers for the jihad, not refugees."

"We can get in touch with the ISI. We can learn what's happened. For all we know the KGB has taken the land."

"Then why were we released?" Abdur asked, turning his head to face the eastern horizon. "My instincts tell me that we've been liberated."

"Wait until Mosa comes back. We'll see what he has to say." During the discussion, Benazar lay unconscious.

"How will we move him?" Timur asked regarding Benazar. "We have no food, no decent clothing, no means of transportation, and nowhere to go. We'll die out here."

"If that's God's will," Abdur said, not taking his eyes of the skyline. He crouched down and shoveled a handful of snow onto his palm. Putting it into his mouth, he savored the water that ran over his lips.

A little over an hour passed and Mosa returned from his scouting mission. He had climbed a rocky hill to observe the distant movements of the Soviets near the prison. After descending the treacherous slope he told his comrades what he'd seen. Mosa had witnessed the Russians packing up as much as they could from the compound and loading everything onto trucks and armored transports in what he interpreted as a hurried manner. Their departure was toward the north, and he was sure that what he'd seen had been a retreat.

"So there it is," Abdur said. "Those KGB dogs are running back across the Oxus. Our next move should be to reestablish contact with our brethren. I say we take the course I suggested earlier." He looked at Timur, whose face seemed disbelieving, as if he knew something Abdur didn't. The look did not sit well with Abdur.

"I still think we should head for the border," Timur insisted. "Look how close we are already. To push forward in this weather in the condition we're in would be a death sentence. We don't know for sure that we've driven them out completely. This could all be some kind of trick."

"You're reaching, Timur." This came from Mosa. "Don't forget, we were winning before we were captured. Whatever we've suffered is insignificant if we've managed to eradicate the communist regime. Islam's prevailed; you must feel it."

Abdur watched Timur carefully. Timur had never been a man of much faith, and he looked conflicted now. But considering what the four of them had endured for the last two years, he was willing to give Timur the benefit of the doubt.

"And what of Benazar?" Timur asked.

"He comes with us, of course. We won't abandon him."

"He can barely move," Timur said, gesturing toward the heap at his feet. "He'll never survive."

"He'll survive," Abdur said with conviction. "He always survives."

CHAPTER 20
February 7, 1989

The men managed to hold a slow but steady pace for three days before hunger and fatigue started to wear them down. There was enough snow on the ground to quench their thirsts, but they were suffering for lack of sustenance. The nights were bitterly cold, and they would huddle together at dusk to conserve body heat. The situation looked grave.

One small blessing working in their favor was that the terrain they needed to cross was mostly flat. They were able to keep their bearings by keeping a constant watch on the distant mountains. For the first day, they took turns carrying Benazar on their backs. On the second day, he had come around enough to limp along with his arms around his comrades' shoulders. Although it appeared he was making a slow recovery, his three companions recognized the reality of their situation, and the implications began to oppress them.

"Why were we allowed to go free only to be left to certain death?" Timur had cried out on the second day. Abdur and Mosa didn't voice their own fears, but both knew the odds were not in their favor. Benazar said nothing. The other three had seen no evidence thus far that he was even thinking clearly. If they were all doomed, then he would surely be the first to go.

On the third day, they were given a small glimmer of hope. "There!" cried Mosa, pointing. It was a Russian jeep, or what remained of one anyway. It was charred black and covered with sand and dust. Mosa almost hadn't spotted it behind a low rise.

As the men drew closer they saw the remains of two corpses slumped over against the jeep's dash. KGB soldiers, no doubt, burned black but not quite decomposed enough to be considered skeletal. The jeep remained intact, but whatever had smashed into it had incinerated its occupants.

"What do you think hit them?" asked Timur.

"RPG, mortar, flamethrower," Abdur said, setting Benazar down on the ground to lean up against an undamaged back tire. "Doesn't matter now, does it?" He picked up the corpse in the driver's seat by the collar and tossed it on the ground beside the jeep. Mosa did likewise with the body in the passenger seat. The two began to strip the jeep.

The search ended fruitfully. The jeep yielded a few blankets, a military first-aid kit, an AK-47 rifle with several magazines of ammunition, a loaded Beretta .9 mm pistol, a canteen, and a field rations survival pack that would last the four of them for at least a few more days. Most of what they found had been stored away in compartments or underneath the seats and had not been destroyed by the fire that had scorched the vehicle.

"We'll camp here for the night," said Abdur. "We can reevaluate our situation now that we've been given some room to breathe."

Mosa tore into the rations pack and ate. "I'm going to scout ahead a half a klick," he said, pointing to the northwest. He cradled the AK-47 in his arms as he moved out.

Timur, too, was eating from the food supply. He looked down toward the ground to offer some food to Benazar and found his comrades eyes locked on the face of one of the corpses. *We're losing him,* Timur thought to himself. Benazar hadn't been able to speak beyond a faint whisper since their journey had begun, and he had said little in that time. Timur stopped stuffing canned fruit into his mouth and crouched down next to Benazar.

"Benazar, here, eat something," Timur said, scooping out a piece of a pear and putting it on Benazar's tongue. Benazar struggled in his effort to swallow it, but he managed to get it down. Timur continued to feed Benazar, a process that required some patience, and he noticed that Benazar was looking him up and down, wearing one of his unsettling frowns. This was not the first time Benazar had looked at him this way, but this was by far the most intense gaze he'd been subjected to, and the scrutiny made him feel uneasy. Benazar's silence added to the discomfort.

"Benazar, rejoice," Timur said, more to alleviate the tension he was feeling than to lift Benazar's spirits. "We've been given a moment of solace. We've been blessed with good fortune."

An explosion sounded from somewhere nearby and a tremor ran through the ground. Abdur, Timur, and Benazar all looked in the direction Mosa had gone and saw a thin plume of dark gray smoke climbing toward the sky. Abdur, who had been futilely tinkering with the jeep's two-way radio, launched himself off of the jeep and pulled the pistol, snapping of its safety.

"Pull him around to the other side of the jeep, and stay low," Abdur commanded Timur. "Plan an escape for him and yourself if I don't return in ten minutes." And with that he was off, sprinting in the direction of the explosion.

Benazar felt himself being dragged by the tattered collar of his tunic as Timur sought cover for the both of them next to the jeep. He laid Benazar on the ground and peered toward where Mosa had apparently been attacked. Benazar felt something wooden and hard beneath him and rolled onto his side.

Abdur's sprint picked up speed.

"If they're using explosives, what can he hope to do?" Timur asked himself aloud. Benazar's attention remained fixed on the wooden panel he'd discovered, four feet by four feet, and about an inch and a half thick. Timur glanced down at him, his attention suddenly divided. Benazar used his right hand to brush the sand off of the board. He gathered his breath and blew the remaining dust off. Timur felt apprehension. It was a sign. On the sign was red paint. The symbol on the sign was of a skull and crossbones.

Benazar croaked something inaudible and Timur dropped to his knees and placed his face close to Benazar's. "What?" he asked.

"Stop Abdur!" Benazar said.

Another explosion, similar to the first one but much closer, boomed through the air. Timur turned his startled face back toward Abdur and found that he was missing. In his place was a cloud of gray smoke rising from a black spot in the ground about two feet in diameter.

"Help me up," said Benazar.

*   *   *

It took Timur three minutes to help Benazar walk the distance Abdur had covered in less than one. Timur hadn't wanted to rush in too hastily, pleading with Benazar to let them circle around the immediate area. Benazar, however, had instinctively known where not to step.

They found Abdur a good distance away from where the mine had detonated. He was in shock when they found him, shaking violently and rambling. Blood was flowing freely and quickly from his neck and from the stumps of his severed right arm and leg.

"Set me down next to him," Benazar told Timur in a raspy voice. Timur obeyed.

"B- B- B- Be- Be- Be- Ben-," Abdur blurted as he tried to sit up. His mouth was full of blood and it was garbling his words.

"Don't try to talk." Timur said.

"I never thought ... I never thought ... I never thought...," Abdur continued, his pupils dilating and his spasms beginning to slow down.

Benazar leaned close to Abdur so that his mouth was next to his ear. "Abdur," he said in as soothing and comforting a voice he could muster, "Abdur, it's your time." Abdur looked into Benazar's eyes and accepted the truth. As he leaned his head back to the ground and resigned himself to death, Benazar placed the palm of his right hand against Abdur's throat, gripping his neck at the carotid artery. He applied just enough pressure for Abdur to lose consciousness. Blood continued to soak the ground underneath the two men, and Abdur's body gave two final jerks as life left it.

Timur sat down on the ground and covered his face with his hands. Benazar lifted his head and looked outward toward the horizon, his eyes slowly moving from left to right and then back again. Death continued to follow them, and they hadn't even seen another living soul in days.

CHAPTER 21
February 8, 1989

There hadn't been much left of Mosa. Unlike Abdur, his body had been blown to pieces. It hadn't been the typical butterfly mines that had taken them out. Something far more explosive had killed them.

The AK-47, however, had remained intact and Timur recovered it. Benazar took possession of the scarred but workable pistol. The two men camped that night alongside the jeep, mourning the loss of their comrades and planning for their own survival.

Benazar seemed to be coming around. He was still sluggish, but the rations pack had helped him to regain strength. Now that it was just the two of them, he was gradually assuming the role of decision maker.

"We'll stay the course," he said that morning after Timur had finished his morning prayer. There was no other choice. If they were where they thought they were, then Kandahar was the closest city. And although they had no idea what current state their country was in, failing to reach civilization surely meant they'd die. So their journey continued.

Hour upon hour of contemplative silence hung between the two men. Benazar still limped, wheezing heavily, but he endured his pain and pushed forward. The terrain became rockier. Not even an abandoned village lay across their path. "Why did Abdur plunge ahead so rashly?" Timur asked in the midafternoon. "That wasn't one of the evasive techniques we learned when under fire."

"He wasn't thinking clearly," Benazar replied, a note of disdain lining his voice. "None of us are. And I don't recall you trying to stop him as we hid behind the jeep."

"I thought we were being attacked. Abdur should—"

"What's done is done, Timur," Benazar barked. "There's no changing it now. You were familiar with Abdur's scars. The burns. The bruises. All that suffering, and he still responded the way any true Mujaheddin warrior would have. Honor his sacrifice."

The silence resumed but Benazar was now troubled. Something he himself had said troubled him. He lifted his hand to his mouth and put his index finger to where his two front teeth should have been. He traced his hand over the scars that ran along his face and neck. Abdur had been similarly disfigured. Then he looked over at Timur.

There were blue and black circles under his eyes. His face was sunken from malnutrition. Other than that he appeared unmarked. He seemed to sense the weight of Benazar's stare and made eye contact with him, then quickly turned away and returned to their trail.

*   *   *

It was approaching dusk yet again, and the mountains didn't seem to be getting any closer. Benazar passed the time wondering where his place would be in Afghanistan after his two-year absence. Once they regained contact with the rest of the world, he would send word to his brother that he was alive. What he would do after that he could not even guess.

There was every reason to believe that they'd won the war. They had been set free before the Russians had packed up and left, and the beating he'd taken the night before indicated that they were retaliating from a wounded pride. What he could not understand was why they had not just been brought out to a ditch and executed. He was sure he would find out if he ever made it out of the desert alive.

"What will you do when we return?" Timur asked, as if reading his thoughts. Benazar had once told Timur not to stick his nose into his personal affairs, but he considered all they'd been through together and decided he owed Timur at least this much.

"I'll find my brother. If the violence has finally ended, then perhaps I'll finally become the man my father always wanted me to be. Perhaps as a liaison. I may even try to open channels back up with the CIA; over ISI's head, of course."

There was a long pause. Timur seemed to be searching for the right words, and Benazar began to suspect something.

"The CIA?" Timur asked.

"Yes. Perhaps even Flanigan is still running operations here," Benazar said, revealing none of his other thoughts.

"But, Benazar, surely you must see the dangers he faced once our strike team fell. You said it yourself, we never had ISI's support. They probably didn't even learn of our existence until after we were imprisoned."

Benazar came to a sudden halt. Timur stopped and turned to face him, an anxious look on his face.

"Meaning what?" Benazar demanded.

"What do you mean?"

"You know what I mean. What did you tell them?"

"Tell who? ISI?" Timur asked, his face beginning to flush.

"No. Not ISI. I'm talking about the KGB." Benazar's anger was gaining momentum.

"What did I tell them about what?" Timur said, feigning ignorance.

"You know what!" Benazar shouted. "About Flanigan. About us. About what we were doing. What do they know?"

There was silence, and Timur's eyes grew wild. "Everything!" he spat. "They know everything. Who we worked with, who armed us, who supplied our intel, even where we were based. They know it all."

Benazar was stunned. So, he was right about Timur's lack of scars.

"How could you?" Benazar asked. "They were our allies."

"They were the ones who let us walk into a trap." Timur retorted. "They were the ones who made sure that we rotted in darkness for the last two years. We owe them nothing, Benazar. Nothing. And don't think for a minute that they'll be waiting for us with open arms *if* we make it back, because I can assure you that they're long gone."

There was a return to silence. The tension remained, but the need to find a place for the night was growing more and more important. About forty minutes passed. The sun descended.

"Should we set up camp before it gets too cold?" Timur asked.

"Yes." Benazar responded indifferently.

"Where?" said Timur.

"There," said Benazar, pointing far off to his right. Timur turned to face the direction he was pointing. Benazar drew his gun and shot Timur in the back of his right leg, right at the knee joint. Timur let out a terrible scream as the bullet tore through his meniscus and sent pieces of ligaments and tendons flying. Timur went down and landed on his back. His pain must have been excruciating, but he still managed to reach for the assault rifle. Benazar slammed his boot's heel down on the AK-47 just as Timur tried to lift it. He pointed the pistol right at Timur's forehead.

"Don't! Please don't!" Timur begged. He looked away and covered his face with his hands. He received no response. "Why? Why are you doing this?"

But from Benazar's point of view Timur was not deserving of an answer. Timur had betrayed one of his people's oldest virtues, and now he was going to die for it. He never heard the bullet that killed him.

CHAPTER 22
February 11, 1989

Benazar realized that now that he had only himself to rely on, he would have to take greater precautions to ensure his survival. The first order of business was to give his body more time to heal. He needed to remain where he was for a few more days. Next he needed to set up some sort of camp, with a makeshift shelter to protect him at night from the elements. He had gasoline that had been siphoned from the jeep and a blanket as well. There was a dead tree close by to provide fire wood. For the time being it seemed that he was safe from freezing to death.

Food was another matter. His body was strengthening day by day, but he was down to the last of the rations from the jeep, and he still had no idea how far he might still have to travel. On the third day after setting up camp, he found a temporary solution.

It was early afternoon and the sun was still high in the sky. Benazar had dragged Timur's body out over the sand and away from the rocks where he camped. He left the body facedown about a hundred feet away. He returned to the boulders and sat down leaning up against one of them, nearly concealed by the shade. The vultures that had been circling for a few days now and had been warded off by Benazar now became bold and descended on Timur's remains. They slowly moved in and began to pick away at Timur's rags.

Benazar wouldn't wait long for them to commence their feeding. He adjusted his rifle so that it was on single-fire and took careful aim. His shot echoed loudly as one birds' neck exploded. It fell dead as the remaining scavengers took to the air. Benazar stood up and went to claim his meal.

*   *   *

That night he feasted. He had broken branches off of the tree and made a spit. He cut the vulture up with a shard of glass broken out of the jeep's window and then skewered the meat. As he watched the flames flicker and illuminate his kebab, he found he could not remove the image of the hungry vultures setting down on Timur. There was something metaphorical to be taken from that image, some meaning that eluded him. Gradually, it came to him. A troubling truth sank in.

When he was growing up, he had often been told that his father had been visited by visions. Some men were foolish enough to convey it through ridicule; others had confided in Benazar with the utmost respect. His brother, Mussar, had never taken such statements seriously, but Benazar had often wondered if there was something to them. The visions didn't seem to entail hallucination, and they didn't necessarily predict future events. What was clear, however, was that his father was able to discern meaning from the stimuli that fired his imagination. Benazar wondered if he, too, might have been visited by a vision.

He believed in Islam; that was true enough. Even during the seclusion of his captivity he had managed to find out the direction Mecca lay and kneel to say his daily prayers. But he was not the devout Muslim his father had been, and couldn't understand why he should be similarly visited. Surely, Mussar, regardless of his skepticism, was a more qualified candidate for God to bestow wisdom upon.

It didn't matter now. What mattered was that he needed to survive. He needed to share his message with someone. He wasn't meant to carry it alone. *I must reach Kandahar.* He wasn't even sure if that was where he was headed, but he would keep moving.

He would leave before dawn. He was healed enough. It was time to find out what had become of his country.

*   *   *

He extinguished the fire and gathered his gear. He had enough cooked meat for another day's meal, and then he would have to discard what remained. The eastern horizon held the slightest shade of pink. He turned and faced north. There was no telling how far he had to go, but he had to take the chance. There was no other option. He threw the blanket that held his meager possessions over his right shoulder. He closed his eyes and took a deep breath. Opening his eyes and exhaling the morning air, he stepped forward and resumed his long trek across the wasteland.

CHAPTER 23
FEBRUARY 13, 1989

More than a week had passed since he'd been set free, and now Benazar Rashid accepted the fact that he was going to die. It was amazing he'd lasted this long. The nights and even some days had been so bitter that chilblains began to stab at his hands and feet, yet he did not succumb to hypothermia. His body required far more proteins than he'd been able to consume, and his struggle against the harsh environment had drained his strength. He'd survived, yet one could only go so far on force of will alone.

Nature, an enemy that had always been secondary in his soldier's life, was against him, and now it appeared that nature was formidable enough to do him in. He hadn't underestimated it or failed to respect it. He'd just always assumed he'd die at the hands of another man.

No! This is ridiculous! They should have shot me, those rotten Roussi dogs. I've bled for this sand. I've earned a better death than this. And then there was the matter of telling his story, of sharing with his people what he'd learned by the light of his campfire so that they too could be prepared for the trials to come. He was sure that the turmoil that had eroded his nation would continue.

It didn't matter now. As he fell to his knees, shivering, he accepted his fate. He hunched over, rubbing his chest with his hands. His forehead hit the dirt, and he rolled onto his side. He curled his body into a ball, shaking uncontrollably. The fetal position. Not even yet a wailing infant, but a fetus. *How ridiculous!*

Let not my final thoughts betray my anger. God, spare my dignity. As it happened, he was able to let go of his seething anger before he lost consciousness. Curiosity got the better of his thoughts as his right cheek pressed against the cold ground and he looked onward. If he hadn't been convinced that he was hallucinating, he would have sworn that only a few hundred meters always lay a gravel road. His eyelids fluttered, and then closed.

CHAPTER 24
MAY 2, 1992

"It's been three years, Benazar. I think that you're ready to return to the world," said Nawaz Saleh from across the fire. He handed the smoking wooden pipe to the man next to him, who took a long inhalation of the opium and then passed it on to Benazar. Benazar pulled the smoke into his lungs and closed his eyes. He held it for a few seconds, exhaled, and returned his focus to Nawaz, who waited patiently for a response.

"And so why now?" asked Benazar.

"When we first found you, you were half dead. After we revived you, I realized how strong your will to live is, but I also saw in you a darkness like a cancer. You still have a long path ahead of you and a great deal of work to do. But you were a broken man, and I needed to help you find an inner peace that you didn't have. To let you walk out of here as you were would have been the same as killing you." Nawaz took the pipe once again.

Benazar remained silent. His eyes, fixed on his companion, reflected the nearby flames.

"The nation has changed," said Nawaz. "You'll find out for yourself when you return to Herat. I believe that there you'll find the answers to your questions, but first you needed to see the world through different eyes."

"And you believe that I'm now at peace?"

"There are still men out there who will die at your hands. Of that I have no doubt. But this war has twisted your mind. You needed to be reminded of what it is you're fighting for." Nawaz's words were not condescending, but rather filled with compassion.

"There was a time," said Benazar, "just before I joined with the American, when I gazed toward the setting sun. The sight was spectacular, but I refused to let it move me. I think that part of me has changed."

Much had changed about him in the last three years. His body was stronger than ever. He had learned to dull his pain with opium and heroin. He had relearned how to appreciate beauty. He had been with women, the first since his son's mother. Perhaps most importantly he had learned patience.

By no means had he ever been their captive. Not technically. But Nawaz had refused to grant him passage out of the mountains, always telling Benazar that when the time came and he was ready, he would return him to Herat. It appeared that that time had finally come.

He would be forever indebted to Nawaz and his people. Represented by tribes all over the country, they were now nomads who had taken to the mountains and redefined their concept of home rather than becoming refugees in Pakistan. Their austere nature was the basis of their survival: Islam had little to do with their asceticism. The leaders of the group, with Nawaz at the head, sustained their lives through drug trafficking. And now Benazar had thrown in his lot with them, the Golden Crescent.

There had been one occasion when a former soldier had recognized him and gone straight to Nawaz, telling him that Benazar was one of the most celebrated killers among the Mujaheddin. In another instance Benazar overheard one of Nawaz's minions ridiculing him, saying that he had the name of a woman. The Benazar of old would have smashed their faces in. But the man he had become simply dismissed it. Nawaz had reprimanded them. Benazar, he pointed out, was their guest, and now he was one of them.

He had undergone a rebirth of spirituality, and he had Nawaz to thank for that. Many long nights he and his new companions sat around this same fire, and he had told them with no ego the tales of his time on the frontlines. He had earned their respect. He fascinated them. They were not warriors; they were survivors trying to live their lives as their country tore itself apart.

"You must make a promise, Benazar, one more to yourself than to me," Nawaz said.

"And that is?"

"That you won't despair. The Russians have left, but many feel our victory is temporary. We will continue here in these caves with our day-to-day lives. It is you who must cope with what Afghanistan has become."

That had frustrated Benazar to no end in his first days here. Nawaz had provided him with few details about what had happened to the country these last five years, claiming that to dwell on such knowledge would stunt his inner growth. And perhaps he had been right.

A small voice always spoke to Benazar in the back of his mind, leaving him uneasy. A dead man's voice. Timur's voice.

"As you say, I may yet have to kill," Benazar replied. "I am, after all, a soldier. But anything I do will be for the right reasons, and I'll never lose sight of what all this bloodshed has been about." He reached to the right to receive the pipe once again.

"Very well," said Nawaz. "God delivered you to us for a reason. I look forward to a day when we may return to our villages and reclaim our homes. With your help we can rebuild what's been destroyed."

"Thank you, Nawaz." He stood up and turned to retire for the evening.

"Just one more thing, Benazar," Nawaz said. Benazar turned around. Nawaz tilted his head to meet his eyes. His lined face lit by the fire seemed to accentuate his wisdom. "Be careful whom you trust. Warlords, not *Roussis*, may be the new enemy."

Benazar nodded. He turned and disappeared into the darkness of a cave. Tomorrow he would return to the city he had once called home.

CHAPTER 25
MAY 10, 1992

Benazar's tea was comforting. It soothed his palate and warmed his body. He sipped it more and more frequently as his brother got deeper into his story. It wasn't as though Mussar's words surprised him. He was only reiterating what Benazar had already feared, but the details, as they just kept coming and coming, seemed to stab at his very soul.

The country was in shambles. Herat, the city he'd grown up in, the city revered by artists and intellectuals from all over the world, was in ruins. The sadness of that irony, that perhaps the most cultured city in all of Afghanistan had suffered the most during the Russian occupation, was particularly depressing to him.

Mussar sipped his tea. Ten years Benazar's senior, he might have been his twin had not time put streaks of silver and gray throughout his hair and beard. In addition, Mussar carried himself with a certain aura of elegance that a hardened fighter like his brother could never project. Mussar sipped his tea and then paused, silently contemplating his next words. "Strange ... the timing of your return," he finally said. "Stalin's legacy is dead. We've run them out. And yet as you can see...," he trailed off, letting his unfinished rhetoric sink in.

Benazar brought to mind recent images of streets, of homes, of people. Then came the words he'd known were coming, yet hadn't wanted to accept until he'd actually heard them. Mussar said, "We're on our own. The United States embassy has been closed. About four months ago there was a pledge made. The United States no longer supports us; Russia no longer supports Najibullah."

For a moment Benazar thought he saw Timur's ghost pass by the kitchen window. He sat silent. Everything he'd fought for, had bled for, had been for *this*? This was victory? He was speechless. He stared down at the table at patterns in the pine that he was oblivious to, lost in thought.

For a long time nothing was said. Then Mussar volunteered more information that Benazar only half heard. "Your release was an unofficial prisoner trade. But those treacherous dogs turned you out into the desert, which was almost the same as killing you. Almost."

Benazar was going farther and farther away. Mussar was saying something about finally accepting Benazar's death when a thought came to Benazar that brought him back. "How did Morodov know we were coming?" he asked.

By the way Mussar stiffened, Benazar knew his brother had the information. He waited patiently for an answer. Mussar met his eyes and said, "You have to understand, when some within our circles learned of the extreme secrecy of your alliance with Flanigan, they feared Hekmatyar was mobilizing secret forces against Massoud and leaked the information to him, regardless of the fact that America favors Massoud. But it wasn't supposed to result in Morodov's awareness of your advance on his position. The whole affair got out of hand and turned into a nasty double cross."

"Just tell me who," said Benazar, his voice hoarse. He had no desire to consider the motivations of traitors.

"The Qazi brothers," Mussar said. "All three of them can be held accountable."

"And have they?"

"Not yet."

"And what have you tried to do about it?"

Mussar did not like the challenge in Benazar's accusing tone.

He straightened his posture and narrowed his eyes. "I've handled my affairs the way I've always handled them, Benazar, the way Father handled them." The words rolled off of his tongue in such a way that the implied meaning was clear: *I'm the older brother, the diplomat who secured your release. You're the neighborhood thug, the kid with anger issues who went astray.*

"I apologize, Mussar," said Benazar. "Please forgive me." Mussar hadn't been expecting that. Perhaps Benazar had grown in ways he hadn't foreseen. Nevertheless, the revelation had run its course and led Mussar to his next topic. He nodded in acceptance of Benazar's apology and waved a hand in dismissal.

"I have to go to Pakistan," Mussar said. "I don't know for how long, but I know I can't take Hakeem with me. I'm going to have to turn him over to you. I'll set you up financially, of course." The last part was lost on Benazar. He was ashamed to admit to himself that he'd thought little about Hakeem over the years. He would be fifteen by now. The truth was that Benazar didn't know Hakeem. Mussar had been the boy's surrogate father from the time he was an infant. Duty had called Benazar away.

"You'll be proud of him," Mussar continued. "He knows the Koran backwards and forwards. Three years ago I took him to Mecca for his pilgrimage. He is incredibly bright and gifted. The poetry he writes underneath that mulberry tree would bring tears to your eyes."

Benazar wondered if that was possible. He let Mussar finish telling him about the important business he had to attend to. Then he said, "Unless I'm to understand that he'd slow you down in Pakistan, it sounds like he'd be better suited to your task. At this point in life, what can I possibly hope to offer him?"

Mussar had his response ready quicker than Benazar would have thought. "Because I've done a good job keeping him sheltered from all this madness. *Too* good a job." When Mussar saw that his message had fallen short, he elaborated. "He's soft, Benazar. Only you can show him how to be a man. The way of the politician no longer exists here. It's your world now."

"So I take it you won't be returning," Benazar said. He and his brother were patriots. Fleeing had never been an option as it had been for others. That was why Benazar couldn't believe Mussar was leaving.

"My leave is temporary," Mussar said. "If I stay now, however, I'll be stripped of all influence or perhaps killed. Neither possibility holds any appeal for me." His smile was grim.

So after all these years, Benazar's son was being turned over to his custody. *Strange timing indeed, my return.* He had just now found out that he would be raising a strange adolescent within moments of finding out that everything he'd done in his life may have been for nothing.

He suddenly got lost inside his head again. Memories new and old collided. *I can truly say that I draw inspiration from the history of your people.* A man slumped against a wall, tattered rags covering his battered form. *We will stand firm in our objective.* A once warm and cozy house reduced to rubble. *How do you feel about accepting the help of an unbeliever?* A street corner cast in darkness, the electric source of its lighting long gone. *You're going to win this war, Benazar Rashid. You'll be seeing your son soon.*

Mussar's words bounced around inside of his head. *Stalin's legacy is dead.* The collapse of the Communist Party. Benazar seethed. *Objective complete.*

He remembered the vulture had looked in his direction before he'd shot it, raw human flesh hanging from its beak. Benazar knew what he had to do.

"Tell me about Hakeem," he said. "Tell me everything."

*   *   *

Mussar knocked on the door to his nephew's room, and Hakeem admitted him. Stepping inside, Mussar was feeling pangs of regret that he knew were a sign of weakness, yet he simply couldn't ignore them. Hakeem had no idea what was coming.

Mussar crossed the bedroom and sat on a wooden stool near the window. He gestured toward the chair at Hakeem's desk. When Hakeem sat down, his trusting eyes fixed on his uncle, Mussar's regret intensified. His nephew had grown a great deal in the last year. Adolescence was filling out his once-bony frame with lean muscle, and his face had thinned out around the cheekbones as the stubble running along his jaw line grew thicker. Hakeem had dark, clear eyes in which one could discern both an adult's reason and a child's naïvete.

What hurt Mussar the most was that it was Hakeem's most promising qualities that would ultimately drive the two of them apart. *This* world didn't have a place for a boy such as Hakeem. Not anymore.

"We need to talk," Mussar said with a heavy heart.

"What is it, Uncle?" Hakeem asked, now apprehensive.

* * *

Had Hakeem heard his uncle correctly? His father? His father was alive? Hakeem was already sitting, but he felt the need to clutch the wooden armrest on his chair. He leaned forward and tried to draw a deep breath. He knew he'd heard something about Uncle going off to Pakistan. Indeed, he'd already known about this trip and had been awaiting an invitation to accompany him, but now it would seem that there were other plans.

He stared at the floor and tried to focus. His father was a great patriot, of this he'd heard plenty. All of the men who'd been in Uncle Mussar's circles had assured him of that when he'd been introduced to them. But he'd heard other stories about his father, stories from his peers who were either privy to or eavesdropping on their parents' gossip. Stories that left him sitting up at night thinking. Stories that bothered him. Stories that—

"Hakeem, do you hear me?" Mussar asked.

"Yes, Uncle," Hakeem managed to mutter. "I ... I mean, I think so. I mean, I don't understand."

Mussar sighed. He sat down next to his nephew and patted his arm. "Hakeem, please believe me when I tell you that you're one of the brightest, most gifted pupils I've ever instructed. You make me proud. But up until now, and I'm ashamed to say this, I've kept you sheltered from the true horrors that exist beyond these walls. I know you've heard the bombs at night, the gunfire echoing throughout the streets, and I don't mean to underestimate any trauma you may have suffered as a result. It's just that…," he faltered, searching for the right words. "It's just that our ways are changing now. There's a world out there that only your father can show you."

There was a long silence. Hakeem finally broke it by asking, "And what of my education?"

"This will *be* your education," was Mussar's reply.

More silence. The more Hakeem contemplated his uncle's surprising line of thought, the more dumbfounded he became. He was *shocked*. He began to sweat and tugged gently at his collar. "They said he was dead," he whispered, more to himself than to his uncle. "I thought he was dead."

"I thought so, too," said Mussar gently.

"And so," said Hakeem, meeting his uncle's eyes, "perhaps now you can tell me whatever became of my mother."

Mussar's eyes narrowed, and his tone took on any icy edge. "Your mother," he said with strained patience, "was a harlot who ran off with some vagabond musician while you were still feeding from her breasts. And that's all you need to know about her. If you want to hear more about your father, the man who protected your life and those of thousands of others, then ask."

"Uncle, please," Hakeem said, afraid to meet Mussar's eyes.

"No, Hakeem," said Mussar, grabbing Hakeem's wrist for attention. "You will be meeting him in a few moments. You better show him the respect he deserves. I don't care what you've heard about him from the other boys while flying kites. *He*'s your guardian now."

And that was that. Hakeem was being placed in the care of a man he couldn't remember, whose name couldn't be mentioned without some hint of infamy surfacing. It felt as though some part of him had just gotten up from the chair he was seated in and walked out the door, taking away his hopes and dreams for the future. There was nothing left to be said.

"Sit tight," said Mussar. "I'll have him come to you."

*   *   *

The door creaked and Hakeem looked up. Standing in the doorway was perhaps the most ghastly figure he'd ever laid eyes upon. Standing about six feet tall, the man had tan leathery skin that looked like it had been repeatedly blistered in the sun. Running diagonally across his right cheek were two deep, jagged scars that left the right side of his face appearing sunken, and his beard was missing patches. Another scar ran from behind his left ear and across his neck. The man didn't smile but his mouth was open wide enough for Hakeem to see that his top two front teeth were missing. Despite the simple brown robes he wore and his recently groomed hair and beard, the man's appearance betrayed years of suffering.

"Hello, Hakeem," the man said. "I'm your father.

*   *   *

The last time Benazar had seen his son, Hakeem had been an infant cradled in his arms. Now Benazar beheld a confused-looking young man with neatly trimmed black hair falling just short of his brow and a patchy teenager's beard.

Hakeem wore a loose gray tunic, black pants, and sandals. His clothes were neat and clean. To Benazar he looked like a young man from a previous generation, a young man oblivious to the pain and suffering that would soon be coming in the form of Russian tanks.

Benazar's mind was divided as he outlined the details of his life since he'd fled Herat. As he told his story, he studied his son, observing how much Hakeem looked like his mother. Hakeem listened attentively and respectfully, but with noticeable anxiety. When Benazar looked into his son's eyes, he saw a frailty within them—they seemed to show a lack of fortitude. As Mussar had explained, it would be Benazar's job to remedy this.

Hakeem squirmed uncomfortably when Benazar gave an abridged accounting of his time in the Russian prison camp. Surely Hakeem knew about all of the suffering and dying. Benazar knew the boy must have witnessed at least some of the violence caused by rockets and gunfire at the height of the Russian occupation, and yet Hakeem wasn't visibly weighed down by it. It was as though it had never been real, as if it had all just been some nightmare.

How long has Mussar kept you hidden away in this room?

It was all so pathetic. Benazar was now going to show his son just how real the devastation was.

* * *

"How did the reunion go?" Mussar asked, his face showing no hint of irony.

"About as well as can be expected," Benazar said. "We still have much catching up to do. You and I, as well, for that matter." He turned and looked out the window. Mussar could see how thoughtful his brother was at the moment and decided to wait him out rather than push the issue. Then he turned back to Mussar. "He has his mother's eyes."

"Yes, I know," Mussar said. "You've said so before."

"Have I?"

"Yes. Long ago." Mussar ran a hand through his thick beard. "Well, at any rate, we have the next four days for the two of you to get acquainted."

"No, not quite," said Benazar. "I'll be leaving tonight and returning the day after tomorrow. I have some business to attend to. We'll take advantage of whatever time remains after that."

Mussar looked at his brother. The skepticism was not lost on Benazar. "What are you thinking?" Mussar queried.

"Don't concern yourself," said Benazar. "The less you know the better."

CHAPTER 26
MAY 11, 1992

Nightmares rarely visited him. Karim Qazi awoke and realized that he actually did smell smoke. He tried to sit up in bed and was stunned when he realized he was tied down.

A wave of panic hit him. *What's happening?* He attempted to cry out for help. He looked at his door and saw that smoke was creeping up from underneath it. He began to sweat. Where were his men?

"Help! Help!" He continued to scream until he was out of breath. Soon the struggle became too much for him. He began to cough violently as his eyes teared from the acrid smoke. Once more he flexed and pushed against his bindings with all of his strength, but the ropes held firm and the effort exhausted him.

He knew the fire was no accident, but he could not imagine whom he might have wronged to deserve a death such as this.

＊　＊　＊

The door to Omar Qazi's room burst open, and two of his most trusted bodyguards came in shouting. "Sir! Sir! We have terrible news. Your brother Karim's estate has been burned to the ground. We fear he was assassinated."

Omar had been asleep, and the words confounded him. Karim dead? But no one could kill his older brother. Who would dare put out a contract on his life? As questions and possibilities raced through Omar's head, somewhere of in the distance an alarm was raised. All three men in the room suddenly froze.

The bedroom window suddenly shattered, and Omar's senior bodyguard slumped to the floor. As his other bodyguard turned to face the curtains now billowing in the wind, Omar reached for the pistol underneath his pillow. When he withdrew it, he saw blood spurt out from underneath his second bodyguard's turban before he too fell. Omar dove off the bed and began to crawl toward the windowsill. Sitting up he braced his back against the wall. He was too terrified to steal a glance into the darkness beyond and at whatever awaited him out there. He took a minute to think of his next move. Just as he resolved to rush for the door and make his escape, a grenade came flying in through the window, bouncing off the bed and settling on a wide crack in the wooden floor just a few feet away.

* * *

Kamal Qazi woke slowly from his slumber. He turned his head and looked at the faintly lighted clock on his nightstand. It was close to dawn. Something elusive was bothering him at the subconscious level, like a bad taste in the mouth, and he was sure this is why he was now awake.

He supposed it was paranoia. One didn't live the life he did without taking certain measures of protection, and he considered it mere collateral damage that he should suffer a sleepless night on occasion to ensure his survival.

Although not the most physically imposing, as the oldest of the three brothers he had been their leader for many years now, and whereas the other two had become complacent over time with the power structure they'd built around themselves, Kamal was sharper than ever. He protected himself with the manpower only money could buy, and if he was less intimidating physically, then at least he hadn't dulled his wits by—

Then he remembered. He hadn't gone to bed. He had only been getting ready for bed when something pricked him on the neck, and then ... and then ... and then *what?* He tried to reach over to his nightstand and light the lantern when he found that he couldn't move. He was tied down to the bed but couldn't see anything in the darkness. Suddenly, a match sparked and the lantern was lit. There was a shadowy figure looming over Kamal. Kamal tried to speak, but his tongue was still too heavy from whatever had drugged him. A loud moaning sound was all that escaped from him.

A covered face moved into the light, and hatred in the stranger's eyes was searing. This was no gun for hire. "Don't bother screaming," the man said. "Most of your men are dead. So are your brothers." The stranger moved to the foot of the bed. He was dressed in dark military fatigues and armed with grenades and bandoliers of large caliber ammunition.

Kamal wanted to speak, but his panic delayed him. It wasn't too late to negotiate his way out of this, but he needed more information. Then the man removed the cloth covering his head and face and underneath was one of the most gruesome visages Kamal had ever seen. And Kamal had seen his share of disfigurements. "I don't know you," he was finally able to say.

The man reached down to his belt and unsheathed a knife, a large, sharp knife. Kamal was now petrified. He needed to think of a solution quickly, but he was still sluggish and unable to move. Who could want him and his two brothers dead? Who could have pulled it off? How had he wronged this man? He had no idea where this man had—*oh no!* Kamal now looked at the intruder more carefully. And now he was even more afraid. "I *do* know you," he croaked.

The man, Benazar Rashid, came around to the other side of the bed, running the tip of his blade over his gloved fingertips. "Tell me something, Kamal," he said.

"Wait!" Kamal said, struggling mightily against the ropes that held him down. "Wait! Don't do this!"

"Tell me, after all these years, after so many of our people have starved, how is it that you've obtained such generous proportions?" Benazar used his knife to gesture toward the paunch of Kamal's stomach, dangling the blade just centimeters away.

"Wait! Just wait!" Kamal pleaded, sweat forming at his brow. He shook the bed violently, but in vain. Benazar stabbed the headboard and Kamal cried out in alarm. The knife rested there as Benazar withdrew two more cloths from a backpack. He grabbed Kamal's jaw, pried his mouth open, and shoved one cloth into it. Then he used the other one to tie the first securely in place, efficiently gagging his victim. Kamal tried to scream for help through the cloths and thrashed violently as Benazar retrieved his knife from the headboard. The muffled screams intensified when Benazar leaned over Kamal and sank the knife down to its handle into the soft flesh of Kamal's stomach. He then slowly pulled the knife deliberately across Kamal's belly, and watched the crimson exposure of his entrails.

The disembowelment didn't kill Kamal right away. It would be an agonizing while before death claimed him, plenty of time for Benazar to watch him slowly die.

CHAPTER 27
MAY 12, 1992

I'm strong. God gives me strength. I won't despair. I'll overcome any obstacle. This is simply a new challenge I must face, one that I knew was coming. This is a test. God is testing me. I have no intention of failing.

Hakeem's life was about to change completely. He was about to cross over into another world, one he knew little about. He thought about his uncle's admission that he'd kept him sheltered from that world, and now he regretted that Mussar had. Perhaps if he hadn't, Hakeem might not be feeling the fear he felt now.

Deep down, part of him knew that it was for the best. Afghanistan was changing in ways no one could have predicted. His father was a survivor. He would teach Hakeem to survive in the world outside Herat.

Then he felt a different kind of regret. He had carried with him aspirations greater than mere survival. He was a gifted individual. He'd been told so by his uncle and many others, and now his talents might go unused. A lump formed in his throat. *I have to be strong,* he told himself. He would not be telling his father about any of these former aspirations of his, because they were no longer real plans, just painful memories. He belonged to his father now, and although when he looked at his father he saw what might have been construed as love, he also saw disappointment there. He would have to locate the root of that disappointment and weed it out completely. He guessed that it had something to do with the impractical lifestyle Uncle had provided for him until now.

He would need to toughen up, and that required a mental discipline he was trying to manifest right now. If he was going to learn how to survive in a war-torn country, then he was going to have to learn that from his father.

He had said so many prayers today, more than ever before in a single day, hiding in his room as if to hold at bay the time until his father's return. He had prayed for strength and guidance. He didn't know what else to pray for.

The door to his room creaked open, and his father stepped inside the room. He had a duffel bag slung over one shoulder. He looked tired.

"Hakeem, have you packed up all of your belongings?" he asked.

"Yes," Hakeem replied. He still didn't know how to address this man.

"Then go and get them. We're leaving."

CHAPTER 28
APRIL 11, 2002

Zack admitted to himself that the lasers were pretty cool. But the strobe light was starting to get to him. And the smoke machine, fog machine, whatever the hell it was, was starting to make him dizzy. *Stupid fuckin' raves,* he thought to himself. *Your days are numbered.* There was just that one beat, incessant, hammering away at his skull. How did people do this night after night?

He adjusted the way he was sitting in his chair. He wondered if people were looking at him, wondered if they noticed. He rubbed his hands together in his lap, and then started rubbing his legs, which were warm but starting to shake nonetheless.

"Hey, come dance with me," said Jacqueline, walking up to the table from the dance floor.

"Can't," Zack said. "Don't know if I can even get up yet. It just started kickin' in."

She looked down at him, squinting her eyes a little. "Oh, my God. Yeah, it did. You took two, didn't you?"

"Yeah," he admitted.

"I told you that I was only going to take one," she said frowning. She looked more hurt than annoyed.

"And I took two," he said, nonchalantly. "I'll be fine. I'm havin' a blast. Go have fun."

"All right, just hang out here and let me know if you need me." With that, she turned and disappeared back into that cauldron of movement.

Zack wondered if maybe he was in over his head. He wasn't terribly worried, but this whole scene was just too much for him. Strange. Most of these people who were on ecstasy just as he was might not have come if they *hadn't* taken it. He wondered why he felt apart from the crowd. The problem, he decided, was that these weren't the Mitsubishis he was used to taking, and the pressies he'd eaten simply didn't make him feel all that upbeat. He felt heroin-high while his retinas were being assaulted by lasers and strobes, his nostrils by that acrid smoke.

Goddamn house music. He was really rolling now, and wasn't sure how much more of this he could take. Just as he made the decision to go get some fresh air, someone appeared at the table in front of him.

"Holy shit," said the newcomer. He was about six-one, Zack's height, but more powerfully built. He was wearing a Yankees hat low, and it was hard for Zack to make him out at first. "Two of the last people on earth you'd expect to find in a place like this, bumpin' into each other after ... what is it, three, four years?" He raised his head.

"Ah, shit!" said Zack, smiling. Joey. Joey Sisco. Joey, about two years older than Zack, had been a senior in high school when Zack was a sophomore. Zack had run with him for a little while and learned a lot from him. Last Zack had heard, Joey had been in some trouble with the law, had beaten some guy up badly. That had been about two and a half years ago. Zack stood up to embrace his one-time friend.

Zack held Joey for a moment too long and said, "Whoa, easy there, fun-boy. I'm not *that* happy to see you."

Zack took two steps back and then fell back into his chair. "Have a seat," he managed to say.

"Goddamn, what the hell did you take?" Joey asked him, eyeing him carefully.

"Noth- it's ... it's nothin'," Zack got out.

"Your jaw, your whole mouth looks like a runnin' cement mixer."

"Heh-heh."

Joey looked around. "So seriously, what are you doin' here? I didn't think you went in for this whole warehouse scene."

"I don't, but Jacqueline," Zack nodded toward the outskirts of the dance floor, "let me drag her to the Mobb Deep show a few weeks ago. I'm just paying my dues. Question is, what the hell are you doin' here?"

"Same reason, more or less. Did you know Maggie and I had a baby girl?"

"No, man. That's great. Congratulations. What's her name?"

"Alexis. She's home with Maggie's mom tonight. This is one my final hoorahs before I ship off."

"Ship off?"

"Yeah, man. Damn, it has been a while. I'm a ranger. I'm off to Afghanistan."

"Really?" Zack didn't hide his surprise. If the military could make a ranger out of Joey Sisco, then anything was possible.

"Yeah, y'know I needed that kind of discipline in my life," Joey said. "I have a daughter to think about now."

"You in the army. Shit, who would have thought?" Zack was sweating heavily now, and suddenly wished his reunion with Joey were under different circumstances. Intuition told him where this conversation was going, and he wanted to steer it as best he could.

"I know," said Joey. "Crazy, huh? I'm not expecting to see too much action in the first few months, but after a while we'll be cave-cleanin', one by one. Bombing just isn't working. They're dug in too deep."

"Oh, you mean Operation Let's Get 'Em." Zack wished he'd kept his mouth shut. It wasn't so much what he'd said, it was the dismissive tone he'd used. Looking across the table and seeing the irritation on Joey's face confirmed his comment had not been well received.

There had been a time where Joey might have smacked Zack for his smart mouth. Instead, he said, "Yeah, that's right. Correct me if I'm wrong, but I woulda thought you'd have a vested interest in this."

So Joey had heard. No matter. "Yeah, well, believe it or not, I'm actually up to date on my current events. And even though I could probably bust a nut thinkin' about what I'd like to do to those brown bastards, I'd just as soon forget about it."

"And so, what? If we go over there and take care of business, you won't feel that's righteous?" Joey asked him, folding his arms on the table.

"Not as much as I'll feel regret that this whole fuckin' mess could've been avoided in the first place," Zack said, gradually able to fight through the effects of the ecstasy to make his point.

"What's that supposed to mean?" asked Joey. Joey was obviously annoyed with Zack's viewpoint and had not been expecting it. He wanted to know where it was coming from. He didn't remember a Zack who was so self-assured.

"I'll give you one example, and that'll be the end of it," Zack said. He leaned forward in his chair. His throat was tired from yelling over the woofers. "Back during the Monica Lewinsky scandal, when Clinton was gettin' his knob slobbed and this whole fuckin' Hollywood-obsessed country became a media-crazed circus, the CIA was *beggin'* for permission to take out bin Laden and his network. I'm talkin' one fell swoop, not cave-to-cave raids. But because Clinton was under the spotlight, and the media made it so that he couldn't make such a big decision without potential backlash, he pussied out. And here we are."

"So you're sayin' things woulda been different."

"I'm sayin' we wouldn't be havin' this conversation."

For a long time, neither spoke. Zack closed his eyes and tried to keep his teeth from clenching too tightly. Then he heard Joey ask, "Damn, Zack, when did you become some such a smart ass?"

"I've always been a smart ass."

"Well, what's done is done. We can't change it now. But we can't let these little fuckers run amok. Even the ones here within our borders. I don't wanna sound like a racist, but these Middle Easterners, they're like wired differently or something. They're fanatics. And if you don't kill them, lock them up, or at least keep them on the run, they'll keep bringing it back to your doorstep. And even though it might seem easier to just turn your back on the whole deal, I know you don't wanna go through that hurt again. I know you're hurtin' now."

The pills made Zack feel like he was wrapped in a down comforter, but the cold still found its way into the pit of his stomach when he heard Joey's words. It felt as though Joey was trying to awaken a part of him that he did his best to keep buried. "Be careful over there, Joey."

"Shit, you ain't gotta worry about me," Joey said, the mood lightening a little. Zack rubbed his hands together and fidgeted some more in his seat. He wanted out of this place. "Better reel in your girl," Joey said. "That dude over there's freakin' on her pretty hard."

Zack only half heard him. "Yeah, well, she's not really my girl anymore." He turned his thoughts elsewhere. He practically forgot about Joey sitting across from him.

Zack was such a simple kid, he thought, just as ordinary as the next guy. Why did he have to concern himself with such matters? How had this become his reality?

Zack was suddenly angry with Joey for coming back into his life, with his patronizing disposition and newly found world view. "I need some air," Zack said. He got up and headed for the door.

CHAPTER 29
April 13, 2002

"Well, you know that one year I lived in Crested Butte I think we might have only had like four or five days that weren't sunny," said Anna, a long time friend of both Miranda and Derek. She and her boyfriend, Luke, were hosting dinner for the McCradys. Anna took another sip of her Nero d'Avola and said, "You two are going to love Colorado."

"I think so, too," Miranda said with a smile.

"And so you're still shooting for the end of June?" asked Luke. Miranda glanced quickly over at Derek before proceeding.

"Yeah, we're hoping we won't have to push it back again. I mean, we'll both be finished with work here regardless. There are just a few loose ends to tie up."

"I know how stressful a move can be," said Luke. Derek nodded. He had been quieter this evening, busying himself with the chicken marsala in front of him. Luke thought he might be able to guess what was on his mind, but thought it was better to leave the subject alone.

Anna, however, was not so hesitant. "Any luck changing Zack's mind?"

"No, he's convinced himself he's better off here," Miranda said.

"He thinks it would be running away. He thinks *we're* running away," Derek said, more bitterly than he wished.

"That's silly," said Anna. "He knows you two were planning to move before the tragedy."

"I don't claim to understand how he thinks," said Derek, raising his eyebrows. "I just wished he'd consider college. His SAT scores were impressive."

"Well, what *will* he do?" asked Luke.

Derek was afraid of his answer. "I don't know."

Luke sensed that they'd touched on a sore subject and wished that Anna hadn't raised it. This was obviously something that Derek was concerned about, and he and Miranda had been trying to get out of New York for a long time now. Luke and Anna understood, as much as they'd miss them. There were just too many painful memories for them here.

Now that it was out there, Derek went with it. "I always thought it was foolish of Jenny to give Zack the amount of freedom that she did. He's reckless by nature. It surprised me, because she was always more level-headed than me."

Miranda came to his side. "Well, Derek, we've talked about this before. You three were orphans. She knew you guys had to grow up faster than normal. Zack's had it hard, baby. You all have."

"I know," said Derek, a little exasperated. Maybe it was the wine. "It's just this whole 'fuck the world' attitude; it worries me. And I'm not his father."

"But you are the closest person to a father he's had," offered Anna compassionately.

"Thanks, Anna," Derek said, settling down a little. "Anyway, it doesn't matter. He's definitely not going with us. He's way too immersed in the New York lifestyle to want to leave. This place will always be home for him. And he's eighteen now. I can't tell him what to do."

Trying to improve the mood a little, Miranda suggested, "Well anyway, we've got Morgan to look after him. Zack couldn't be in better hands."

"Zack isn't Morgan's responsibility," Derek said. He obviously hadn't caught Miranda's meaning.

"Why don't we change the subject?" Miranda said. Anna and Luke had been kind enough to have them over for dinner, one of the few such social occasions left available to them with what little time they had left. She refused to let Derek make their hosts feel awkward. There were obviously issues that needed to be resolved between Derek and Zack, but that could wait for some other time.

Anna was understanding. "Hey, it's okay," she said. Luke lifted his glass of wine off of the table and raised it for a toast, although nothing was said. The four simply smiled at one another and touched their glasses, the clanking sound bittersweet in both Derek's and Miranda's ears.

*　　*　　*

It was cloudy and windy in Battery Park at dusk. Morgan Hutton pulled his trench coat around him even more tightly. It was particularly chilly on this April day. Morgan stared out at the water toward Ellis Island.

"Hey," Zack called from behind him.

He turned to face Zack. "Rubbing my nose in it a little, aren't you, Zack, making this our meeting place?" Morgan said. "Why here?"

"I don't know. Why'd you bring your mistress here?" Zack said casually. "Cause it's private."

"Not private enough," Morgan said with scorn.

"You got my papers?" Zack asked, ignoring the remark. Morgan leaned his briefcase on the railing and opened it, withdrawing a brown folder. He handed it to Zack and then turned his eyes back to the water. He couldn't even look at Zack, at that smug expression on his face.

"Your parents would be appalled," Morgan said over his shoulder. Zack didn't take his eyes off of the papers he was examining.

"Yeah, well, I'm sure the same goes for you, too."

Morgan's response was bitter. "I guess we've all got our faults. We'll have to just work at it a little harder."

"Sure, whatever," Zack said, uninterested in Morgan's attempt to vent his guilt and scatter blame.

There was a long silence as Zack made sure that everything was in order. Then he said, "I'm sure I'll figure all this out later."

"Why do you come all the way down here, Zack? Is it because it's close to Ground Zero?"

"Go fuck yourself, Morgan."

"Life sure has dealt you a lousy hand."

"Yeah, it sure has," Zack shot back, refusing to be baited by reverse psychology.

"Is that why you're doing this to me?"

"Look, Morgan, the only reason I'm doin' this, the *only* reason, is to get by. To survive."

"Bullshit."

"Believe what you want. I honestly don't care." Zack loaded the papers into his backpack and got back on his bike to go. "I'll see you around, Morgan. You take care." He made it about a hundred feet when Morgan called out behind him. What he said made the cold hit Zack harder than ever.

"You've become a rotten person, Zack."

CHAPTER 30
April 15, 2002

"I think something bad's gonna happen," Zack said.

"Why do you think that?" Ms. Shearer asked him. She had agreed to meet with him when she had time between two students who still actually attended the school.

"I feel like all I want to do is forget about it and move on, but instead I keep getting dragged through it. It's startin' to get to me. I mean, I think I've done an all-right job up until now, right?"

"I'd say so," Ms. Shearer said. She wanted to maintain some semblance of control over this conversation. She didn't know if Zack knew that she'd overstepped her professional bounds by continuing to meet with him like this. They weren't talking about college, and they weren't talking about a job. They were just talking.

"So, I mean," Zack continued, "there's only so much a guy can take before he snaps. And I feel on edge right now."

They had drifted into dangerous waters. She had to bring them back. Before he could continue, she interrupted. "Zack, we can't have meetings like this anymore."

"Like what?" Zack asked, thinking that she sounded strange saying that. He found her attractive, but they'd never met outside this office.

"Like *this*, Zack."

"What are you talkin' about?"

She leaned forward in her chair and rested her folded hands on the table. "Zack, I was your guidance counselor. And you're not a student here anymore. You graduated."

Zack didn't try to hide his surprise. What was going on here? "Wait, so you think that I think I'm like Tony Soprano and you're my Dr. Melfi? I don't come here for you to be my therapist. I come here because I thought you were my friend."

He sounded hurt. She tried to repair the damage. "I *am* your friend, Zack. But these meetings we're having might raise questions with the administration. I'm not certified to offer you the kind of advice you're looking for."

"Oh, so you're worried that you might lose your prestigious job?" he asked nastily.

She blinked. She would have thought that it would be obvious. "Of course that's what I'm worried about."

Zack thought it through and sighed deeply. "I guess you're right," he muttered.

"Zack, there are still certified professionals you can talk to. With what you've been through, you—"

"Goddamned bureaucratic bullshit," he interrupted. "Goes to the very root of my problem."

"Zack, listen—"

"I tell you that I think something bad's gonna happen, and your administration's spooked you so bad that you can't even wait long enough to hear me out?" He ran his hands through his hair. "Goddamn."

She became sterner. It was time to play the maturity card. "First of all," she began, "don't speak to me that way in my own office. Second, someday soon you're going have to realize that just because you've had it bad doesn't mean that you can just shape things up the way you want them to be. That's not how the world works."

Zack stood up from his chair. "I'm gonna go."

"Zack, please, let's talk and we'll work this out."

"I gotta go," he said. He went out the door.

＊　　＊　　＊

Zack did his deliveries for the remainder of the day. In the early evening he found himself with some down time and spent it in the back of Marco's shop, smoking pot and playing pinball. Marco and Jamar didn't know about how much Zack's meeting with Ms. Shearer had bothered him; they just noted how aggressively he played pinball, shaking the machine and swearing.

"Take it easy on my damn machine," Marco said over his shoulder to Zack. He was currently Jamar's blackjack dealer and was annoyed with the distraction. "I thought you ate Xanax." He looked to Jamar.

"Hit," Jamar said.

Marco flipped the card. His whole face seemed to pucker with exaggeration. "Ooooooh, sorry. Bust," he said.

"Goddamn it." Jamar said.

Marco ran his hands over the cards again. "Okay, here we go."

He waited for Jamar to place his bet. Putting his chin to his left shoulder, he said to Zack, "Hey, man, I heard you talkin' to your brother earlier on the phone. How the hell you gonna talk to your older brother like that?" Back to Jamar. "Thirteen."

"Hit," Jamar said.

"What can I say?" Zack said. "The guy goes out of his way to piss me off."

"No, man," Marco said. "He's your older brother. Respect his experience. You're too quick to write him off." He looked back to Jamar, who told him he'd stay at twenty. Marco flipped his cards.

"Fourteen. Sixteen. Twenty. Tie goes to the dealer."

"Motherfucker!" Jamar yelled. He scattered the rest of the cards to the floor.

Marco was a hard individual, but not without a sense of humor. "Now, now," he said to Jamar. He loved patronizing Jamar. "Let's not blow our stacks. Not very becomin' of one of my top earners." Just as he said that Zack grew frustrated at losing another ball and slapped his hand down on the glass top. "Lotta angst in this room," Marco said. He stood to his full height and turned. "What'd I just tell you? Take it easy on my goddamn game! They don't make Grand Lizard anymore, and it's special to me."

"Sorry," Zack said.

"Now answer my question," Marco said.

"What question?" Zack asked.

"Where do you get of talkin' to your brother like an arrogant little bitch?" Marco demanded.

"What is this?" Zack said. *My life is just one big open-fuckin'-book.* "I got trust issues. I can't trust him like I do you guys."

"And that's some of the dumbest shit I ever heard come out of your mouth," Marco said, snorting. "That's your blood, man. That's family." He pounded his fist against his chest for emphasis. He glanced down at Jamar, sulking on his wooden stool. "It's guys like me and Jamar you gotta worry about. We're the ones who'll let you down."

"Speak for yourself, Mr. Smart Ass," Jamar said. "I don't gotta tell Zack. He knows I got his back."

"Yeah, well you two will be the death of each other," Marco said, looking back and forth between both of them. "Mark my words."

"That's fucked up," Zack said.

"Call it what you will," Marco said. "But I've met your brother. I'm sure he has nothin' good to say about me, but he's definitely got his head screwed on straight. You oughta follow his example."

"Yeah?" Zack asked, pretending to take Marco's words to heart.

"Yeah," Marco said. He raised his right hand and rotated his index finger as if to take in the whole room. "I know this is cool, us spending our days here and all. We have good times." He lowered his hands and locked eyes with Zack. "But you can have more than *this*, man."

Zack stared back blankly.

CHAPTER 31
APRIL 16, 2002

Connie Hutton hadn't liked how long her grocery list had been before she'd left work. Even though the store was only a block and a half away, she knew she'd have her hands full. Myles offered to help her when she got to the door of her building, but she was a fully capable woman and relieving her of this particular burden wasn't in his job description. It had been a short walk, but a cold and windy one, and she was grateful she'd been able to hook three heavy plastic bags onto each arm and make it home without mishap. Her chestnut hair had been blown free of its pins, and it hung in her eyes. She thanked Myles graciously as he called the elevator for her.

Putting the grocery bags on the floor of the elevator, she raked the hair away from her forehead. She looked at herself in the elevator's golden mirror and then put her hands on her hips. This new jacket *did* look good on her. She pushed her hips to one side, putting the weight on her right leg. Pursing her lips, she looked at her mirror image and kissed the air. *Still got it,* she told herself.

She'd been planning this dinner for a while. There was no special occasion; she was happy nonetheless. It was just one of those cold, rainy days that when you got home from a long day at the office, you just wanted to kick of your shoes, jump on the couch, and have a glass of white wine while waiting for Morgan to come home. She knew how much Morgan liked to contribute to the cooking effort, so she'd wait for him.

As she got off of the elevator and headed for their penthouse, she thought of how well they'd done since the kids had gone off to college. The empty nest had been a tough reality to cope with in those first days, but she had to admit to herself that the change had had its benefits. She and Morgan had enjoyed some wonderful evenings at home.

Arriving at the door, she put the groceries back on the ground and fumbled for the keys in her pocket. Digging them out, she went to insert one in the lock when she heard singing in the apartment. *Bad* singing. Had one of them left the television on this morning?

Opening the door and crossing the foyer, she headed down the hall. Getting closer to the source she realized it was Morgan who was singing and that his speech was seriously slurred. Still though, she could make out the lyrics as she reached the living room.

"*You have loved lots of girls in the sweet long ago,*" Morgan sang with a heavy tongue. "*And each one has meant heaven to you.*" She stood dumbfounded. He was sitting on the ground slumped against the windowsill, his forehead resting against the glass. His left arm was also lying across the windowsill, a glass full of whiskey in his hand. She knew it was whiskey not only because Morgan only drank Jack Daniel's but also because he had a mostly depleted bottle gripped in his right hand resting on the floor. A light drizzle of rain peppered the outside of the window. That and his singing were the only sounds, and he was utterly oblivious to her presence. "*You have vowed your affection to each one in turn, and have sworn to them all that you'd be true.*"

"Morgan, what the hell are you doing?" Connie asked. Startled, Morgan jerked his head back. She took him in. He was a mess. His shirt was untucked and his collar hung open. Both had absorbed spilled whiskey. His tie sat on the floor next to him. His eyes were bloodshot, his salt-and-pepper hair was matted, and there was a sheen of perspiration on his forehead and stubbled face.

"Connie," was all he said, and she heard sorrow in her name.

"Morgan, what's going on? Why aren't you at the office?"

"Oh God, Connie," he said, inebriated.

"And why are you shit-faced?" she asked, pointing at the bottle on the floor. "It's five-fifteen in the afternoon."

"Connie, I have ... I have to—"

"Morgan, what is it? Tell me what's wrong."

"I have to tell you something." His words were so desperate that he seemed more able to articulate now. "And it's not going to be easy for you to hear."

"Morgan," she said, kneeling down to his level and placing her hands on his shoulders. "Morgan, tell me."

"Okay," he said, as if ready to be rid of some great burden. He ran his hands through his hair, combing it back. "Okay, here goes."

*   *   *

He and Jamar had done it. They'd gotten everything moved into their new Brooklyn apartment. There was still a lot of work to be done, but Zack was happy with how the day had turned out. It was only 6:30, and all the hard tasks were over with. Now, back in Manhattan, all he had to do was get all of his stuff out of the old apartment, and he had all the time in the world to do that. He decided that he would head back there now and make a list of everything he'd be keeping and everything he'd be selling.

He took the train to Marco's. He picked up his bike there and headed home. He called both Jacqueline and Jamar to tell them to come and claim their belongings that they'd left behind. He was going to go home and replay some old memories in his head.

It had gotten dark by the time he arrived. He looked down at his key ring and frowned. Why had he removed the bike-lock key again? He couldn't remember. He picked up the bike and hauled it up the stairs, bringing it into the hallway. He leaned it against the wall and went inside the apartment. He turned on the lights and looked around.

What had been his choices? Rent this place out and make money, saying good-bye to one of the last pieces of proof that he'd once belonged to a family? Say good-bye to all those good times with his friends?

Or stay here and continue to hang on the painful memories that accompanied the good ones, keep hauling all that emotional baggage around? Refuse to let go of the past?

No, it was a no-brainer. He would have to wash his hands of this place. He wanted to grow. He wanted it just as badly as all of those who watched him and wanted him to mature. And hanging on to this place would stunt his growth. He wouldn't have to do it tonight, or tomorrow for that matter, but he would have to do it eventually. And he was okay with that.

That didn't change that it was hard. When he had been in here with his loved ones there had been no world outside these walls. Everything had begun and ended in here, and Zack hadn't been burdened with a reality beyond this place. But times had changed, and it was time to move on.

He made his list. The stress level of the move was proving to be low, and he was grateful for that. He found a half-smoked joint on the coffee table and lit it. As he got stoned, he debated whether or not to sell the coffee table. It was awfully run down. *Oh, shit!* He realized he'd left his bike out in the hallway. He picked up the U-bolt lock from the floor and went to get the bike before someone helped himself to it.

Stepping out into the hall, he froze. Someone *had* helped himself to his bike. *What the fuck?* Who possibly could have grabbed it? He bolted outside to the top of the stone staircase. It was dark out, but he could make out a figure pedaling away from him heading east. He jumped down the flight of stairs and hit the ground hard, but he was up and running in no time. He sprinted after the thief, who didn't know he was being pursued, yet was still trying to make a speedy getaway. Zack summoned all the speed he could, but it was useless. The bike thief was getting smaller by the second.

When he resigned himself to the fact that his bicycle had been stolen, he screamed something unintelligible and threw the useless U-bolt on the ground. The thief heard Zack's voice and looked over his shoulder. Zack still couldn't make out the person, who was now pedaling much faster.

Zack seethed. His Diamondback was gone. Just then Jamar rounded the corner, right in front of the guy.

* * *

Jamar had received Zack's voicemail telling him to come over and claim whatever items he might have left floating around the apartment. Since he was already in the neighborhood, he figured it would be better to do it then and get it out of the way.

He had just rounded the corner of Zack's block on his skateboard when he thought he heard Zack shout something. He looked down the street and saw Zack throw his bike's lock on the ground. Zack saw Jamar and shouted his name pointing at the man on a bike, *Zack's* bike, coming right at him.

Jamar had already been speeding along, and his current trajectory had him and the stranger on a collision course. Jamar didn't think. He just acted. He gave two strong pushes of the street with his left leg, picking up more speed for good measure.

Jamar kick-flipped his board up and into his right hand in a move that an observer would have been impressed by if circumstances had been different. The stranger tried to pedal away from Jamar, but it was no use. Jamar grabbed the board by its trucks and brought it back over his right shoulder. He swung the board at the stranger, the wood smacking right into his forehead. He fell backwards off of the bike and hit the street, stunned.

Jamar stood over the guy. He didn't want to act until he had discerned how badly he'd hurt him. Jamar took a good look at the person before him. He thought he knew him. He did. It was that little shithead Mo, from the basketball court that one day. *The balls on this prick!*

Zack had apparently identified Mo too by the time he arrived judging from that wide-eyed look on his face. He had picked up the lock from the street. It was hanging from his right hand.

"Are you kiddin' me?" was all Zack said. Mo, dazed, had managed to lift himself into a sitting position. Jamar was worried how Zack would react, and just as he was processing that thought, Zack, gripping the lock by the curve of its U-shaped bar, swung it horizontally, smashing the heavy locking mechanism into Mo's skull, right behind his right ear. The thud that sounded from the blunt contact made Jamar wince. He heard Zack yell something unintelligible as Mo went down for the second time. Blood began to trickle from his head, and Jamar knew it was time to go.

Jamar practically dove into Zack. "Get the bike. Let's go," he said, grabbing Zack by the hood of his sweatshirt. But Zack didn't move. He just stood over Mo, breathing heavily. Maybe Zack was still a little angry, but he was definitely a little scared. "C'mon, c'mon, let's go!" Jamar said again, picking up volume. Zack snapped out of it and grabbed his bike and started heading back in the direction of the apartment. "Yo, where you goin'?" Jamar asked, exasperated. He wanted no part of the events that would soon follow. They needed to take off.

"Gotta lock the apartment," Zack said. Jamar took a worried look around and followed Zack on his skateboard, leaving Mo on the ground, bleeding, clutching his wounded head in his arms.

Jamar caught up to Zack and said, "Zack, what the hell did you do that for?"

✻　✻　✻

Zack knew he'd been asked a question by Jamar, but he hadn't heard what the question was. He was pedaling back toward the apartment at a furious pace. He didn't want to be seen on the street. He looked into Ms. Goldcamp's apartment. No lights. That was good. He looked to the upper balcony … and found Mrs. Pezeshk looking right at him, her hands over her mouth and nose, tears gleaming on her lined face in the fluorescent light. He wondered how much she'd seen.

I'm fucked, Zack thought to himself.

CHAPTER 32
MARCH 2, 1998

Hakeem Rashid stood at the southern perimeter of the farm, holding his AK-47 ready in his right arm, its barrel pointing toward the sky. He rested his left hand on the wooden post of the chicken wire fence he'd installed years earlier. He scanned the land before him only briefly before he turned his attention to the electric wire that ran along the top of the fence. It was functioning normally.

The fence was there to keep the livestock in, not to keep intruders out. Intruders, if they were foolish enough to try to trespass, would be blown to bits by the dozens of land mines that surrounded the farm. The whole property was booby-trapped with mines, wired grenades, flares, bear traps, and even pits. His father had shown him how to install these security precautions.

Hakeem, now twenty-one, had been trained by his father to protect the farm at all costs, by any means necessary. Sniper tactics and demolitions also played their parts in this defense. He'd also learned hand-to-hand combat techniques, including some martial arts his father had mastered during his time spent with the Golden Crescent. No one would survive an attack on this farm—Hakeem would make sure of that.

At the moment, the responsibility was on Hakeem alone. His father was incapacitated, his Uncle Mussar had returned after many years of being away, and it was entirely possible that Mussar had been followed here by one of the many enemies his family had made.

Mussar's business had taken him to Pakistan before Hakeem had been turned over to his father's custody. His business trip had turned into his exile. Hakeem didn't know all the details, but he knew it had had something to do with the retribution his father had sought on some men who'd betrayed him many years ago. He didn't know if his uncle had truly been involved; he only knew Mussar was not welcome in Herat, and that there were individuals all over the country who would kill him if they could. Mussar had taken a great risk coming here, and Hakeem was grateful his uncle had responded to his call.

It often frustrated Hakeem that his father chose to share with him some of the most harrowing details of his past, yet oftentimes he left him in the dark about others. He supposed his father weighed the facts in his head and decided what was and what wasn't important, but Hakeem sometimes felt that he was only seeing the side of his father that he was allowed to see. Not far from the son's mind were all the stories he'd been told before he'd been re-introduced to Benazar. Those stories seemed to match up with what Hakeem had come to understand about his father's past, but Hakeem had yet to see the connection for himself.

Hakeem would have liked to think he'd grown into a man his father could be proud of. The boy he'd left behind in Herat was gone. It seemed like a lifetime ago; so many years had passed that the memories might have belonged to someone else. He'd grown up fast in those first few days with Benazar. It wasn't until then, after seeing how ravaged the country was, that he came to terms with the fact that the hopes he'd had for the future had been unrealistic. His uncle had chosen the life of a peaceful negotiator, and even he had managed to get a price put on his head. This was not the time of the diplomat. And yet ... and yet, there was still a feeling of great loss that came with that realization.

He hoped that Uncle would be able to get more information from his father than he had been able to. Benazar had been rambling incoherently when Hakeem had found him on the outskirts of the farm, soaked to the bone and shivering. Hakeem had set out searching hours before, leaving the farm unmanned and unprotected. When he found him, he helped him back to the farm, where he drew Benazar a warm bath and got him into bed. Then he'd sent word to Mussar.

He'd spent the next few days awaiting Uncle's arrival and pondering his father's motivations. Wandering off to into the desert without telling Hakeem was not something he'd have expected from Benazar. It troubled Hakeem deeply.

In all of his father's mumbling after he'd been found, one word had stuck in Hakeem's head: *vision*. Uncle had once told him that his grandfather was said to have been prescient, supernaturally so. Mussar gave the claim little merit, for he'd never seen anything that would make a believer out of him. Hakeem had barely acknowledged the notion, filing it away in his mind as part of the legend that seemed to grow around his family.

He knew his father had endured more pain and suffering than any human being should ever have to. He prayed that Benazar had not had a breakdown.

He hadn't thought it possible. Just looking at his father's accomplishments since they'd arrived here, and the contacts he had made, would bring one to the conclusion that Benazar was of sound mind, a man calm and calculating. One would never suspect the trials that he'd been through. It was on those nights when they would sit in complete silence that Hakeem could look upon that unfocused, unblinking stare and watch his father get lost inside his head. It was unsettling to observe.

Hakeem turned and headed for the barnyard to kill some chickens. He had grown to six feet tall and had a strong build, wiry but powerful. His beard had filled in nicely, long and thick. He didn't wear a turban but rather a green military-style cap. There were those who would ostracize him for his choice of head gear, but those were men who wouldn't dare speak out if they came here visiting. And those who visited only came on matters of business.

One could come here and purchase horses or other livestock. The money would support his father's agenda, which had yet to be revealed to Hakeem, but selling animals was merely their front.

One could also come here to purchase drugs. From opium to heroin, the drug trade supported them more than livestock ever could, and his father had befriended some powerful men in the business. Hakeem was aware of the toll the drugs that came from that association were taking on his father physically, but recognized that someone like Benazar occasionally needed an escape from his pain. Hakeem was aware that he and his father might have been contributing to others' misery, but the trade had made his father some unexpected allies. And it wasn't as though his father's situation was unique. Even Massoud was said to have a hand in the narcotics that flowed through Afghanistan.

And then there were the guns. Hundreds of guns. Since he and his father had first set out together all those years ago, they had been gathering guns of every kind and stockpiling them. His father had an uncanny knack for recovering them, often from battle sites, and they all eventually found their way here. They even had precious stinger missiles in their arsenal, which the Americans had attempted to buy back in recent years all over the country. Behind the barnyard was an underground cache, which was also a hidden bunker. He and Benazar had dug it themselves.

To the naked eye it appeared as though a father and son were merely trying to get by in a war-torn country. And Benazar liked it that way. He didn't want the wrong people to come knocking at his door. Loyalties and alliances were forever changing throughout the country, but Benazar's personal politics were always at the forefront of his business. *No one* with shifting allegiances purchased animals or contraband here. And in a country where no one could ever be sure whom to trust, his father had grown better at trusting his own instincts.

Benazar had once told Hakeem of a personal betrayal he had experienced that had changed his whole way of thinking, his whole way of life. Hakeem had first thought of all the men who'd turned up dead on the same day his father had come for him. But later he came to the conclusion that it was a wound that ran deeper than that. Benazar had promised to elaborate on it further for him one day, but now Hakeem was twenty-one, and nothing more had been confided to him.

Hakeem hadn't needed to do a whole lot of guesswork. It was the Americans. It had to have been. Benazar had memories from another lifetime as well. His torment at Soviet hands was rarely mentioned. It was alluded to, really, only when used as a reference for Hakeem's lessons in survival. Something had gone wrong during the time his father had trained with the Americans.

Anti-American sentiment was spreading everywhere. Whereas over a dozen years before, citizens were fleeing the country in droves, now it seemed as though there was a large influx of idealists who'd come to train with the Saudi Arabians, who'd found a haven here through apparent political asylum.

It was hard for Hakeem to keep up on current events. He'd spent the last six years here in virtual isolation with his father, gathering secondhand information from those who came calling. This only contributed to his regrets, but he buried the pain. It was useless now to wonder what might have been.

He knew that there might be more to their time spent here than merely trying to get by. His father had intentions, but Hakeem wasn't sure what they were.

There were times when Benazar seemed unbalanced, yet existence in a land such as this was demanding, and his father had taught him to be strong. Something he'd come to understand was that Benazar was not nearly as radical a Muslim as those who flooded the camps. He was a pragmatist. Islam provided him with a guide for living life, but not a blueprint. Hakeem often wondered how many times his father, locked away in that dark cell for those years, had questioned his faith. Hakeem couldn't walk in Benazar's shoes. Thinking about the atrocities Benazar had endured made Hakeem shake his head.

He looked over to the house from the barnyard. He hoped Mussar could get to the bottom of the present situation. He feared Benazar might finally be falling apart. And if this was the case, he wanted to know what his own destiny was. He may have been willing to abandon romantic ideas of rebuilding a nation in favor of a more direct approach to the problem. However, it was something else entirely to follow a madman into the abyss.

*   *   *

"Benazar." Benazar heard his name spoken and opened his eyes. His brother was sitting in a chair next to him. Extending a steaming cup of tea to Benazar, Mussar said, "Here, sip this."

Lifting his head from the pillow, he asked, "What are you doing here, Mussar?"

"Hakeem contacted me. He said you left him here without telling him you were leaving. He also told me he found you nearly freezing to death in a heap on the ground, babbling like a madman."

Benazar said nothing. He was used to his brother's short temper. It was better to let Mussar's frustration run its course.

Exasperated, Mussar continued. "What if there had been an attack? Hakeem would have died thinking you'd abandoned him. All of the noble acts of your life combined couldn't excuse you for that."

Benazar finally spoke. "What makes you so sure Hakeem would die?" Mussar closed his eyes and took in a deep breath. It was obvious he was travel weary and irritated by the possibility he might have come here on a fool's errand.

As if reading Benazar's mind, Mussar said, "I've risked my life coming back here, Benazar. It would be a sign of respect to me if you'd tell me why you did what you did."

Benazar could see Mussar visibly brace himself, as if he knew what Benazar was about to say. There was no sense holding anything back. "I had a vision."

Mussar gritted his teeth and looked out the hut's window. "And?" he said. Was he going to play along this time?

"And time is short," Benazar said.

"We're going to be attacked?"

"We're going to be systematically wiped out."

"I see." It was obvious to Benazar that Mussar didn't see. "The Americans?" he asked. "Why would they do that?"

Benazar stiffened and said, "Because those camps are swelling with infiltrators, and soon they're going to do something unthinkable."

"And you'll have your chance at revenge."

"I'll have my chance to set matters straight."

"Well, we've seen how well it's worked out for both of us when you've set matters straight," Mussar said with contempt.

"You're missing the point," Benazar said. "Whether we get involved or we sit here on our hands, they're going to come for us. You and I will be at the top of their lists. There's nothing we can do to change what's happening, even though there are millions of people who feel as we do."

"This is what your vision told you?" Mussar asked, incredulous. He took Benazar's silence as a confirmation. Then he said, "Is it possible that perhaps this was a hallucination brought on by your painkillers rather than one of the visions that couldn't save even our father?"

So, it appeared that Benazar had lost some credibility with his brother, or Mussar's respect, or maybe both. He didn't want to argue the point that he'd greatly reduced his drug use in recent months. Instead, he said, "Again, you miss the point. What is relevant is that I know what I have to do now."

"Which is?"

"Prepare my son."

"I thought that's what you've been doing all these years," Mussar said.

"You don't understand," Benazar said. "It's more than mere survival. He has an important job to do."

Now for the first time Mussar seemed to be listening intently. "Really?"

"Our time is past," Benazar said. "But Hakeem, he has the potential to make the whole world open their eyes to what's been happening."

"And we need to put him on this path?"

"Yes."

"This is what you saw in your vision?"

"Yes."

There was silence as Mussar considered what his brother had told him. After a minute he said, "Once again your timing could not have been odder."

"What does that mean?" Benazar asked.

"It means I have information that you don't, and we both have an opportunity to seize."

"Tell me," Benazar demanded.

"First, I need to know if you're serious about this."

The question was an insult to Benazar. "When have I ever been known to be halfhearted about anything?"

"You're changing in front of my eyes," Mussar said. He pulled back the cot's covers and grasped Benazar's left wrist, exposing the blackened blotch over the veins on the inside of his upper forearm. "Ten years ago I wouldn't have considered this a possibility."

Benazar said, "I'm your brother, Mussar. You can trust me to do what's right."

Mussar wasn't so sure. But something he was sure of was that events were already being set into motion, and it was better to be part of the change involved than simply to stand by and watch it come to pass.

CHAPTER 33
JUNE 15, 1998

The jeep slowed as the terrain became rockier. When Benazar decelerated, the man sitting next to him found that both the engine noise and the dust had decreased. He had a pad and paper in his hands and he turned and asked Benazar in English, "So this was the road they used to advance on your position?"

"Correct," Benazar responded. The man left it at that. There would be plenty of time for questions once they reached their destination. The three of them continued the journey in silence.

For the briefest of moments Hakeem glanced into the rearview mirror and locked eyes with his father. He had no idea what his father was up to, but he was sure that, as with everything else concerning Benazar Rashid, it would be made clear in due time. For the moment, Hakeem just kept quiet.

Saying something wrong was one mistake Hakeem probably wouldn't have to worry about. Benazar had been explicit in his instruction to remain a careful and quiet observer. The stranger had no idea that Hakeem spoke English. And of course Hakeem was to respond when spoken to in whatever harsh Dari the man remembered from his time spent here. By now the American surely knew that Hakeem was Benazar's son. But Hakeem had been told to blend into his surroundings and file away as much information as he could.

"Make him forget you're even here," Benazar had told him. "Take note of his mannerisms, the way he moves and speaks. Don't allow him to know that you understand what we're saying."

Hakeem tried to sort his way through the confusion by making a mental list of what he *did* know: First, all the strange behavior between his father and his uncle had started soon after that dumbfounding morning he'd found his father shivering and rambling west of the farm. Second, his father and his uncle were planning something. This was apparent to Hakeem after Mussar had extended his stay in Afghanistan, risking his life. Third, his father had a hidden agenda on this trip they were on. He had come to know Benazar, and he was sure that Benazar was not a man who would give guided tours of battle sites— *especially* not the ones he himself had bled on, and *especially* not to an American. Fourth, the American had been born here. He was about the same age as Hakeem, and his surviving family had fled the country during the Russian occupation. Having just graduated from some American university, he was now returning to the land of his birth with all the hopes of an aspiring photo journalist. He was apparently working on some reflection piece and had been brave enough to risk the journey here. This was admirable in Hakeem's opinion, but he wouldn't dare share this with his father.

Hakeem grew apprehensive the more he thought about it. Benazar hated Americans. Hakeem could not imagine one plausible scenario in which this situation they were now in could ever have developed to this point. Hakeem had been commanded to remain aloof, yet he had a million questions to ask the American. *Just do as you're told, and you'll get all the answers you need.*

After weaving their way up past five switchbacks, the trio reached their destination. The jeep came to a halt, and the impatient reporter jumped out. Benazar stepped out of the vehicle and Hakeem followed suit. The American's camera was already out and in use. Benazar and Hakeem started unloading their gear.

"We'll camp here tonight," Benazar said in accented English.

"Very good," the American said. Hakeem began to busy himself with setting up camp. Aside from keeping quiet, he had other responsibilities and knew what was expected of him. The American pointed up the rocky slope and asked, "Is that the bunker there?"

Benazar nodded. The two started toward it and Hakeem resumed his duties unpacking. He heard his name called and looked to Benazar, who was nodding upwards and gesturing for Hakeem to follow.

The men reached the bunker, a mass of dusty rubble. "I'm sorry it's not intact for you," Benazar said, and Hakeem thought he heard strained sincerity.

"This is fine. This is perfect," the grinning American said. He reached into his backpack and retrieved a miniature tape recorder. As Hakeem watched him he realized that he and the American, without the glasses and beardless face, looked enough alike that he almost saw himself, or what he might have been if fate had allowed him the life he'd sought earlier. Familiar pangs of regret sprang up within him, but he mentally seized them and sent them back down into that dark place where they festered.

"I'm standing on a mountaintop about ninety miles southwest of the city of Herat," the American said into his tape recorder. Hakeem had to pay attention to keep up with his rapid English. "I'm standing with Benazar Rashid, one of the most talked about soldiers for the Mujaheddin. We're at the remains of what once was a bunker."

Hakeem didn't need to hear it. He'd been here many times before. In fact it was a back-up cache, with a hidden bunker, so that in the event that he and his father were overrun from the farm they'd have a refuge to fall back on. Hakeem feared this might become their home if his uncle and his men were attacked while guarding the farm. He'd feel much more confident if he and Benazar were defending their land.

"The bunker was of vital importance during the Soviet-Afghan conflict because of the strategic value of its location, as well as the timing of the final battle," the American said, pausing. Then he turned off the recorder and turned to Benazar. "Before we continue, let's go over what happened."

Benazar dove right into it. "We occupied it, but we were forced out. Then we returned and killed everyone in it. We managed to keep them from sending a distress signal. Then we waited."

"When was this?" the American asked.

"In December of 1985."

"This was roughly a year before you began working with the CIA?"

"Yes," Benazar said. Hakeem didn't like the sudden look in his father's eyes. He'd seen it times before when his father went swimming in his sea of memories, and it always made Hakeem uneasy.

"And so...?" the American prompted.

"And so there were about six of us packed in there. A Soviet truck carrying about twenty troops arrived, taking us by surprise. We managed to surprise them too, and we opened fire on them."

"You didn't know they were coming, and they didn't know you were there?"

Benazar nodded.

"And so what happened when you opened fire?"

"We managed to take down about three or four of them before they scattered and dug themselves in. The blanket of snow was thick. We took out the truck with as little ammunition as was necessary. We had no rockets and only a few grenades. We had a brief firefight and then we waited."

"How long?"

"Two hours."

"Then what happened?"

"They called in an air strike. The second we heard those jet engines we poured out of the bunker. We expected to be picked off one by one by the soldiers as we did."

"What happened?"

"We lost one man. The bomb they dropped on the bunker served us in the end. It scattered the enemy, and the five of us that survived rushed and killed every single one of them."

The American remained perched on a rock, looking thoughtful. Hakeem looked at the pile of rocks his father had just been talking about. He'd heard the story before, but never like that.

"I'm glad to hear it," the American said, writing something down on his notepad. Hakeem detected the false empathy, as if this man and his father had fought side by side.

Benazar stared at the back of the American's head. Hakeem thought his father looked disgusted. Whatever this charade was, he doubted Benazar would be able to keep it up.

The American turned the recorder back on and began to speak into it. Hakeem knew it was his job to listen to what the man was saying, but for a brief moment he was startled to see what might have been taken as an expression of sadness on his father's face. Then, as quickly as it had appeared, it vanished.

* * *

The sun had set and the temperature was dropping rapidly. The men ate some jerky and pomegranate for dinner, and then built a fire that would struggle to survive against the frigid mountain winds.

"Hakeem will take first watch." Hakeem rose, cradling his rifle.

"Is there always a need to stand watch?" the American asked.

"I don't let my guard down, if that's what you're asking," said Benazar. Hakeem was still sure the American thought him ignorant of the dialogue with his father.

"Life must be difficult. Not ever knowing who your true enemies are, that is," the American said. Benazar stared back at him with years of bloodshed contributing to the fury in his eyes. The American suddenly grew visibly uncomfortable, but didn't break eye contact.

"That was a problem for me once," Benazar said. "But not anymore." A long silence ensued, one of the typical silences that usually followed one of Benazar's references to his past. Fortunately for Hakeem, he'd grown accustomed to them. Grabbing his poncho, he turned his back on his father and the American and headed for a cliff's overhang where he could monitor the switchback.

"I'll relieve you in four hours, Hakeem," Benazar said as his son departed.

"All right."

*   *   *

The American had asked enough questions for the day. He was tired and eager to start fresh the next morning. After nightfall there was no reason for him to stay awake. He took off his glasses and crawled into his sleeping bag. Running a hand over the stubble of his jaw, he imagined that he might look just like the soldier's son if fate had not taken his family out of this godforsaken land.

Well, he had every intention of bringing this story back to America with him. It would put him on his career path while at the same time it would pay homage to his heritage. As grateful as he was to his new country for taking in a desperate refugee, it sometimes sickened him how easily this place had been forgotten there in recent years. Wounds this deep did not heal so easily.

Hopefully, he had the power to raise awareness. He had taken a great risk in returning here. But it would all be worth it. He had a bright future ahead of him.

He drifted off to sleep with these thoughts.

*   *   *

The American woke up. He was groggy and didn't know what had awoken him. He stuck his head out of the sleeping bag, and tried to adjust his eyes. His vision was blurry and light was scarce from the diminished fire, but he could see enough to know that Benazar was standing over him. He groped for his backpack and pulled his glasses out of one the compartments.

He put on his glasses … and found himself staring at the shiny silver barrel of a Desert Eagle pistol. He struggled to rise and found himself half jumping, half crawling backwards, his movements made clumsy within the confines of his sleeping bag.

"What … what are you doing?" the American asked in Dari. Benazar took two quick steps toward him, closing whatever meager distance the American managed to put between them.

"Please! Please don't!" His terror grew with each passing second as he took in the flames flickering in the whites of the Benazar's eyes. There was a detachment in those eyes that he had not seen earlier.

In a low tone that was barely audible, the soldier said, "I want you to listen to me very carefully."

*   *   *

Hakeem dreamt of a time that he could not possibly have remembered, a time when he was merely an infant. The streets were soaked with blood. Buildings were burning. People were screaming.

It was the revolt of Herat in 1979. It had been described to Hakeem often enough so that he recognized it when he saw it. That fact didn't make the dream any less horrifying. He supposed he should've taken comfort in the fact that he was watching his side win. But watching the rebels butcher the wives and children of the communist political advisers made him want to scream. When he tried to scream within his dream, however, there was only silence. Or maybe his voice was simply drowned out by the booming of gunfire or the wailing of the victims.

There was a man crouched down on the ground alongside a dead body. His back was turned to Hakeem and he was busy at work. Hakeem was afraid to look but couldn't force himself to turn away. When the man stood up, Hakeem's fears were confirmed. The man was Benazar Rashid, and in his right hand he held a Russian politician's decapitated head by the hair. He looked right into Hakeem's eyes. Taking a few steps to his right, his father found a pike of rebar protruding from a mass of smashed concrete as if it had been awaiting a trophy. He walked over to the pike and impaled the dead man's head on it. Blood dripped down the metal pole, and in his dream Hakeem managed to close his eyes.

Stop it! Stop it! Stop it! Stop it! Stop it! Stop it! Stop it! Stop it! Stop it! Stop it! Stop it!

The scene changed. He was still standing in the middle of the street in Herat. But now it was daylight and all of the people were gone. All but one.

There was a man slumped against a wall on the far side of the street, and he was moaning. Hakeem hurried toward him. The street was still in shambles, but, except for the moan, all was now quiet. He drew nearer, and the man raised his head to look at him. To Hakeem's relief he realized he didn't know this man. It was just another broken civilian.

The man had a lined face and tears in his eyes. His age was impossible to determine. He opened his mouth to speak and Hakeem braced himself.

"Gaaaaahhhhhh," was all the man got out. Hakeem looked down at the man's exposed right forearm. His left hand rested on a hypodermic needle that was piercing a vein. The skin surrounding the puncture was black with infection, a small crater of swollen skin surrounding the needle.

Hakeem wanted to vomit, and not simply at what he saw before him but also because it forced him to be honest with himself, and that hurt more than merely bearing witness to another man's ruination.

The man's eyes rolled back in his head, and all Hakeem wanted to do was run, but the dream held him frozen in place. Then he heard the scream of jet engines, and he looked up over the tops of the buildings into the sky just in time to see two Russian planes pass overhead. A bomb fell almost in slow motion and landed not far from where Hakeem was standing. The terrible explosion gave of a blinding white light that seared his eyes and—

Hakeem's dreams ended. He was grateful and terrified at the same time. He was grateful that his drifting off into sleep had gone undiscovered and frightened by the prospect of what might have happened had he been discovered.

He was ashamed of himself. As hard as he tried, he just couldn't live up to the expectations his father had for him. What would it take to make him a man?

He realized he was shivering violently and checked himself over. He was drenched in sweat. He didn't remember the details of his nightmare, but he could still feel a ripple of the fear he'd just experienced moments before.

The rifle! Where was his rifle? In a panic he threw his poncho off and scanned the area for his AK-47. He found it near the cliff's edge where it had almost gone over. How in God's name would he have explained that to his father?

Hakeem checked his military-style watch. His father should have relieved him by now. Maybe Benazar had discovered him sleeping. *No.* No, that couldn't be it. So where was he?

Hakeem had a difficult choice: abandon his post and risk his father's wrath, or stay here and ignore the fact that something might be terribly wrong where he'd left the other two men. In the end Hakeem chose the former. If his father told him he would relieve him in four hours, then he would have relieved him in four hours.

He left his post.

*   *   *

The fire offered comfort as Hakeem drew nearer, and soon he could see the form of his father on the far side of it. He had to walk around the pit to clearly take the man in.

Benazar was sitting cross-legged in one of the meditative postures he often held, eyes closed. *What now?* Hakeem thought. He had been so preoccupied on his journey back with solidifying his argument for returning here that he hadn't thought much about what he'd find when he arrived. And *this* was not what he had expected.

Suddenly, fear born of experience rather than instinct arose, and Hakeem looked down to his right and saw an empty sleeping bag.

A shiver ran through Hakeem, and with his eyes fixed on that spot he heard himself asking, "Where is he?"

Benazar did not open his eyes, but opened his mouth to speak. "Down the south face, into the southeast canyon."

Confusion outweighed Hakeem's trepidation. "Why would he flee?"

Glowing embers were floating up from the fire and illuminating Benazar's face. With eyes closed, his facial expression remained neutral as he said, "Because he knows I'll kill him if I find him."

Hakeem looked off into the darkness. At the moment he was too afraid to delve into the details. He knew something like this was all to commonplace for his father. He was surprised it had been this long before he himself would have to experience something like it. He simply said, "Well, if he ran then he's dead already."

Benazar finally opened his eyes and turned his head in Hakeem's direction. "That's something you're going to make sure of."

"What?" was all Hakeem could say.

Benazar rose and walked over to his son. "Do you have your knife?" he asked.

"Of course," Hakeem said while trying to contain his growing fear.

"And your pistol?"

"Yes."

"Now take this," Benazar said, unslinging a rifle from his shoulder and exchanging it for his son's AK-47. Hakeem reluctantly took it into his arms. It was a sniper rifle, one of the very same buffalo guns Benazar had used to take out Russian targets in his time with the Mujaheddin. "I know how accurate you are with this," Benazar continued. "I want you to follow his trail. I want you to find him and I want you to kill him."

Hakeem's jaw dropped. "But why?"

"If and when a time comes when I feel it's necessary for you to know that, then I'll tell you." His voice dropped and his stare grew fierce. "Now prepare yourself and get going. He already has more than an hour's head start on you."

But Hakeem just stood where he was. Benazar's eyes narrowed and he said, "What are you waiting for?"

Hakeem looked down at the rifle cradled in his arms and grew fearful. He knew what he did next would be just as hard as what Benazar was asking. "No."

"What?" Benazar snarled.

Hakeem started to tremble when his father unsheathed his own knife, the blade shining in the firelight. But he held his ground.

"No, you tell me why. You tell me what he did."

Benazar lifted the knife and ran the tip through the hairs of Hakeem's beard. Hakeem continued to visibly shake, and his breathing had grown rapid, but he stared straight ahead. For several moments Benazar looked over his son's face as if he were studying Hakeem for the first time. What Hakeem would never know was that his father held a secret admiration for the courage his son was showing in making this stand. There was hope for Hakeem yet.

"Very well," Benazar said in a dull whisper that Hakeem could hear. "He left with secrets. Secrets about us. About what we've been doing. He's going to take them to the wrong people, and he's going to share them. He can't be allowed to do this. He simply can't be allowed to live. Now, do you feel enlightened?"

That was a strange question, and Hakeem knew that not everything added up. But if Benazar was telling the truth, then he had a valid argument. It was entirely possible the American could get both him and his father killed. Then everything they'd been doing would have been for nothing. *As if I have any idea what exactly it is we've been doing all this time.*

In the end it came down to another important decision: put faith in what his father was saying and hunt down the American, or refuse and perhaps be killed right here on the spot. And at that moment Hakeem wondered whether his father *could* find it in himself to kill his own son.

"What will you be doing?" Hakeem asked. "Why aren't you coming with me?" He looked around. "How did he even escape in the first place?"

"You're running out of time," was Benazar's answer. "If he reaches a village or even crosses the border, and there's a good chance he will, I cannot emphasize enough the danger we'll be in."

There was nothing more to be said. Hakeem would carry this burden. He had no other choice. He donned his backpack, already prepared for survival, and started down the southern slope of the mountain.

"Don't radio me until the job's done," Benazar called to his son.

*   *   *

The American fell to his knees. His lungs burned. He was covered with bruises and scrapes from trying to navigate his way through the canyon in the dark. He was exhausted, battered, and still panic-stricken.

But Rashid's words kept going through his head: "Run. Run that way. If you follow that canyon it will lead you to a settlement. If you stay here, I'll kill you. If you don't flee fast enough, my son will kill you. There are no tricks here. If you reach civilization, you'll live. Leave right now if you want to increase your chance of survival. Otherwise, you have exactly one minute before I shoot you."

He still couldn't believe the situation he found himself in. He had known before coming here about the dangers he would face, but this ... this was a manhunt, a situation beyond belief.

He didn't necessarily believe what Rashid had told him about letting him live if he somehow reached a village, but if Rashid or his son didn't kill him, a rugged, rock-strewn landscape surely would. He needed to keep moving.

He reached the mouth of the canyon, which opened up into an even larger ravine. Despair almost took over before he realized that he could edge his way around it. He took another moment to catch his breath, and then resumed his jog.

One misplaced step was all it took to bring him down again. This time he fell hard. He banged his head on a rock and cracked the right lens in his glasses. Taking them off and examining the damage, he realized how much visibility he'd just lost, and how hopeless his situation was becoming. He began to sob and slumped against a rock. He couldn't find it in him to get up and start moving again.

*   *   *

Hakeem moved quickly along the edge of the top of the canyon's eastern wall. There was no method to his tracking. He'd been told which way his prey had gone, and he simply followed the established trail. He supposed he had some advantage knowing the layout of the canyon. This would give Hakeem time to catch up with him.

Then Hakeem would have to … he'd have to do his duty. This man he sought was apparently an enemy, just so. And he needed to be dealt with accordingly. So why couldn't Hakeem hold his fear at bay?

Perhaps it was because his father had played judge and jury, and given him the burden of being executioner. And how could he carry out his task without a certainty that justice accompanied it?

These were legitimate concerns, but with additional consideration, he became aware of what frightened him—killing. Taking the life of another human being. He wanted nothing to do with what might be murder, yet this was the situation he found himself in.

At one time he considered himself to be one product of a wounded nation, his father another. But more and more he considered the possibility that he and his uncle's kind had no place left here. This land's conflict would get to you eventually, whether it killed you, changed you, or chased you out. Uncle, father, and son were all victims.

Hakeem reached the end of the canyon. He began to formulate a plan for what he would tell his father if the American escaped. He'd be just as well off killing himself.

The starry night provided faint illumination of the landscape. He looked down to the land below. If the American had accidentally plummeted to his death, Hakeem would technically be relieved of his burden, but he would never be able to provide proof that he'd carried out his task.

He lifted the rifle to his cheek and looked through the night-vision scope. He started to have doubts about whether the American had even made it here. Perhaps he'd doubled back in frustration.

A moment later Hakeem spotted his quarry. He was hunkered up against a boulder, shivering and with his face buried in his arms and knees. Hakeem flattened himself instantly. There was almost no chance of the American's spotting him, but the reflex was second nature. He crawled forward slowly.

There he was, right in Hakeem's line of sight. Hakeem could end this right now. The American would never see or hear death coming. It was almost a mercy killing.

The black crosshairs drifted over the American's balled-up form as Hakeem tried to control the shaking in his hands. He took a deep breath and reminded himself that it wouldn't get any easier than this. This was it.

The shaking slowed and Hakeem managed to calm himself. The crosshairs remained fixed on his unsuspecting target. He could do this. He'd rehearsed it a hundred times before, just as Benazar had said. He was ready to fire. His right index finger rested on the trigger. *Just squeeze the trigger and it will be over. Just squeeze the trigger. Squeeze the trigger!*

He vomited. Bile spilled out of his mouth and splashed off his left forearm onto his poncho and rifle. Nausea remained with him. He rolled over onto his back, forgetting all about the man he had just been ready to kill. He tried to decide which he hated more—himself or this world he'd been born into.

* * *

The American awoke with a start, trying to remember where he was and what he'd been doing. When the reality hit him like a splash of icy water, he took off moving fast, finding a replenished store of energy that came from his will to survive ... and from fear.

It took him just under an hour to make his way through the rocky terrain. It was another hour before he found himself crossing open desert. He had his compass, thank God, and he headed west.

The attack he'd expected had never come. Perhaps this had all been some sick game from the beginning.

Relief washed over him when he finally saw lights. There were thousands of them, giving evidence that he was near the Iranian border.

He was going to make it. Iran was right in front of him. Just a little farther. He quickened his pace.

He'd gone about ten paces when something stood out in his field of vision. It was a black silhouette set against the canopy of Iran's brightly lit streets and buildings. Tall and still, there was no mistaking that it was the shape of a man.

The American just barely had time to register this and feel again his sense of dread before he saw something on the silhouette flash.

Blood geysered from the American's chest as a bullet pierced his sternum and passed through his heart. His entire spectrum of hopes and fears ceased as his brain shut down and he fell forward, dead.

* * *

Benazar walked over to the American to make sure that he was dead. When he was sure that he had killed the man, he picked up his body and hefted it over his shoulder. He started back toward his truck.

CHAPTER 34
APRIL 17, 2002

Derek received the first phone call around 3:45 just after he'd left school. "Hello?" What Derek heard was a strained female voice, one that had been worn thin probably by yelling or prolonged crying. And it was a voice he recognized.

"Derek, it's Connie. Listen, do you have a moment to talk?"

"Of course. What's wrong? You sound upset."

"I just … oh, God."

"It's okay, it's okay. Just take your time."

After a long pause Connie spoke, now sounding collected. "It's about Zack, Derek, about what he's been doing to our family. And this isn't going to be easy for either of us."

* * *

Derek spent the next forty-five minutes deciding what action he should take, and what actions he had the *right* to take. The second phone call came in around 4:30.

"Hello, Derek? Judy Goldcamp here. I'm sorry to call you so late in the day with this, but I wanted to make sure you were out of school for the day."

"No that's fine, Ms. Goldcamp," Derek said, his interest piqued suddenly just from who it was that was calling. "What's going on?"

"Well to be truthful it's really none of my business," she began. At other end of the phone, Derek rolled his eyes. "But I've been talking to some of our neighbors, and it sounds like Zack was involved in some kind of brutal fight. He and that black guy he hangs out with put some poor kid in the hospital. They're saying it's some kind of hate crime."

*　　*　　*

Zack was at a friend's house when his cell phone rang. Caller ID told him it was Derek. "What's up?"

"Where are you right now?" Derek asked.

"Over in Flushing. Why?"

"Good, then you're close by."

"What's goin' on, Derek?"

"You get on the next bus, and you get your ass over here."

"I've gotta lot goin' on."

"Right now, Zack!"

Zack was taken aback by Derek's tone. "Can't you at least tell me what this is about?"

"I'll tell you when you get here. Now get moving!"

*　　*　　*

Derek opened the door and Zack entered the house. Zack got down on one knee to greet Bella, and Derek closed the door and simply stared down at his brother. Zack looked back up at him.

"What is this, Derek? I had a lot to do, but now I'm *here*, and I wanna know why."

"Judy Goldcamp called me and told me that you and Jamar put some kid in the hospital," Derek said. It was straightforward and simple and prompted a stab of fear in Zack.

Zack looked back at Bella. He suddenly couldn't face Derek.

"Yeah, he probably is in the hospital."

Derek waited. When nothing came, he said, "And?"

"And the fucker stole my bike. I caught him red-handed. The two of us have been goin' back and forth for weeks now. It was only a matter of time before somethin' like this happened."

"I heard it was excessive," Derek said. "I heard it was *awful!*"

"Yeah, well, if you heard it third-hand from that mouthy broad, then you probably heard a lotta things."

"Goddamn it, Zack! She told me Mrs. Pezeshk saw it all. Judy's spoken with her and she's horrified. Mrs. Pezeshk thinks you did this as some kind of revenge."

"Well, who cares what Mrs. Pezeshk thinks? You know the truth now."

"I care," Derek shouted. "I won't have you dragging our family's good name through the mud. You're going to go over there and explain the situation to her, and you're going to apologize."

"I can't go back over there."

"Why not?" Derek asked.

"Because the cops are probably lookin' for me."

Derek put his right hand to the bridge of his nose. "Jesus Christ. It's never ending with you."

"Okay, I'll do it," Zack said, reconsidering. There might be a warrant out for his arrest, but he did not want Derek trying to bring Morgan in on this. "All right, I'll go over there and apologize. I'll even do it now." Zack turned to go.

"Wait a minute. We're not done here," Derek said. "Judy Goldcamp wasn't the only one who called today."

Zack froze on his way to the door. *Who else had called?*

"I know about the situation with Morgan, Zack. Connie knows, too, and she told me everything. So I guess your blackmail game is over."

Zack closed his eyes. In a voice barely above a whisper he said, "Motherfucker."

Whereas Derek had previously felt anger at the whole Mo fiasco, now he just seemed bitterly disappointed. "How could you, Zack? To our father's best friend, of all people. Our *family's* best friend.

"Who wants a lawyer with virtues like his? He turned his back on me when I needed him most."

"To help you hold on to a goddamn apartment? Take a look around, Zack. There are millions of apartments, and none of their tenants have their lawyers payin' the rent."

"Look, Derek," Zack said, "I'm sorry Connie had to find out. I am. Believe me. I never wanted her to know." He sighed and paused. "But as far as Morgan's concerned, I don't feel the least bit guilty about it."

Something inside of Derek snapped. He lunged at Zack and grabbed the collar of his jacket. He pushed Zack back against the front hall mirror so hard that Zack's head cracked it. Bella began barking loudly, and pieces of glass shattered on the floor. Derek had his right forearm pressed so firmly against Zack's throat that all Zack could do was try to pry Derek's arms away from him. Zack went red in the face.

"Tough-ass, little street thug, huh?" Derek said with contempt. "So this is the only way you can communicate, eh? Well, when was the last time you could take me, Zack? C'mon, hoodlum, fight back!"

"F-fuck you!" Zack got out through strained breaths.

"Thought you could cash in on all your personal pain and suffering—was that it? Thought you could turn people's pities and sympathies to your advantage?" Derek was relentless. Bella's barking continued. Miranda, who had promised earlier not to intervene, had heard enough. She came barreling down the stairs.

"Stop it! Stop it now!" she yelled. "Derek, let him go!" But Derek would pound some sense into his brother if he had to, and he held Zack's head pressed firmly against the broken mirror, his lower back twisted against the oak table underneath it.

Then, in the midst of the struggle, some flow from that deep well of pain Zack kept buried came to the surface. Derek saw it when Zack's eyes began to tear up. He released his grip on his brother, and Zack slid off the table to the floor.

"Derek, what the hell is wrong with you?" Miranda cried.

Derek ignored her. He looked down at Zack and said, "Do whatever the hell you want. I'm through trying to show how simple it is just to do the right thing. I don't know what Jenny ever saw in you that she put such faith in you. If she could have seen what I see right now, she'd have been disgusted."

Zack was too humiliated to face his brother or his sister-in-law. He picked himself up of the ground and went out the front door.

*   *   *

Zack was apprehensive about returning to the scene of the assault, particularly because he still had deliveries to carry out before the end of the day. But now he wanted to give the apartment a once-over because he would not be returning anytime soon. He could stop by Mrs. Pezeshk's first. Even though his deal with Derek seemed void at this point, he actually *did* feel remorse for her having seen the altercation. He wanted the chance to explain himself, especially since the word on the street was that it had been a hate crime.

He didn't know how circumstances would change now that Connie knew about the blackmail. He supposed he would have to start thinking about a new place to live. He didn't think the apartment would be an option for him anymore. Even if he could have stayed, the place was now tarnished with enough bad memories to rival the good ones.

It was of little concern now. He wanted a chance to clear his conscience, and he could only concentrate on one action at a time. He went upstairs and knocked on Mrs. Pezeshk's door.

He hadn't rehearsed what he was going to say. He had no idea how this was going to play itself out. He had always been under the assumption that Mrs. Pezeshk had gone a little batty in her old age. He doubted he would even be able to have a rational discussion with her. He hoped that maybe Nomar had returned from his trip a little early so that he could act as some kind of go-between, and Zack needed to be in and out of here quickly.

The door came open with the chain still in place, and Zack could see Mrs. Pezeshk's lined face through the crack. She looked frailer than ever, and startled.

"Zack," she said.

"Hi, Mrs. Pezeshk," he began. "Look, I know this is awkward, but I wanted to apologize for what you saw, and maybe get a chance to tell my side of the story."

He took note of how sad she looked in her reluctance to accept, but she said, "All right," and closed the door to unlatch the chain. She opened it again and told him to come in. Zack stepped into the apartment and looked about. Nomar definitely kept this place well maintained. Or maybe she still did. Either way, the extravagant Persian rugs and furniture along with the lush plant life gave the place an exotic yet cozy kind of feel. He stepped past the foyer and crossed the carpet into the television area by the balcony. Mrs. Pezeshk closed the door and turned to face him.

"First off, I just want to say that what happened between me and Mohammed has nothing to do with where he's from," Zack said. "It was about personal differences that he and I have."

"An ambulance came and took him away," was all she said in a scratchy voice of accented English.

"I know that I overreacted," Zack said, bringing up his hands together in a gesture that suggested reconciliation. "I can't defend what I did, and I can't take it back. All I can do is say that I'm truly sorry. For some reason I have trouble findin' peaceful ways to deal with these situations I find myself in."

She sighed and Zack suddenly feared that there might be some kind of story coming. He was right. She said, "My family fled to Pakistan when I was a little girl. This was a long time ago. I'm sure you can imagine. We fled there because of all the violence. My parents wanted a better life for me and my sister. But violence found us in Pakistan, too."

Zack waited for her to continue. He was suddenly interested in what she had to say. "So we came here to the country that everyone comes to in search of a better life, a country that is based on ideals we could not find anywhere else. We came in on a boat, passing by the Statue of Liberty, just like you have seen many times in the movies and on television. And for a time we found what we were looking for."

She paused with a melancholy expression in the way her jaw was set. "But, violence found us here, too. Sometimes it had to do with who we were and where we were from. Other times it did not. That was when I realized that violence had not found us yet again, we had found *it*, again and again. Violence does not stay inside borders or boundaries." She brought her right hand to her heart. "Violence stays inside *here*. And it only comes out when people let it. And the more people there are who let it out, the more awful situations there are for everyone to have to go through."

Zack never suspected that this little old lady could be so articulate or have such insight. "I hear what you're sayin'. We have to try and fight the worst parts of our nature."

"But there is more to it than just that," she continued. "We cannot let the pains and sufferings we have had excuse us from the wrong that we do."

"And when you say we...?"

"People," she said. "Not Americans. Not Middle Easterners. Just people."

Zack wished that he could listen to Mrs. Pezeshk at length. She was an interesting woman with probably a hundred stories to tell. But just then he glanced out the window and saw a police officer getting out of a squad car. He began to cross the street, heading for the entrance to the building.

"Mrs. Pezeshk," Zack said, his mind whirling frantically, "can I use your bathroom?"

"Of course," she said, pointing to the hallway. "Right over there." Zack headed in that direction, trying not to move too quickly. More likely than not the cop expected Zack to be in his apartment and not Mrs. Pezeshk's, but the timing of the cop's arrival was far too convenient. He suspected that Ms. Goldcamp had a hand in this. And if that was the case, then the cop wouldn't even need to be buzzed into the building. She'd be waiting for him to let him in.

Zack closed the bathroom door and locked it. He went for the window over the toilet. He didn't know how he was going to explain *this* to Mrs. Pezeshk, but at the moment he had more pressing worries. He had a lot of drugs on him that didn't even belong to him, and a lot of cash. He could not be taken into custody.

He lifted the window and stuck his head out. He peered over the fire escape and saw an abandoned Chevy Malibu just sitting in the alley, its beige paint job flaking of and rag-top torn up. Seconds were precious. He would jump from the fire escape onto the car's hood and run out of the alley. He'd come back for his bike later.

Just then he heard a knock at the front door. "Mrs. Pezeshk, this is Officer Sanchez of the NYPD. Please open the door." Zack panicked. It was time to go.

He started to climb out of the window when he spotted another cop in the alley. The cop saw him and spoke into the two-way on his shoulder. "I've got him," the officer said. "He's trying to make it out on the fire escape."

Zack backed himself up, back into the bathroom, where he was essentially trapped. Ms. Goldcamp *had* thrown him to the wolves, damn her. He heard the front door being opened by Mrs. Pezeshk. *Think, damn it. Think!*

Under the sink was no good. There was a steel hamper built right into the tiled wall, but it didn't feel secure enough to him. Running out of options, he started to grow panicky. But then when he glanced up at the ceiling he got an idea. It wasn't like the ceiling in his bathroom downstairs. This one had acoustic tiles, like in his school or in office buildings. *Perfect.*

Taking of his backpack he jumped up onto the sink's counter, pushed the tile up, and slid it over. He tossed the backpack up into the darkness and replaced the tile. Then he jumped back down.

It was time to own his actions. It had been stupid to come here. He should've known better. Now he was going to pay for his stupidity. He opened the door and stepped out into the hallway.

"Zack McCrady?" the heavyset officer asked.

"That's me."

"I'm going to need you to come with me. You're under arrest. Stand over here and put your hands against the wall."

Zack sighed. "Why not?" He did as he was told, and the cop came up behind him.

"Spread your feet," the cop said. "Now, you don't have any sharp objects like needles in your pockets that I might prick my hands on, do you?"

"No," Zack said. He glanced over his shoulder at Mrs. Pezeshk. She looked torn.

"Eyes to the wall," the cop said, putting his right hand on Zack's head and turning it.

"Hey, take it easy," Zack said. "I'm tryin' to cooperate."

"Officer, please," Mrs. Pezeshk said.

"It'll be all right, ma'am," the cop said. "This'll be over in just a minute." He reached for Zack's wrist. "Okay, now I'm going to take your right hand and bring it behind you so I can cuff you. Just keep the rest of your body still." But Zack risked another glance at Mrs. Pezeshk. She looked more than just upset. She looked ill. "What did I just tell you?" the cop said, raising his voice.

"Hey, somethin's wrong," Zack said, his eyes fixed on Mrs. Pezeshk. Her hand was on her chest, and she slumped down on one of her couches. The cop turned to see what Zack saw.

"Oh, no." The cop went for his two-way. "Mercer, we're going to need an ambulance over here. We've got a possible cardiac arrest in the apartment. I'm going to need you up here now."

While all this was going on, Zack's eyes were on the small, round dining table where the cop had put his wallet, keys, and phone. Mrs. Pezeshk's keys were there too, right next to his stuff. Zack took a big risk in what he did next.

"Maybe I can help," Zack said, going to the table. "I can call a doctor who lives close by." It was a complete bluff, but he managed to get close to what he wanted.

"No. You stay right where you are," the cop ordered. He went over to assist Mrs. Pezeshk. The front door was ajar, but Zack didn't dare make a break for it. Besides, the cop from the alley was most likely on his way up right now, and even if he wasn't, they already knew who Zack was. They'd get him eventually.

Zack used the distraction to take Mrs. Pezeshk's apartment key from her key ring. He quickly clipped it to his. This was no easy task, but Officer Sanchez had his hands full at the moment. Zack finished the switch, and, ignoring what the man had told him, he went over to assist in whatever way he could.

The other cop arrived, an ambulance came, and Mrs. Pezeshk was sent to the hospital. Zack was taken to jail.

*   *   *

"Yeah?"

"Jamar, it's me. I'm in jail. You gotta come over here and get me out."

"What? Where did they get you?"

"At the old place. I made a stop and they snagged me."

"Why the hell did you go back there? That was stupid."

"Look, we'll worry about that later. Just come down here and get me. My bail's ten thousand dollars, but I already called a bondsman. I just need you to bring a grand."

"Ten thousand? Did you get popped on your route?"

"No, but I got my stuff stashed and I need to get it back. I need you to get me out of here right away so that I never have to explain this to the boss."

"Can't you just call Morgan?"

"Is that supposed to be funny? What the hell is wrong with you?"

"All right. Just sit tight."

"I'm not goin' anywhere."

"Which precinct you at?"

CHAPTER 35
JUNE 16, 1998

Hakeem returned to camp just before dawn. Hours before at his sniper position, he had spent a long time just lying on his back in self-reproach. Afterwards, he turned his gaze back down the rocky slope to where the American had been resting, only to find that he was gone. Then came another period of waiting in fear, but this one was a little different.

There was no way for Benazar to know of the opportunity Hakeem had had and passed up. But the end result was the same for Hakeem: he'd failed, and now he had to go to his father and report his failure.

The sky was showing just a faint sliver of pink when Hakeem finished his climb, which was especially difficult because he had not gone down the same face as the switchback. He was drenched in cold sweat and removed his poncho first, then his herringbone vest. That was when he noticed the body.

He was too startled to yell. He stepped back and closed his eyes as if he could ward of the vision, but when he opened his eyes not only was the body still there, but so was his father. Benazar was sitting just a few feet away.

Hakeem was speechless. All his mind could process was how sickening it was to see this man, whom only hours ago had been walking and talking, now dead at the hands of his father. The

American's body was flat on its back, with its hands bound over its head against a log.

Hakeem would take what was coming to him like a man. Perhaps not the man his father wanted him to be, but a man who would accept his fate. Benazar was looking right at him. The sky was growing brighter, and as Hakeem looked at his father, it was harder than ever to read that stony expression. Benazar had a blanket wrapped tightly around him so that only his face showed.

"You failed," Benazar said matter-of-factly, with just a touch of what Hakeem might have called regret.

Hakeem found it in him to reply. "Did you think that I would succeed?"

"You had a lot working against you," Benazar conceded. "But I always held out hope."

"Working against me in here," Hakeem said, touching his hand to his chest, "or out there?" He used the same hand to wave the view around him.

"Inside," Benazar said.

Hakeem felt short of breath. "This was all a test, wasn't it?" he asked. "For me, that is?"

"Yes," Benazar said.

Hakeem felt that nauseous feeling in the pit of his stomach again. "Did he need to die?" he asked, desperately needing to better understand what was happening.

"Yes," was all that Benazar said.

"And this test, what was it all about?"

"To spare you from what has to happen now." Benazar stood up and removed the blanket. "Come here."

Hakeem didn't move. His mouth opened ever so slightly, but that was the only motion other than his heavy breathing. "I'm not going to harm you," Benazar said. "You're still my son. The life I've been living may have ruined the better part of me, but I would *never* hurt a member of my own family."

Hakeem found the strength to step forward. Benazar may have been hard to read, but Hakeem had learned he was a man of his word. He went over to his father's side to look down at the body. There was a gaping dark red hole at the center of his chest, but not a great deal of blood. Hakeem reminded himself that this was a sight few people here in Afghanistan didn't have to see. Taking this in might even make him stronger.

Hakeem's aching desire to trust his father evaporated instantly when he saw three objects lying to the right of the dead body. There was a hacksaw, an axe, and a machete. Hakeem's breathing grew rapid once again. He was certain about what was to come next.

"I need you to cut off both of his hands, and then his head." Hakeem stared straight at the tools. "Hakeem, I know this is hard for you. But you must do as I say."

Hakeem stared, enduring further silence.

"Hakeem, if you don't—"

"Why?"

"Hakeem, I told you once before—"

"No! You tell me why! I deserve to know *why.*"

Finally, Benazar said, "Hakeem, you're a good son and a good man. You're right. You *do* deserve to know what this about. And I promise you that I will explain everything in due time. But for right now all you need to know is this: for every duty I put before you that you fail to fulfill, there'll be an even greater repercussion as a result. Believe me when I say that it'll have nothing to do with me. I'm trying to save you from the forces gathering here."

"You're not making any sense," Hakeem said.

"That doesn't change the fact that you need to trust me. And it will make sense, I promise you."

Once more, Hakeem stared at the tools. He didn't move.

"Hakeem, please, you have to prove to me that you can do this. He's already dead. Just do as I say."

Hakeem picked up the machete. He moved as fast as he could so that he wouldn't have to think too long about it. He held the blade over his head and brought it down on the dead man's wrists with all his strength. His senses exploded. The sight was overwhelming. The sound was sickening.

The body's left hand had come off completely, but the right one still dangled by some loose flesh. Another swipe of the blade took the hand off.

Hakeem kept going. He brought the machete down on the dead man's neck, but the spinal column proved too tough. Hakeem didn't move to the axe however. He just kept hacking away.

He grabbed the head by the hair and gave a hard yank, but it remained attached. Hakeem threw down the machete and picked up the hacksaw. He lined up the jagged edge of the blade and drove it back and forth, back and forth, until the head came free. The left hand that held it by the hair kept pulling, and when there was nothing left to hold it in place, the force of the pull as the two objects separated made Hakeem lose his footing. He fell on his back, covered in blood, staring up at the sky. He suddenly remembered the nightmare he'd had earlier.

Benazar knelt down next to Hakeem. He got both of his hands under his son's arms and helped to lift him up. He only managed to get Hakeem into a sitting position. Hakeem kept staring straight ahead, saying nothing. The corpse's bloody hands were right in his line of sight. He had no idea where the head had gotten to.

Benazar went over and picked up the dismembered hands. He walked them to a large cooler and opened the lid. The cooler was filled with ice, and Benazar put the hands in a plastic bag before burying that bag in the ice, his own hands turning the water in the cooler a deep pink. Then he took an even larger turkey bag from inside the cooler and went to retrieve the head. All the while Hakeem kept staring at the mutilated torso.

"I know how difficult that was for you," Benazar said over Hakeem's shoulder, placing the bloody head in the turkey bag and returning to the cooler. "I once saw it done to a living man."

Hakeem didn't care what his father had seen or done in his day. He didn't care at all.

CHAPTER 36
JUNE 17, 1998

Hakeem rested his forehead against the cold glass of the truck's window. His father was driving, and the two had ridden together in silence for an hour. Hakeem just stared out at the dusty landscape. His mind reeled.

He'd changed in the last twenty-four hours. No longer was he the man he'd once been, and he certainly wasn't the man he'd hoped to be. He was his sick father's puppet. His life wasn't his. He wondered why it had taken him so long to realize this.

"It won't be much longer now," Benazar said at last.

"Where are we going?"

"To Pakistan."

"It's hundreds of miles from here," Hakeem said hoarsely. In the past he might have been excited to finally see what lay beyond Afghanistan's borders. Now he couldn't bring himself to think about what waited for him there. Instead his thoughts returned to the dead man's remains in the back of the truck.

"We're headed for an airfield," Benazar said.

Hakeem didn't know why he'd even asked where they were going. He didn't care. There was little he *did* care about at this point.

Benazar sensed his son's psychological turmoil. In a low voice, he said, "Hakeem, I want to tell you something I've never told another person. It's something I've always known I would tell someday, I just didn't know to whom until now."

Hakeem said nothing. All his father was to him now was a stranger who'd been broken by a war many years ago.

"After my release," Benazar continued, "when I was struggling simply to survive, I used the dead body of one of my comrades to lure in some vultures so that I wouldn't starve to death. That was when I had an epiphany like the ones your grandfather was often said to have had."

Hakeem closed his eyes.

"I had never put much faith in those stories back then, but this vision hit me with such clarity that I suddenly let my doubts leave me." Benazar paused to choose his words carefully, and part of Hakeem was becoming interested in what he had to say. "When that body was invaded by the vultures, I realized that that's what we as a nation have become—a carcass whose bones are being picked clean.

"Our day is done. Our people fight one another and kill each other. They live in a constant state of fear. Our land was the object for conquest long before you and I were ever born, but this time it is different. We've been defeated. Nothing we can do now will ever restore what's been lost, what's been taken from us.

"But there is a way to make it right. There's a way we can tell our story to the world. There's a way to make those who've exploited us see the price they'll have to pay for having used us with such malice."

"You mean the United States," Hakeem said, still looking out the window.

"I value the education you've received under your uncle's tutelage. You know what a cold war is."

Hakeem only nodded.

"Well, there are many ways to achieve one's own ends in a cold war, with objectives greater than racing to see who can be the first one to reach outer space.

"You and your uncle spent many afternoons playing chess, yes?"

Hakeem nodded.

"We were used, Hakeem, used like pawns on a chessboard. The Americans were all too happy to see us bleed until we finally drove the *Roussis* out. Then they returned to the 'free world,' leaving us with damage control."

Hakeem turned and looked at his father.

"Look at us now, Hakeem. Look what we've become. Our homes and our villages have become havens for the most fanatical interpreters of Islam. The whole country is a military zone now. There's nothing left to be done here."

Hakeem groaned. Was that true? He just didn't know anymore. "What does any of it have to do with me? What would you have me do?"

Benazar didn't have the intention of dodging his son's questions, but he needed to state his answer in such a way that Hakeem could perhaps see through his eyes.

"Do you remember when I said that I regretted that your uncle sheltered you from all the horrific acts that have transpired here?"

Hakeem nodded.

"Well, I'm guilty of the same," Benazar said. "I took you in because you're my son and I wanted to protect you. But there *is* no protecting you, Hakeem. Never."

Hakeem stared at his father.

"I don't fault you for not being able to find it in you to kill that man. Taking the life of another is not desirable, but in this case it was necessary. If you had been able to kill him, then perhaps my instruction would have been enough. But now I realize my guidance alone won't help you with what you need to do."

"What *do* I need to do?" Hakeem asked, trying to keep the pleading out of his voice.

"Rise above all of this," Benazar said. "You were meant for a more meaningful life than cutting men's throats. But you'll never survive if you don't learn how to do what needs to be done."

Hakeem pondered his father's words.

"Another time, another place and you might have found a life that suited you. But not here, Hakeem. Not now.

"We didn't know one another until you were in your teens, but I swell with pride when I remind myself that you're *my* son. You're intelligent and gifted, and passive in a way that humbles me when I consider the environment you've been raised in. But—"

Hakeem had known there'd be a *but.*

"Unfortunately, your options are limited. Look at your uncle. One of the most distinguished intellects from Herat, living like a fugitive. I won't have you go through that, Hakeem."

"What are you planning for me?" Hakeem asked, far too many thoughts racing through his head to pinpoint what he was feeling at this moment.

"Those you encounter on your journey, many of them will have power over you," Benazar said, this time deliberately dodging. "But you must never let yourself forget the power *you* have within you. And you must never let them see it, either. Your strength will come from your ability to conceal it, to blend in with those who think themselves your better."

Hakeem stared at his father, the look in his eyes practically begging Benazar to tell him something, *anything*, that would let him believe that Hakeem wasn't a doomed man.

But apparently Benazar had thought he'd given Hakeem sufficient cause for trust. He said nothing more. Hakeem could only take so much at once; the more he learned, the worse his torment.

Minutes passed. "You may hate me for what I'm putting you through," Benazar said. "You may hate the men who are tearing this country apart. You may hate the Russians, the Americans, or anyone else who is causing you this pain. But never allow yourself self-hatred, Hakeem. You can always count on yourself. Be who you are. Your means to achieving your ends may be changing, but that doesn't mean you have to change who you are."

Hakeem tried to imagine all the different possibilities that might have been if he'd remained with his uncle when he was fifteen, or if he'd just gone off on his own. He wondered if his situation would have been better or worse than the one in which he now found himself.

His father was a far cry from the run-of-the-mill, transient warriors for Islam who seemed to be flooding the madrassas and camps. This was *his* land, and most of them were just opportunists, men here to relieve themselves of their own burdens. They had old scores to settle, ones that had nothing to do with Benazar.

And yet it still made them allies, didn't it? How did that old cliché go? *The enemy of my enemy is my friend.*

"So what this all comes down to, really, is revenge?" Hakeem said, looking out his passenger-side window, his head resting on the glass.

Benazar was a man who was solid in his convictions. It surprised Hakeem when it took him a moment to answer. "Restoration of the balance," he said finally. "Everyone knows what needs to be done, and there's only one way to do it."

Hakeem still had no single detail of what the future would hold, but he could guess what the end would be. It wasn't as though he'd been deaf to all the talking among those who dealt with Benazar. "The repercussions," Hakeem said, "I can't even begin to think…"

"That's what I've been trying to make you understand," Benazar said. "Events have already been set into motion. What has to happen *will* happen, with or without us. We choose to act, trusting our instincts and following our consciences."

"You think my conscience is clear?" Hakeem asked.

"If it isn't now, then it soon will be."

CHAPTER 37
April 18, 2002

Zack was out of jail and he needed to move fast. He'd be able to explain to Marco why his deliveries hadn't gone through, but he'd never be able to explain that he'd lost Marco's product. He needed his backpack right away.

He felt guilty that Mrs. Pezeshk's hospitalization made it easier for him to sneak in and out of the apartment. He ought to have checked up on her first to see how she was doing. But priority one was squaring up with Marco, who was still in the dark about all of this.

Jamar had gotten him out, and had even gone back to Marco's shop to try to smooth everything over. Zack ran the whole eleven blocks back to where he'd gotten arrested. It was almost midnight, so he hoped it would be nice and quiet.

He stopped by his old apartment to pick up a Mini-Mag flashlight. Then he crept up the stairs to Mrs. Pezeshk's and got his keys out of his pocket. He did everything stealthily so that he'd go undetected by that rat-bitch, Ms. Goldcamp. He opened the door, stepped inside, and closed it behind him.

No police notices. No lights. Nothing to suggest what had happened here yesterday. Zack looked over at the couch that Mrs. Pezeshk had fallen into. He hoped she was all right. He left the lights off and headed into the bathroom.

He got the flashlight out of his jacket pocket and turned it on. Once again he climbed back onto the sink's counter and stood up to push back the plasterboard ceiling tile. He scanned the immediate area and didn't see his backpack. He tried to remember throwing it. He *had* heaved it pretty hard.

Could it have gone over some obstruction? At the moment, that's how it looked. *Shit!* He put the flashlight away and jumped up to grab the edge of the bathroom wall. He kicked lightly off of the medicine cabinet, thankful that it didn't collapse under the weight, and managed to prop himself up on his elbows. He got his right foot up onto a concrete slab, and was now lying on his stomach in complete darkness.

He took the flashlight back out and twisted it on. There it was, sitting a few feet to his right on a tile over another room. He reached over for it, but he was too hasty. He tried to regain his balance, but he overcompensated, losing his hold on the concrete. His left arm kept him from falling, but he'd almost gone over, and his right arm went through the tile closest to him down to his elbow. The tile broke and disappeared. So did the Maglite, which had been in his mouth.

Shit! He looked down and saw where the flashlight lay, still lit. He made a second grab for the backpack, this time more carefully, and pulled it to him. He looked at the opening he had made in the ceiling. He couldn't just leave it as it was. Sighing, he returned the bathroom tile to where it belonged, lowered the backpack into the bedroom on the other side of the wall, then dropped down next to it. He landed softly on carpet and looked for the light switch.

The lights came on and Zack squinted slightly. *This must be Nomar's room.* The first order of business was fixing the tile. He picked up two broken pieces which fit like a puzzle. This wouldn't be too hard. He stood up on Nomar's bed and tried to put them back the way they'd been when they were still joined. It actually worked. He'd be able to cover his tracks after all.

He brushed off whatever white dust had showered down onto Nomar's bed. He picked up his backpack and put his arms through the straps. It was time to go.

He began to open Nomar's door, which had been locked, and then stopped. He took in the room. Nothing was out in the open. There were no objects lying around, nothing he could hold in his hand, just a bed, a bureau, cabinets, a closet, a desk, and a safe. About the only tangible items Zack could have picked up were the bed's pillows and down comforter.

Zack moved toward the foot of the bed. He tried the closet. Locked. So were the bureau drawers, the cabinets, and, of course, the safe. But the top drawer in the desk did slide open. Inexplicably, it had been unlocked.

His interest was piqued. There was a beige lock-box inside. *You are a stubborn bastard, Nomar, aren't you?* He took the box out and placed it on the desk. He noticed another object in the drawer and picked it up.

It was a stainless-steel handle, and at the top was a button. He suspected he knew what this was, and part of him grew excited. Holding the handle to one side he pressed the button. A spring uncoiled and a shiny metal blade came flipping out. It snapped into place with a click and Zack smiled. He'd been right. It was a military grade switchblade. *Oh, yes.*

He took a few seconds to get acquainted with the weapon and figured out how to retract the blade. This was definitely going with him. He put it in his left jacket pocket, and turned his eyes back to the lock-box.

His grin faded into a frown. What was happening here? The obvious effort for secrecy in Nomar's room made Zack uneasy. He didn't want to give in to rising suspicion. The thoughts he was suddenly having were too big for his head. Everywhere he looked there was a lock. There had to be some explanation.

Then a realization hit him. He knew this brand of lock-box. He had one himself. You could buy them at Wal-Mart for about thirty dollars. All they were good for was protecting valuables from fire; that was about it. He wondered if Nomar knew what he knew—that these lock-boxes all came with universal keys. A key like the one he had on his key-ring right now would open any such box.

He took his keys out and fumbled for the smallest one. He used his hand to brush the hair away from his eyes. He wanted no distractions. He opened the box and looked inside.

There was a pile of folders and papers. He took them all out and placed them on the desk. He took one stack of glossy papers and thumbed through them. They were black-and-white photographs of various people: men, white men, white men in suits, white men in suits coming out of buildings, white men in suits getting into limousines, white men in suits speaking into microphones on podiums, white men in suits with bodyguards, white men in suits who were apparently unaware they were being photographed.

Zack braced himself on the desk and tried to control his breathing. It could mean anything, couldn't it? He pushed away the photographs. What he found next was even more disturbing.

Under the photos were large papers folded into quarters. They were schematics. Zack was stunned. In his hand was a blueprint for the Holland Tunnel. There was another for the Lincoln tunnel. He unfolded one paper after another, growing a little more frantic with each one: the Brooklyn Bridge, the Williamsburg, the Queensboro, the George Washington, the Manhattan, the Triborough, even the Tappan Zee. Zack groaned and massaged his forehead. His mind was so overwhelmed he couldn't even begin to sort through all his thoughts.

"Zack."

Zack whirled and let out a yelp. Nomar was standing in the doorway. Zack couldn't see his eyes through the glare from his glasses in the light, but Nomar appeared to be studying him carefully.

"Nomar. Shit, you scared me," Zack said, breathing heavily.

"What are you doing here, Zack?"

"Y-your aunt, she ... somethin' happened. She had to go to the hospital."

Nomar made no sign of being alarmed. "Yes, I know. That's why I'm back. I'd gotten word that something happened." He seemed more concerned with what Zack was doing here than the well-being of his aunt. "Zack, you don't look so good. Why don't you come out here and we'll talk about what happened."

Nomar was all that was standing between Zack and his escape. The exchange between the two was now like a game of poker, and Zack didn't want to show his hand. What did Nomar plan to do? Did he know how much Zack now knew? Was all this what it looked like?

Zack was sweating. He moved toward the door. He offered no reason or excuse for his presence here in Nomar's locked room, with Nomar's personal belongings out on his desk. He just walked right at Nomar and then past him on Nomar's left. Nomar turned and fell in step with Zack, putting his right hand on Zack's left shoulder. "Let's go sit down," he said.

Zack tried not to panic, and while his mind was busy trying to figure out what his next move would be, Nomar lifted his forearm and smashed his elbow into Zack's left temple, dropping him instantly.

CHAPTER 38
AUGUST 12, 1998

The truck sped along the dirt road under the cover of darkness. Hakeem looked over at Benazar, who was driving the vehicle wearing night-vision goggles, the headlights turned off. The two rode in silence.

Benazar's appearance was fearsome as usual—he was clad head to toe in black. Hakeem's appearance was fearsome as well. His entire head was wrapped in bandages, and to anyone who could have seen him he might appear to be a ghostly apparition. But they weren't going to happen upon someone on this road. Not tonight.

The bandages had come off briefly the day before. Hakeem had thought that the sweat-soaked gauze had been the initial cause of the intense itching, but he had learned soon after removing them that it was the tender condition of his skin that was the cause of the irritation.

Hakeem had made the mistake of letting Benazar catch him attempting to scratch his face. *That* had been unpleasant. He would not make the same mistake twice. There was a difference between doctor's orders and Benazar's orders. New bandages were now wrapped firmly back in place.

Hakeem looked down at his hands, which were bandaged and gloved.

"I know how much discomfort you're in," Benazar said. "Try and offer it to God."

Hakeem doubted Benazar believed in God. In truth, he didn't care much about his physical discomfort at this point. The apprehension he felt was far too distracting.

Hakeem was about to step through another doorway. He'd done it once before in his teens, and he'd been scared then too, but this time he was more realistic in his expectations. This also meant that the stakes were even higher now, and there was little reason to expect a reprieve.

Now that Hakeem understood what his father and uncle had been planning, certain actions made sense, and yet others made none. Hakeem felt more betrayed by his uncle than when he'd been left in Benazar's custody all those years ago. He'd come to expect radical behavior from his father, but not from the man who'd raised him. The Mussar he'd once known had left many years before. All that remained was the cowardly man he'd now been turned into.

Maybe America did have it coming after all. How might it have been different if it had seen a recovery effort through to the end and not turned its back on an exhausted nation that needed time to heal and rebuild? His father might have found a place at Mussar's side instead of the other way around. There might not have been assassinations, public executions, or breeding grounds for martyrs. There might not be starvation. Islam might have been lived in the tradition he remembered, not what it had been warped into. Businesses might have thrived. Women might have been happy.

But not now. Not ever.

The truck, which had been on a steep incline for some time, came to a halt.

"We're here," Benazar said. Hakeem looked out the window but couldn't see much except for the outline of hills. The starry night painted the landscape in silver, but visibility was low. Benazar opened his door and got out. The frigid air crept into the truck.

Hakeem was reluctant to get out. He sat where he was, nervously contemplating his situation, but in a moment of clarity, he decided that his fear was not going to leave him. Fear was an animal survival instinct, as natural as breathing. His intuition told him that more frightening days lay ahead. Whatever it was he had coming to him, he would take it standing on his feet, and if he died … well, everyone dies eventually. At least he could die with peace of mind, knowing that he had met his end without surrendering to his fears. He could die a man.

And then there was another possibility. He could endure this, wherever it led him, and perhaps influence it, guide it. Maybe even lead it one day, give it some sense of legitimacy. He might be able to live a life that had real meaning in a savage world. It was time to accept his place in the grand scheme.

He glanced in the rearview mirror, and saw his father unloading crates from the back of the truck. Hakeem admired the man at the same time that he pitied him. Benazar Rashid was the product of a terrible conflict, and a frightening example to the world of what such trauma can do to a man. But above all else, the man was a survivor. And that's what Hakeem needed to do—survive what was to come. And he would. He'd learned from the best.

He opened his door and stood outside. They were at an altitude high enough that Hakeem could see his breath forming in front of him. Benazar put the crates on the ground and turned his attention back to Hakeem.

"Come with me," Benazar said, walking up the path past Hakeem.

"What about those?" Hakeem asked, nodding toward the crates.

"Leave them," Benazar said over his shoulder.

Hakeem quickened his pace to fall in step with him. They had only gone a few hundred meters when someone shouted. Two men appeared from opposite sides of Benazar and Hakeem's position, effectively flanking them with rifles raised. Hakeem was startled but Benazar simply identified himself. The two men moved in, lowering their rifles.

The newcomer who approached from their left wore a ski mask, as did another man who followed him, with a chained mongrel of some kind. The dog was large and growling. It hadn't barked, but saliva glistened on its bared teeth. Hakeem looked at the animal. It wanted to hurt Hakeem. It had been trained to hurt, trained to please its master.

The man who came in from the right said something in Arabic. Benazar responded in Dari. "This is my son, Hakeem," he said.

The man who'd spoken moved into view. His entire head was wrapped in a single dark sash, which covered his face. He removed a photograph from his jacket and looked at it. "Let me see," was all the man said, moving past introductions.

"Hakeem," Benazar said. Hakeem reached up to his right shoulder and grabbed the end of the bandage where it was tied. He began to unravel it. It took him a few moments to remove it completely.

The man holding the photograph now held it up so that it and Hakeem were in his field of vision. He looked at the photograph, then at Hakeem, and then back again. "Very impressive," he said.

Hakeem had seen his face only a day before in a mirror. There was no disputing that his looks had been drastically altered. He looked like a completely different man. But Hakeem hadn't thought at the time that he'd looked like the American, despite the gruesome model that his surgeon had used. Now, with all the swelling and scarring, he thought he must look repulsive. When he heard the satisfaction in the man's voice, however, he supposed that maybe one day it was possible to grow into that look.

"And the prints?" the man with the picture said.

"The skin was successfully grafted to his fingers," Benazar said. "I paid for the best."

The man with the picture nodded as if convinced. He said something in Arabic to his companions, and the two men and the dog walked down toward the truck to retrieve the crates Benazar had brought. The man with the picture said, "I'll give you two a moment alone." He turned and headed up the path. Hakeem looked past him and thought he could see some kind of steel door cradled in the shadows of converging rocks.

He turned to face his father, with tears forming in the corners of his eyes, but he wasn't crying because he was parting ways with his father. The wind picked up and blew the tears across his cheeks. The bandages that he held in his right hand at his side fluttered as well. Fate had led him to a strange place.

"You're going to need to cover your face back up," Benazar said.

Hakeem's voice held no hint of his apprehension. "I won't be seeing you again, will I?" he asked.

"No," Benazar said. "This place will be your home for many months."

Hakeem didn't flinch. He remained strong.

"How many?"

"That's entirely up to you," Benazar said.

In the past Hakeem might have turned away to avoid eye contact with Benazar. Now their eyes remained locked. "What will *you* do?" Hakeem asked.

"That's irrelevant. What's important is that you know that my hopes and prayers go with *you*."

Hakeem took one last look at the man who'd given him life, then altered the course of it. Did he find fault with the man? *Yes*. But did the man also deserve his respect? *Yes*. "I won't fail you this time, Father," Hakeem said. He turned and headed up the path.

*   *   *

The two guards who'd accepted Benazar's gifts headed back up the path and passed Benazar and his son as they spoke. Hakeem turned and followed the men uphill. Benazar watched his son walk out of his life forever. He felt empty.

He hadn't let Hakeem see his pain. He couldn't let him. If Hakeem had seen that suffering, even for a second, then he would forever live in doubt. And Hakeem needed to know, as Benazar did, that sacrifice was his ultimate goal. A man needs to find the strength within himself to do what needs to be done, whatever the cost. And if Hakeem walked out of his life thinking that his father didn't love him, well that was another sacrifice Benazar would have to make.

"I won't fail you this time," Hakeem had said. Benazar kept his eyes focused on the door as it closed behind the men. *Yes, son. I know you won't.*

CHAPTER 39
APRIL 19, 2002

Hakeem looked down at the unconscious form at his feet. What in God's name was this boy doing here? Hakeem had been contacted only recently with word of Rabia Pezeshk's hospitalization, and he knew that Zack had been present when the ambulance had come. Hakeem had raced back as fast as he could, but the boy *should not* have been here.

Hakeem had been apprehensive enough as it was upon learning the news. The police had been in his apartment. Fortunately, they hadn't felt any inclination to snoop around. But here was the boy, who'd found a way past Hakeem's locked door and even into his personal effects.

Hakeem didn't panic. He'd been trained to deal with split-second decisions in a crisis such as this, but he kept wondering if the boy had told anyone about his findings. If he had, which Hakeem doubted, then this whole charade was already over. He wondered if anyone even knew Zack had come here in the first place.

He considered his options. *Think!* No, the boy was a street thug; trouble. He had come here to burglarize, probably because he'd found a way to enter the day before, when he'd been arrested. Then he'd discovered the truth instead. Well, that problem was easily fixed. He'd kill the boy and dispose of the body. Then he'd cover his tracks.

He went back into his room and unlocked one of the cabinets. From there he retrieved a Beretta nine-millimeter and switched the safety off. He then took a silencer out of the cabinet and screwed it into place. Removing a long strand of steel wire from the same place, he went back out into the hallway.

The boy was starting to stir. He was mumbling some nonsense, and Hakeem could hear the pain in his voice. Zack managed to get himself up into a sitting position, holding his head in his hands. Hakeem lowered the pistol and jabbed it against the back of the boy's head. His finger rested on the trigger.

*   *   *

Zack didn't know where he was. He didn't know much of anything at the moment. All his brain could do for him was tell him how much pain he was in; that message hit home with agonizing clarity. He couldn't see past the tears in his eyes, and his ears rang deafeningly. He grabbed his head in his hands. The pain! If only it would stop. Then it all came back to him in an instant.

Nomar. The pictures. The maps. Zack's attempt to act nonchalant and make his escape. And then…?

He felt something blunt and hard at the base of his skull and his eyes went to the hall mirror right in front of him, where he saw Nomar with a gun pressed right against his head.

Panic. That survival instinct that every animal possesses kicked in with a wave of terror as Zack realized he was about to be executed.

"No!" was all he could blurt out. He was too petrified even to move. The fear for his life was too much. He just kept staring ahead at Nomar's image in the mirror.

Nomar didn't shoot. Zack looked into his eyes through the mirror. There was something there, some hesitation. Nomar looked haunted. It was as if he was there, right now, ready to do the deed, but some part of him had detached from reality completely, and all that was left was a shell awaiting its return.

Zack remained frozen with fear. He was at Nomar's mercy, and too afraid to make a move to save his own life.

Nomar's eyes moved back into focus. He was back and he remembered what he had to do.

*   *   *

Hakeem had had a momentary lapse. He didn't know where his mind had wandered to, but he knew where he was now.

The gun was overkill. There would be blood everywhere, and more trails of blood would follow him once he moved the body. It was messy and unnecessary. He took the muzzle away from the boy's head and placed the gun on the hall table next to him. Zack exhaled a deep breath and Hakeem imagined the relief that was washing over him right now. But Zack had the wrong idea.

Hakeem took the wire and held it in a tight grip in both hands. Zack was no longer focused on him. He was still struggling to maintain consciousness. Hakeem wouldn't have to look the boy in the eye. All he would see would be a sandy mane of curls as Zack died.

Hakeem crouched down and deftly wrapped the cord around Zack's throat. Zack let out a gurgling sound of surprise as Hakeem strangled him. The boy's hands came up and his face turned red as Hakeem pressed his right knee against his back and yanked with all his strength.

*   *   *

There had been a surge of relief when Nomar had put the gun down on the hall table. But that ended in an instant when some kind of wire wrapped around Zack's throat. Zack's hand came up instinctively to his neck, and he actually managed to get his right index finger inside the wire. He tried in his frenzy to pull some slack from it, but the lack of oxygen to his brain was starting to take its toll, and for the second time Zack was in danger of blacking out. Only this time he wouldn't be waking up.

236

Fear and instinct urged his left hand toward his jacket pocket. He found what he was looking for.

The switchblade came out and Zack hit the release. The weapon's spring clicked the knife into place, and when Zack felt it lock he took a desperate jab at his attacker. He felt the blade make brief contact with flesh and heard Nomar let out a startled cry. That was all the distraction he needed.

Placing his foot against the bathroom doorjamb, he used it to push away from the wall and send his body backward. Zack heard the crunch of cartilage as his skull smashed against Nomar's nose, and the hands that had been choking the life out of him let go. Free now, he rolled over on his stomach, panting heavily.

Nomar had been knocked flat on his back and when he lifted his head up Zack could see blood gushing from his nose. His glasses had flown right off of his head. There was also blood trickling from his forehead where Zack had jabbed him with the knife. He suspected that he'd broken Nomar's nose and knew that he'd bought himself a few precious seconds. He tried to get up, but he was exhausted. Nomar was stunned but managed to get to his feet, and Zack could see how enraged he now was. He went for the gun on the table next to Zack.

Nomar got his hand around the pistol. Zack knew there would be no second chances this time. Struggling to a crouch with all his remaining strength he lunged at Nomar.

Zack had switched his grip on the switchblade. He now held it facing downwards, and he used it to stab Nomar. The knife pierced the muscle of Nomar's left thigh, and Zack pushed it in hard enough so that the blade plunged all the way to its hilt.

Nomar gasped with shock. He dropped the gun, and his right foot kicked out, knocking over the table and sending it crashing down between them. He looked down in disbelief at the knife in his leg and let out a shriek. He staggered back a few feet and passed through the doorway to his room, falling backward out of sight. Zack heard his body crash to the floor. The bedroom door bounced back and settled slightly ajar.

Zack didn't waste a second. He grabbed the gun in his right hand and crawled to his left into the bathroom. He closed the door and locked it, then crawled over to the toilet. He pressed his back against the wall so that he was nestled in between the toilet and the cabinet underneath the sink. He pointed the gun at the door but couldn't hold it steady. His hand was shaking too violently.

He waited.

*   *   *

The pain was almost more than Hakeem could bear. He was afraid he would go into shock. *Sloppy.* He had been so sloppy. He could have ended it right then and there. Instead, he had made a decision that caused him to lose control over the situation.

With shaking hands he reached down to the knife, *his knife,* buried in his leg. He trembled as he grabbed the handle. If he pulled it out now he might bleed to death, but if the knife was blocking his femoral artery then he was dead for sure. He chose to pull it out. He took a pen out of his pocket and put it between his teeth, clamping down on the plastic.

He wrapped both hands around the knife and pulled it out.

"Aaaaaaaaaaaaahhhhhh!"

He fell forward. His head hit the floor and he panted. He pressed both hands tightly against the wound, but blood kept pouring out. He was going to bleed to death if he didn't act.

Through his pain he thought he heard something. He lifted his head with sudden attention and listened more carefully. He *did* hear something. It was someone knocking at the front door.

"Nomar! Nomar, are you all right? Open the door! Nomar, please, let me in!"

The Goldcamp woman. She'd heard. She knew something was wrong. She'd be calling the police. It was over.

He sat up and pressed his hands against the wound, applying as much pressure as he could. Then, using the knife he'd been stabbed with, he cut a thick strip from the sheet on his bed. He twisted the strip until it was tight, and wrapped it around his leg above the wound. He then closed the blade and tied the ends of the sheet tightly around the handle. His teeth clenched again as he turned the handle around and around so that it wrapped his leg tightly enough to slow the bleeding. Such a crude tourniquet might result in the loss of his leg, but at this point it didn't matter. His life was forfeit anyway.

The knocking at the door ceased, and Hakeem thought he heard the woman retreating back downstairs. He didn't have long.

He pulled himself up onto his bed. It was time to rely on his training. He knew what he had to do, step by step, but a nagging thought tried to interfere, and he couldn't let it.

He'd failed. Everything to follow would simply be cleaning up after the mess he'd made. He'd failed himself, his people, and his father. The realization was worse than the searing pain in his leg.

No time for that now. Think! Act! He managed to stand. He limped over to his desk and unlocked it. He took out some duct tape and wrapped it several times around the tourniquet so that it was held in place. Then he moved over to the closet. Each step was agony, but he'd have to endure it. He'd been *trained* to endure it.

Unlocking the closet, he reached in and pulled out a loaded twelve-gauge shotgun. He cradled it in his arms. Obtaining guns in this country had always fascinated him. In Afghanistan, one had to seek out someone like Benazar. But *here*, here it was as simple as going down to the local Wal-Mart and purchasing one.

He moved the safety forward on the weapon and placed it on the desk. He used his sleeve to wipe blood from his nose and moved back toward his bed. He lifted the mattress, the weight causing him to cry out, and threw it off of the box-spring.

There it was, the detonator made out of the remote control from a toy boat, also purchased at Wal-Mart, that would ignite the nitric and sulfuric acid hidden underneath the floorboards, leaving this entire building in a flaming pile of rubble.

There would be nothing left for the authorities to examine. This place would be blown sky high, and Hakeem would be gone by the time that happened. He stuffed the detonator into a duffel bag that held everything he'd need.

The last piece of hardware he took was a U.S. Army grenade that one of his associates had supplied. It had been given to him to blow himself up if he ever found himself cornered, but now it looked like it would be put to a different use. The last thing he did was put his cell-phone down on the box spring.

It was time to go. If he was to be martyred, then so be it. That's what had always been expected of him anyway, hadn't it? But he still had work to do.

He limped out of his room, the duffel bag slung over his shoulder and the shotgun pointed straight out in front of him. He inched his way along the wall, leaning against it for support, toward the bathroom door.

*　*　*

Zack had heard Ms. Goldcamp banging on the door, but he hadn't moved. He could have taken the cell phone out of his pocket and called for help, but he hadn't moved. He just sat there, with his shaking hands holding an unfamiliar weapon pointed at the bathroom door. If he heard or saw the lock twist even a fraction of an inch, he'd shoot. If he heard or saw anything, he'd shoot.

He'd never been so terrified. It wasn't just the fact that his life was being threatened; it was this extraordinary circumstance in which he found himself.

His brain gave him an assist. He was consigning himself to certain death if he just sat here on the floor and did nothing, but he was shaking so badly that he wasn't even sure he'd be able to hit a target—if one presented itself—right in front of him.

Fight or flight? Zack chose flight.

He clambered up on the toilet's tank and opened the window for the second time in two days. He kept glancing over his shoulder as he crawled out onto the fire escape. Nothing came through the door. He closed the window and looked over the metal railing. The Chevy Malibu was still there.

He took a deep breath. Same drill as before. Just jump.

*　*　*

Hakeem released a round into the bathroom door. The blast was deafening, and wood splintered and went flying inwards.

Hakeem knew the boy had his pistol, so he took no chances. Putting his back against the wall next to the door frame, he leaned the shotgun against the wall and pulled the grenade's pin. He waited only a second before he tossed the grenade through the hole he'd blown in the door, and ducked for cover in the next room.

*   *   *

Zack had gotten one leg over the railing when a booming sound shook him, almost causing him to lose his grip on the fire escape. A split-second later the bathroom window exploded. Glass, plaster, and brick shot outwards, tearing through his clothes and spearing his skin. The whole foundation of the building seemed to quake as the fire escape rattled. Zack brought up his arms to protect his head, and that motion combined with the explosion thrust him outward. He fell.

He landed, hard, on his right side. His back and right shoulder hit the hood of the car, and his leg cracked the windshield. His momentum propelled him over the hood, past the grill, and onto the ground by the front bumper. Lying on his stomach, he tried to lift his head up and then lost consciousness for the second time.

*   *   *

Hakeem peered into the bathroom. The boy was gone. His eyes went wide and he moved to the shattered window. He stuck his head out but still saw no sign of him.

Then he looked down through the metal grating of the fire escape and saw one of the boy's legs. He was down. He must have been killed. The blast had obviously blown him right out the window.

Hakeem had needed to kill Zack, the only other person to know what had gone on here. Now he assumed the boy was dead, and he had to move swiftly. He was running out of time. Already, he could hear sirens in the distance.

Hakeem turned to go. He went out the front door of the apartment and started down the stairs. Each step sent a jolt of pain through his body, but he'd learned to control his pain.

The Goldcamp woman was downstairs, standing in her doorway in a bathrobe. She took a step back when Hakeem pointed the shotgun at her. She screamed and retreated into her apartment, slamming the door shut behind her. Hakeem hadn't bothered to shoot her. With the explosion to come, she'd be dead soon enough.

He stopped and leaned up against the wall. Blood was still flowing from his leg, and he was getting dizzy. He took a moment to catch his breath. The sirens were growing louder, but no one was around and he still had time. He discarded the shotgun over the side of the stone staircase. It fell into a crevice below street level alongside the lower level apartments and landed with a clatter. He went down the steps and limped diagonally across the street toward the park.

He had one more important piece of business, and now those sickening thoughts of failure started to work their way back into his consciousness.

*　　*　　*

Zack came to. There was blood on the ground from the cuts and scrapes he'd suffered from the blast in the bathroom and subsequent fall. He rolled over on his left side. His right arm was broken. He was sure of it. Something was wrong with his right ankle as well. There was the blow he'd taken to the head from Nomar, as well as injury to his skull sustained from the fall. He touched his left hand to the side of his head and saw blood on it when he took it away. He was bleeding from his ear.

He shouldn't move. He should just lie here until he was found. Someone would find him.

Through the darkness he looked toward the mouth of the alley. The street was lit. He saw Nomar crossing the street, favoring his left leg.

Zack's fear turned into rage. That motherfucker! Here Zack was, having come face to face with one of these devils. Nomar wasn't any different from the men who'd killed his sister, who'd killed thousands, over some problem years past in some land he'd never even been to or ever even acknowledged. This bastard had been living right under their noses, acting neighborly, acting with kindness, all the while trying to figure out ways to kill people like Jenny, Peter, and their unborn child. *He brought bread pudding to my place. Bread pudding. I'm gonna kill you, Nomar.*

He couldn't let this stand. He had to set it right. He hadn't done many good deeds in his young life. In fact, he couldn't think of one particularly decent act he'd ever done for anyone. What he'd done to Mo was despicable; he knew that now. But if he could just get this *one thing* right, then he just might be able to live with himself.

He used his left arm to prop himself up and then crawl along the brick wall of the alley. Miraculously, he found the gun he'd dropped after the fall, and held it firmly in his left hand. He inched himself up the wall and then started to move forward.

His vision was blurry, but he fought through it. He had to. He had to stay conscious. His only fear now was that he might lose Nomar.

He heard the sirens closing in, but didn't know if they'd be here in time. The cops were taking forever. Was this New York City or wasn't it? How long did it take, with all the cop cars in Manhattan, to cover a few city blocks? They'd certainly moved in to arrest him fast enough.

Zack was moving along sluggishly, but then so was Nomar. Nomar staggered over to the park and crossed it. If the lights in the park had ever worked, they certainly weren't working now. Zack managed to cross the street without falling, trying to ignore the pain.

Nomar stopped at a battered phone booth, placing a duffel bag at his feet. He had his back turned to Zack. He picked up the phone and began making a call. Zack crept slowly toward him.

The sirens were loud now, but Nomar wasn't concerned about them.

Zack crept closer. He didn't know whether he had it in him to shoot him in the back, but he was about to find out. He was almost there. Almost there.

*   *   *

Hakeem picked up the phone and punched in the number he'd memorized. This number could only be dialed from a landline, and only from a pay phone. His trepidation, his feeling of utter failure, was overwhelming. This was the worst possible timing for these events to unfold. There was still so much to do, and now he'd endangered their entire operation.

The phone rang twice before someone answered it. "How can I help you?" a voice on the other end said.

Hakeem had trouble finding his voice. "I-I'd like to cancel my order, confirmation number J35677728."

The silence on the other end tormented Hakeem. When the voice returned, it responded in a careful, low tone. "Are you absolutely sure?"

Hakeem closed his eyes. "Yes."

"Well then, consider it canceled. Have a wonderful evening."

Hakeem only heard the underlying meaning: *God be with you on your journey.*

Hakeem hung up the phone and lowered his head. There were only two actions left to take, and one of them he could take care of right now. He could see the police cars pulling up to the building. He was at a safe enough distance to trigger the detonator.

He leaned over, wincing in pain, to grab the duffel bag, but something out of the corner of his eye distracted him. It was Zack, and he brought the butt of the stolen pistol crashing down on Hakeem's broken nose.

Hakeem's hands flew to his face, and he moaned as he fell. He looked up through blood to see the barrel of his pistol staring him in the face. Hakeem was stunned to see that the boy was still alive. Zack must have thought he was now in control, but he didn't know just how intensely Hakeem had trained for a situation like this, or how much physical pain and suffering he could endure. Now Zack was going to find out.

This had gone on long enough. Hakeem used his good leg to kick out, catching the boy in the left knee and dropping him. He thought he heard something snap as Zack fell. The boy was writhing as Hakeem looked around for the pistol. He could hardly see.

He got himself back on his feet and needed to balance himself against the phone booth for support. The gun was nowhere to be seen. He looked down at the injured teenager and kicked him in the ribs. Zack groaned and struggled to roll over. Hakeem could almost admire how tough the boy was, if he wasn't so pathetic.

Hakeem reached down and grabbed a handful of the Zack's hair with his left hand, yanking his head back and exposing his throat. He made his right hand as straight as a dagger, and brought the heel of his palm down as hard as he could on Zack's trachea. Then he let go of the boy, grabbed his duffel bag, and started across the park behind the basketball court.

He could see the red and blue lights of the squad cars now, only a few hundred feet away. They obviously hadn't seen what had just taken place.

When he felt that he was safe from detection, he unzipped the bag and removed the detonator. He took no satisfaction in what he was about to do. He simply knew that it was part of his fate.

*   *   *

Officer Scalini looked up the stone steps as his partner exited the building. "Any luck?" he asked.

"No. She's hysterical. She won't open the door."

"She knows we're cops?"

"Yeah."

"Is this that same lady?"

"Yeah."

"Damn it!" Scalini thought he heard something like a cry of pain across the street. At the same time, another squad car arrived. "Hey, we got backup. I heard something over there I'm going to check out." He pointed across the street. "Just hang tight."

He didn't like leaving his partner, even if backup had arrived. But the details of the call had been vague at best, and it seemed as if their unit was being called out to this location a lot lately.

He crossed the street and snapped on his flashlight. Parks like this always seemed to lose their lights to vandals.

He stopped in his tracks when he saw blood. Lots of blood. He followed the trail to a young guy, lying on his back, his face twisted in pain.

"Oh, God!" Scalini called for an ambulance, and a minute later one of the officers from his backup came to assist him.

It didn't look good. The kid looked like he might be dying, and until medical help arrived there was little the two men could do. They remained with the kid awhile. Then Scalini spotted another trail of blood. "Stay with him," he told the other officer. "I'm going to check this out."

* * *

Hakeem, hidden in the shadows, was looking over to the apartment building, and he held the gun that Zack had dropped. It was hard to see through the chain-link fence of the basketball court, but men in uniform were coming and going regularly now. He checked the battery in the remote control.

This was it. The explosion would be spectacular, but to Hakeem it only meant that he had failed, and that his men would now have to go even deeper underground. This was a major setback, and it was *his* fault.

He pulled the trigger. Nothing happened. Fear began to grip him, and he changed the battery. He pulled the trigger again. Nothing happened. It wasn't working.

No! He'd done it right. He *knew* he'd done it right. He'd done it just like he'd been shown a thousand times before in the camp. *No! No!* He squeezed the trigger again and again but not even a plume of smoke rose from the building.

His ultimate failure. His ultimate disgrace. What would Benazar say? What would he think, if he could see his son right now? He felt sick. Dirty. Vile. He was unworthy of the responsibility that had been bestowed upon him. He wanted to die. And now he was going to die for nothing.

"Hey, you, are you all right?"

Hakeem heard a voice as a flashlight shone on his face. He looked around to see a police officer moving toward him. Obviously, the officer didn't think Hakeem posed much of a threat.

He was tired and only semi-coherent. With his failure he'd lost the will to fight. Nothing mattered now. All that mattered was that he die.

He couldn't even risk shooting the officer. If the officer shot him back and he somehow survived, then he might be taken off to some place like Guantanamo Bay where he would rot in disgrace and torment.

That's the way the Americans work. They're no different from the Russians. That's why I'm here. That's what this has all been about.

Was it? Could he be certain? He wasn't so sure. As the blood left his body and his thoughts drifted, he grew confused. How had he arrived here, in this strange land? It looked like it had a lot to offer, with people living the kinds of lives he'd once wanted for himself. *That's why I'm here. Because they took that from us. They needed to be reminded. Reminding them. That's why I'm here. Isn't it? Isn't it?*

"Hey, it's okay. Just stand still and let me see your hands. Just put the bag on the ground and … Put the gun down right now! Put it down! Now!"

Reminds me of that poem I wrote when I was twelve. The one Uncle liked so much. He raised the gun to his head.

"Put it down! Put it down!"

How many poems did I write under that tree? Was that my best one? He put the gun in his mouth and felt the cold steel of the silencer against his palate.

Scalini took a step forward. "No! Don't!"

Yes, that was definitely my best one. Uncle's favorite. My favorite.

He squeezed the trigger.

EPILOGUE

Zack was sitting at a table on an outdoor patio at a cedar-shingled coffee house. He took a look around. It was one of those quaint, old Colonial New England towns, and the crisp air and beautiful shades of red and yellow from the foliage made it clear that the area was well into fall.

He sipped a hot cup of coffee and looked across the table at his mother and then at Mo, sitting next to her. Mo didn't say anything. He wouldn't even look at Zack. He just looked down at his lap.

His mom was the one who spoke up. "Zack, why is it that you feel you can just go around assaulting people?"

Zack looked back at Sally and could see more hurt than anger written on her face. It was the disappointment that stung him. "No, Mom, it's not like that. I already said I'm sorry."

"Well, it's too late for that *now*, Zack," Sally said, shaking her head. "Now you're going to have to learn some discipline."

"What are you gonna do?"

"*I'm* not going to discipline you. I said you're going to have to *learn* some discipline. I think you need to join the army."

"What? You're kiddin', right?"

"No, I'm not. You're going to have to go with Joey Sisco."

"No. No way, Mom. I don't mean to hurt you. You know I hate to hurt you. But that's just out of the question."

Sally looked over at Mo, who said nothing and kept looking down at his hands in his lap. "He is his father's son, through and through." She turned back to Zack and said, "There is one other option."

"What's that?"

"Come with me."

His mother rose from the table and walked of the patio and out to the sidewalk. Mo got up and followed her. Zack took the last sip from his mug of beer and got up to go after them.

He caught up with Mo as he was crossing the street. Zack followed Mo's gaze to one of the skyscrapers gleaming in the sunlight. It held Zack's attention too. It looked like it was rattling. Zack could hear it and see it shake, but he couldn't feel the vibrations on the concrete under his feet.

"They say that LA could get hit by 'the big one' any day now," Mo said with less of an accent than Zack remembered.

Zack's eyes stayed fixed on the tall building. "This is New York, not LA," he said.

Mo stopped and put a hand up to bring Zack to a halt as well. He looked Zack right in the eyes with a seriousness that compelled Zack to listen. "You've never been to LA," he said in a warning voice. He then resumed his walk and followed Zack's mother across the street.

Zack stared at Mo's back bewildered, and then followed the both of them. He caught up at a grassy field.

"I used to play little league here," Zack said with a hint of nostalgia in his voice.

"No, you didn't," said a sad voice, and Zack looked over to where his mother was standing. She was at the foot of a ditch. He looked around. It was a cemetery.

He went over to join her at the edge of a deep hole. Nervous now, Zack looked down into the hole. There was an open casket, but there was no body in it. He felt an interior chill.

He looked at the tombstone, but it was blank. "Why isn't there an epitaph, Ms. Shearer?"

"This is that other option I was talking about," Ms. Shearer said, looking down into the empty grave. "You need to climb down and lie in there. After you close the lid we'll fill in the hole."

"If I wasn't gonna go into the army, what makes you think I'd get in there?" Zack asked.

"It's all right," Ms. Shearer said. "Your brother will be along in a little while. He'll dig you up and let you out."

"Are you sure?" Zack said doubtfully. "What if he forgets?"

"He won't."

"And what if I run out of air? I'll suffocate."

"You won't."

Zack looked at Ms. Shearer's perfect face. "I guess I can trust you," he said.

He climbed down the hole and into the coffin. He settled down against the silky soft fabric and looked back up at Ms. Shearer. He didn't say anything else. He just closed the lid and waited in darkness.

He didn't know how much time passed, but he opened his eyes when he thought he heard muffled voices. His eyes had trouble adjusting, but now there was a little bit of light in his coffin.

No, not a coffin. A drawer. A drawer of some kind. *Wait a second.* He'd been in one of these contraptions before. It was a CAT scan machine.

He heard an unfamiliar voice say, "...and a hairline fracture right here on the tibia."

What? What's going on? He tried to speak out but he couldn't.

"Zack! Seriously man, climb on out of there! I'm gettin tired of waitin' for your ass."

Zack heard Jamar's voice above him and started up the ladder. He climbed up through the uncovered manhole expecting to find himself in the middle of the street, but instead he was in some kind of basement.

"Not a whole lotta room in here," Terence said to Zack.

"We can make it work," Jamar said.

"Wait a minute," Zack said, "I know this place. I used to come here for Sunday school."

"Oh, really?" Jamar said, the sarcasm pouring off of him. "Why do I give a shit?"

Zack left Jamar and Terence and climbed the stairs to the church. With light from a stained glass window guiding his steps, he hastened to the altar, but it had been stripped bare. There was nothing but a layer of dust.

"Where'd everything go?" Zack asked Joey.

"I don't know, man," Joey said.

"Y'know my mom wants me to go with you over there," Zack said.

"Really?"

"Really."

"I don't believe you. What parent would want that for their son?"

"She wants me to learn discipline," Zack said.

"Heh-heh. Well, I guess that makes sense."

"You got any Xanax, Joey?"

"Nah. Sorry, man."

"It's all right." Zack turned around went to leave the church, but when he got to the vestibule he saw a group of blurry, white objects. His eyes tried to focus, and he realized they were people. People in long white robes.

He was weary once again. He realized he was lying down and his whole body was numb.

His eyes adjusted to the figures moving about him. They were men and women in lightweight coats, holding clipboards and looking at him.

Zack had trouble hearing. His thoughts suddenly seemed muddled. He could hear only one person speaking, an older woman, and he could make out only random, hushed words throughout her monologue of technical jargon: "...no serious trauma to the spine ... third-degree burns ... basal skull fracture ... punctured ear drum ... lacerations ... clean break of the right humerus ... dislocated shoulder ... ligaments torn ... endotracheal intubation ... milligrams of morphine ... long road of recovery ahead ... intense physical therapy ... lucky to be alive ... let's move on..."

Zack watched them go. He was alone in the room. There were no other patients in here with him. For a while he watched the rain outside beat against the window, but eventually he grew tired again and drifted back off to sleep.

* * *

It was night and the lights were turned off when Zack awoke. When he looked down at his body all he could see were plaster casts and all sorts of tubes going in and out of him, including the one attached to the mask he was breathing through. He heard a soft hiss coming from one of the machines at his bedside.

His eyes moved to a lighted hallway. Two nurses were talking. At first he thought they were talking about him, but after listening he realized they were discussing someone else.

"Well, he just woke up a few days ago."

"How is he?"

"He'll be fine. He seems strong."

"It's a damn shame, it is. How can people be so brutal?"

"Well, oddly, he admitted that it was in retaliation."

"Retaliation? For what?"

"He said he stole a bike from the guy who hit him over the head."

"Really? I didn't know."

"Yeah."

"Still, that doesn't justify what was done to him."

"That's where everything gets tricky. I had a chance to speak with his mother. Apparently, he's been behaving this erratically since the end of last year. It's a response to all the hate that's been aimed at him and his family since the attacks."

"Oh. Oh, that's terrible."

"I know. I mean, he's just a kid. People have been telling his family to go back 'home.' He's been verbally assaulted in the street. His uncle's corner store has been the victim of petty thievery and vandalism. She says he was just pushed over the edge. I guess it's just one of those cases of, 'You want me to be a bad guy? I'll show you what a bad guy can do.' The self-fulfilling prophecy. It's all just so sad."

"I keep hearing more and more of this happening all over the country. Granted, it's gotten better since those first couple of days, but it still makes me sick. 'Go back home,' they keep saying. Let me tell you something—unless you're a Native American you have no right to tell someone to go home. These ignorant people are just running around giving our country a bad name. I hope when they catch this guy who hurt him they deport *him*."

"Amen."

Zack closed his eyes. What a conversation to wake up to.

*   *   *

Strange dreams and nightmares kept blending in with conscious thought to the point where there was almost no distinction. It wasn't until he woke up one morning and Derek and Miranda were at his bedside that he knew he was awake.

They didn't say much. They knew he couldn't talk because of the damage to his throat. He couldn't even write. But they just wanted him to know they were there.

He imagined he looked like hell. He couldn't ask for a mirror, and even if he could, he doubted he'd be given one.

The more he was able to think clearly, the more questions kept piling up. He kept thinking about what had happened that night. He wished that whatever it was he was being sedated with would be delivered in stronger doses so that he wouldn't have to think about it. At this point he was totally unable to communicate with anyone. He supposed that's what had kept the police and the reporters away.

Derek and Miranda came every day. They were supportive without being intrusive. They respected his need for rest. Really, the most they could do was to show their love and concern.

Jacqueline came in a few times. She sat at his bedside and held his hand, occasionally reading to him or telling him about what was going on with their friends.

That was when Zack found out there was a chaperone. Every time Zack had a visitor, there was someone posted right outside the room. This person must've known by now that Zack couldn't talk, but he or she was definitely listening to what he was being told. When Jamar and the boys came to visit him, they would laugh and joke in an effort to cheer him up. It wouldn't be long before they would see how tired he was and leave to allow him to rest, or sometimes his doctor would come to send them on their way. In the end, nothing he was told by anyone was of any real consequence.

He knew there were questions, though. He could see it in their faces. And could he blame them? After all, those same questions nagged at him again and again. But for now, all he could do was wait, and he definitely wasn't going anywhere anytime soon.

* * *

A tall man in a dark suit was standing in the doorway. He was arguing with Zack's doctor.

"Look, I appreciate the position you're in, but I have to say no," his doctor said. She looked annoyed. "He's in a weakened state and we can't allow any visitors, even *you*, to upset him."

"And I appreciate the position *you're* in," said the man, "but this can't wait any longer. I don't need him to tell me anything, but I do have information that I need to share with him."

"And I understand that, but as I already told you—"

"Look, Dr. Waters, we can keep going in circles like this all day, or I can go through the proper channels and make this visit official. But either option will be a waste of your valuable time as well as mine, and I don't think either of us wants that. I respect 'doctor's orders,' but I'm only asking for a few minutes."

"You have five, Mr. Branding," Dr. Waters finally said, and then she turned and walked down the hall.

Zack stared at his visitor, who turned and looked back at Zack.

"Hello," the man said, walking over to Zack's bed. He took a metal chair leaning against the wall and unfolded it. He sat down next to Zack. "My name is Agent Branding. I'm with the FBI."

Zack just looked at the man. There was nothing else he could do. Agent Branding appeared to be in his mid-forties with a graying, receding hairline and a long, thin face. He wore thick glasses that rested on his prominent nose. "I know you can't speak right now. Just blink once for yes, and twice for no, all right?"

Zack blinked.

"Very good." He paused. "I'm sure you've been expecting this visit." He waited for Zack to blink. Zack didn't. "Well then, first order of business. Congratulations. You're a hero."

Zack just looked back at the man.

"I know you haven't been able to give an account of your experience, but we've managed to retrace your steps in an attempt to fill in some of the blanks. So, are you wondering what we've put together?"

Zack blinked.

"Well, it seems that you, by what we've figured to be pure accident, have managed to identify a wanted criminal. A terrorist." Zack stared at Agent Branding.

"With all the work that's gone into exposing terrorist plots, it's hard to accept that a man like this was living here in Manhattan right under our noses, but there's a reason he was difficult to spot.

"Mr. McCrady, what you've managed to uncover was the workings of a terrorist sleeper cell, and a unique one at that. Whereas a great deal of our manpower has gone in to identifying those individuals who are new to this country or those who've grown up here and have been known to sympathize with our enemies abroad, this particular sect is made up of men who've actually stolen the identities of some of our citizens."

Branding opened the briefcase he'd carried in and removed two photographs. He held up the first one for Zack to see. Zack saw a picture of Nomar. "*This* is the Nomar Pezeshk you knew," he said, then held up the second photograph of a boy in his teens, "and *this* was the actual Nomar Pezeshk. We've discovered that he disappeared three years ago in Afghanistan. His Aunt Rabia only knew him as a small boy, so the sham was not so hard to pull off."

"The man's real name is Hakeem Rashid. He spent two years in a terrorist training camp and then came here in August of 2000. We don't have too much information about him before then, but of particular interest to us was his father's identity."

He held up a new photo. "This is Benazar Rashid. The CIA trained him during the conflict with the Soviet Union in the eighties. He's currently on Interpol's most-wanted list. And he's one of our top priorities. His son was merely a minion. This man here is a very, *very* dangerous individual."

Zack took in the dark eyes of the man in the photo. He didn't know what to think.

"Thanks to you," Branding continued, "we have a great deal to work with. The apartment building you lived in was rigged with enough explosives to bring the place down, but miraculously it never came to that. We've gathered sufficient intelligence to go after the rest of the cell, and we're confident that we'll arrest them soon."

Zack wondered if Branding could see how confused he was. As if he was reading Zack's thoughts, Branding said, "You're probably wondering why I'm telling you all of this just now."

Zack blinked.

Branding reached into his inside pocket and took out a handkerchief. Removing his glasses, he used his right hand to wipe the lenses. "For several reasons," he said.

"The first reason is that you've earned it. The service you've done this country goes above and beyond what might be expected from a civilian, and the government wants to show its gratitude through an act of good faith."

Zack arched his eyebrows at Branding. *And?*

"The second reason is the more important of the two. I needed to speak with you because I need your vow of secrecy. Yesterday's wounds are still fresh in everyone's minds. I'm sure you of all people can relate to that. I am truly sorry for the loss of your sister and brother-in-law.

"Having this get out would be damaging to this country because of the doubt it would sow in the minds of the people— doubt about their government. The people need to know that we're on top of this, that they'll be protected from future attacks. We can't keep this doubt from forming if they know that this cell exists right here in Manhattan. For everyone's sake, we need to keep a lid on this.

"The third reason is that we need to go after the rest of the cell, and the less information there is floating around out there about this, the easier it is for us to do our jobs. Can you see where I'm going with this?"

Zack blinked.

"I've been authorized to make a deal with you," Branding said, his voice dropping. "If you swear yourself to secrecy on this issue, then I can see to it that any case the state might build against you with regard to the contraband you were carrying when you were brought here will go away."

Zack winced. He'd forgotten completely.

"Unfortunately, as far as the assault charges pending against you go, there's nothing I'm able to do there. I am able to provide you with the names and numbers of some excellent attorneys, but from what I understand your family's lawyer is quite capable. You might consider arranging for his services."

Was he serious? This whole scenario was all so bizarre. For now, Zack was glad he couldn't speak.

"We've already been in contact with the police officers who were at the scene, as well as your neighbor, Judy Goldcamp. Everyone else knows what's expected of them. Do you think you can go along with all of this?"

It was a moment or two before Zack blinked.

"Very good then."

"Mr. Branding, your time's up," Dr. Waters said, sticking her head through the door.

"I was just leaving," Branding said. He took a business card out of his pocket and put it in the drawer of the table holding flowers Zack had received. "This is my contact information," he told Zack. "When you're finally released from here, you'll be contacted by another one of our agents who will arrange a time and a place for you to meet and go over what is and what isn't acceptable for discussion on this matter."

Branding got up and turned to go. Before he left, he said, "Sleep well, Mr. McCrady. You've earned it." Then he walked out.

Sleep well. Zack doubted that.

* * *

Zack's mind kept going back to that moment when Nomar had had a gun pressed against his head. Zack had been certain that he was going to die, but he kept remembering that moment of hesitation. Nomar, or Hakeem, or whatever his name was, had the look of someone who was utterly lost. Zack had seen something in his eyes, but he wasn't sure what it was. He supposed he would spend the rest of his days thinking about it.

Had Nomar been a kid just like me once?

Zack wondered what it took to make such men. Jenny had never done anything to men like that, but they'd taken her life. He wanted to know what kind of backgrounds would enable such people to rationalize the killings. What prompted their actions?

There was a lesson to be learned here, he just didn't know what it was.

Conflict and war had been around since the dawn of man, and it seemed the more man moved forward, the more complicated life got. He didn't for a moment entertain the idea that this was the end of hard times. On the contrary, he suspected that everything was going to get worse, much worse for everyone. He saw no way out of this mess. The government might have made this bed, but everyone had to lie in it.

The world was a nasty place. He'd always known this. But when you constantly brushed shoulders with individuals who choose not to take notice of it, it was easier to be cynical.

He needed to stop feeling so angry and sorry for himself. Everyone who came into contact with him was affected by it. He had family and friends who loved him, and what did he ever do in return but shun them or take advantage of them. He didn't have it as bad as he'd previously led himself to believe. And now, through his own actions, he'd made life much worse for himself and his loved ones.

He needed to change. He needed to stop being so sure of himself, so cynical about others. He needed to stop every now and then and ask himself questions, instead of pretending to have all the answers.

The world was messed up, sure, and it could do irreparable damage to good people, but nothing he'd ever done by blaming it had made his life any better.

Well, that was all going to change. He was going to make that change.

It was time to grow up.

ABOUT THE AUTHOR

©dominikphoto.com / dominik Huber

Douglas Grant is the author of the 2010 novel, *Preemptive* and the 2013 novel, *Imaginary Lines*. He earned his BA in English at the College of Charleston and his MA in Education at Point Loma Nazarene University. He lives in San Diego.

Click here to find Douglas Grant's profile on Amazon.

Please leave a short review of *Preemptive* on Amazon.

Please tweet to your followers that you've read *Preemptive*.

Follow Douglas Grant on Twitter.

ALSO BY DOUGLAS GRANT

DOUGLAS GRANT

IMAGINARY LINES
A NOVEL

This book is available on Amazon

Kyle Conway is about to make a breakthrough for Conway Brothers Construction Co.—a long sought after opportunity for a major real estate score. His wife and two boys will prosper, his brother-partner will do the same. And the Conways are delighted that friend and business colleague, Mauricio Solares, will have the chance to rise higher in society than other Mexican immigrants trying to realize the American Dream.

Yes, Kyle, a bit rough around the edges but a good guy at heart, is happy for Mauricio; but his proclivity for careless, insensitive remarks about or in front of his Mexican friend, causes Cynthia Conway to chastise him repeatedly, a fact that leads to frequent verbal clashes between them. He bristles at suggestions of mistreatment. She wants to enlighten her husband and to preserve the warm friendship that the Conways have enjoyed with the Solares family.

Is there a legitimate cause—perhaps beneath the surface—for tension, or is it a result of imaginations being overwrought? That question becomes critical when a vacation visit to Mexico intended to offer the Conways an opportunity for celebration and a strengthening of their marriage turns into a horror show, one that compounds suspicions and tension. Their journey south of the border turns relaxation and optimism into terror and the possibility for tragedy.